Cathedral of Dreams

By Terry Persun

Edited by Richard Mandel

Jacqui,
All life is a Cathedral
if we want it to be.

Booktrope Editions
Seattle WA
2011

Cover Design: Simanson Design (simansondesign.com)

ISBN 978-1-935961-20-8

DISCOUNTS OR CUSTOMIZED EDITIONS MAY BE AVAILABLE FOR EDUCATIONAL AND OTHER GROUPS BASED ON BULK PURCHASE.

For further information please contact info@booktrope.com

Library of Congress Control Number: 2011910386

Dedication

For Catherine

Chapter 1

DAY 1

Keith rolled his head from side to side on the pillow until he awoke from the bad dream. Sweat beaded his upper lip. He ran a hand over his clammy forehead and through his hair. Although he forgot what had happened in the dream as he became fully conscious, a feeling of dread lingered. He had to calm down, but how? He held back tears and tried not to think about what could happen next. He feared the system would recognize his emotional peak. He stared at the ceiling for a few minutes, then closed his eyes to see if any part of the dream emerged. If he knew what the feeling of dread concerned, perhaps he could shake it. No luck.

After lifting his head from the comfort of his pillow, Keith swung his feet over the side of the bed and let his toes enter the plush softness of the warm carpet. He rubbed his face, pushed the heels of his hands into his eyes, rolled his neck, sat up straight. He stretched his back until a small snap brought relief from the night's immobility. A sound sleeper, he moved very little throughout most nights.

When he glanced toward the clock it shifted into the next digit and a sweet voice said, "Keith, it is time to awaken." He stared at the clock a full three minutes until it repeated the message, this time raising its voice as it said his name then dropping back to normal for the remainder of the sentence. He ignored further attempts to recall the dream and continued his morning routine, stretching his arms over his head, twisting his back, and rising to a standing position. The third time the clock sounded its voice was raised for the entire sentence. Keith reached over and flicked the alarm off even though he liked hearing the pleasant voice.

He trudged into the bathroom to relieve himself. Passing the mirror, Keith noticed how he had plumped over the past year. A slightly rounded stomach had appeared where it used to be flat. He knew he should expand his morning exercises beyond stretching while seated on the edge of his bed, but there was little reason to do so. There was no woman in his life to impress. Perhaps if there were he would have more incentive to stay fit.

He reached over and pushed the shower button, then stripped away his pajamas and stepped into water spraying toward him from several directions. Set at the perfect temperature, Keith experienced a familiar relief while standing there.

When the feeling of dread swept over him again, he poked his head out of the shower to see if something in the bathroom was amiss. His own face looked back at him from the mirror over the sink. He smiled at himself and noticed the way his wavy hair fell flat against his head. He had full lips and strong cheekbones. Even his eyes drew you in, he thought. He was handsome enough. Perhaps he needed a girlfriend. Maybe he should put in for one? Again he thought that a woman might provide incentive for him to stay in shape, give him a reason to exercise more often. He was getting used to the idea.

He finished in the shower, shaved, and brushed his teeth. He dressed comfortably for work. The sense of dread had waned, but he knew it would be back. The trick was to hold it at bay, not let it grow too strong. Not allow a dream, which he couldn't remember anyway, to cause the police to show up at his door. That would only perpetuate more dread feelings, which could transfer into more dreams like it had before, months ago. He still didn't recall where the police had taken him or what happened while there. He only remembered waking in his own bed on a Tuesday, just in time to prepare for work.

Breakfast for Keith was a quick cup of coffee and an egg sandwich that made its way from the refrigerator into the microwave and onto a plate without much thought or fanfare. He ate the same, or similar, breakfast every day. Few of the ingredients were changed and the flavors had become comfortable if not tasty.

After placing the dishes into the cleaning receptacle, Keith went to open the door to his apartment when a knock surprised him. He stepped back, "One moment."

"It's the police," a man said in a gentle, non-threatening tone.

Keith put a hand over his heart as though to still it. He stepped backward. The door was unlocked. They all were. He couldn't stay the inevitable. When the second polite knock came, he advanced and opened the door.

The officer in front of him looked familiar in the way that a man looks familiar if you met him only once at a gathering. His uniform was stiff and creased in all the right places. His hands were folded in front of him. They were soft hands, which made Keith wonder if he shouldn't put in for a man instead of a woman. The nametag over the officer's breast pocket read, "Hello, my name is Richard." He had a nice smile, as though he were about to deliver wonderful news. Two officers stood behind him and smiled as well. They were all very pleasant and kind. Very proper.

"May we come in and talk with you for a moment?"

"I was just heading to work."

The familiar officer, Richard, glanced over his shoulder and one of the other men began typing into his wrist computer. "Taken care of," Richard said. "You'll receive full credits."

Keith stepped back and allowed them passage.

"You are feeling something..." Richard paused for a moment to emphasize the next word or to consider exactly which word he would use and then said, "unusual this morning?" A smile plastered across his lips, Richard continued to look into Keith's eyes. He didn't look around the room or glance away for a moment.

"Nothing like before," Keith said, knowing that there must be records of his episode. "I had a bad dream. That was all. I had no recollection of it when I awoke this morning. Nothing to worry about, I'm sure." He hoped that Richard did not sense the shakiness in his voice.

Richard opened a wrist computer and glanced over some information. He typed and spoke at the same time, "No recollection," he said. He looked up at Keith. "We received a very slight reading, and wanted to be sure that you're feeling all right." He hesitated as he had earlier in their conversation, as though he had to think of what to say. "May I ask, is this the first time since several months ago? Have you had other feelings that seemed odd or unusual in any way?"

Keith thought back, but didn't put too much effort into it. His biggest concern at the moment was to get through this confrontation, no matter how pleasant, and to get on with his normal life. "This is the first. And I had all but forgotten it until you visited." As he said this, the feeling of dread made itself known, like a shadow slipping across the floor in the corner of the room. Keith hoped that Richard could not detect the wave of emotion on his wrist computer, if, in fact, that was what the data portrayed.

"We are very sorry for bothering you, but it is our duty to make sure that every resident is completely happy with his or her life, is satisfied with accommodations, and has no reason to strike out at anyone in any way." Richard reached to shake Keith's hand.

Keith accepted the gesture. "All is fine here. I appreciate your concern."

"It is the concern of all of the Newcity Police, young man," Richard said.

The use of the words "young man" reduced the handshake to official business and far from friendly. Richard, if familiar, was now a member of the Newcity Police force just doing his job. Keith sensed a separation of emotion between them whether real or imagined.

Richard's two associates never came very far into the apartment, and now they backed into the hall. Other people walked by, residents. Keith nodded to the ones he recognized. Everyone was on his or her way to work, as they should be.

As though Richard knew Keith's thoughts, he said, "You have an additional thirty minutes due to this inquiry. Relax." The men turned sharply to leave, then stepped away as though they had another important call that they were already late for.

Keith thanked them for their concern as he closed the door.

The room enlarged now that it was empty. Being a rather bulky man, Richard had taken up a lot of space. Keith glanced around in an attempt to find something to do for the extra time he had available. He could switch on the news, but disliked the noise in the morning. No music either, for the same reason. He sat on the sofa and crossed his legs. What was that dream about? Closing his eyes brought nothing into view, no change in emotion, thank God.

He got up and paced to the kitchenette and pressed the coffee button. A cup slipped into place and coffee and creamer entered the cup simultaneously, in the exact amounts that he liked it. He took the cup back into the small, efficient living room and sat down again. It was curious how he thought about the police a little while before they arrived. Did that happen to anyone else? He couldn't have known about them arriving. He set the cup down, then picked it back up and sat holding it in his lap. He hardly drank any of the liquid.

He decided that he didn't know that the police were coming, but naturally feared that they would arrive after his dream. It was coincidental that they arrived just as he was leaving for work. He nodded to himself, satisfied with his conclusion. Still he wondered, why must he make more out of things than what they are? He never used to do that.

It was times like these, no matter how few they were, that Keith wished he had a close friend—or a woman—to talk with. He could contact a neighbor, and there were workmates, but no one who lived with him.

Time moved so slowly when he sat alone. He opened his mouth to start the television, but nothing but an "Oh" came out before he changed his mind and clammed up. No noise.

Could he request a woman that was not noisy in the morning? The women he had requested in the past talked too much when they first woke up. And, there was that one time when he was requested and stayed at that woman's residence—what was her name?—no matter, she talked almost constantly. That is what prompted him to be removed from the companion list for a while. Now he thought that a quiet woman might be the answer. Perhaps there was a woman in the system who would want only a short relationship, several days perhaps? Someone who was quiet, even shy, would do.

Keith got up and poured the remaining coffee into the sink. The cup went into the cleaning receptacle, and he opened the screen on the terminal next to the refrigerator. He used a finger to flip through the pages until he reached the Companion site. He voiced his request in single words as the screens passed through their sequence. He didn't concern himself with physical matters, but requested only those women who wanted a short relationship and were quiet in the morning. That should open the possibilities and increase his chances of approval. Before closing the terminal, he requested that the person come by a half hour after he was home from work. That would give him time to freshen up. He didn't mention sex in his request, but considered that as an option dependent on how well the two of them felt matched.

His request had passed the remainder of the half hour perfectly and he walked around the counter and out the door. Few people were in the hall now that the morning rush was over. He walked to the end of the hall where the space opened into the central dome. He lived high into the residencies and stopped briefly, as he often did, to glance down into the metropolis that was Newcity. From his vantage point he could see thousands of individuals wandering the streets, taking elevators, riding in travel carts. The corridors appeared to be full, even though many residents were at work by now.

This area of Newcity was the most recent of the livable residencies. Keith had been here for close to thirty years, but hardly remembered anything prior to his sixteenth birthday. The celebration included a lot of people he recognized as family if he thought about it, but few people he could actually name. Even the mental images he had of his parents were questionable. From then on he had been alone and found that as a preferred state of living.

Many of those who wandered past him on their way to work or home or somewhere else said hello. He had no obligation to return the greeting, but often did so knowing that it was the polite thing to do. The faces he saw this morning were different than those he usually saw and recognized from many years of occupying the same time space: they who went to work at the same time and came home at the same time ad he. There was a similar effect to his lunch hour, only with different faces. Although he had become friendly with a few people, relationships with Keith didn't appear to last long or become very deep.

This morning, though, he wished he would run into a few of those familiar faces. The short half-hour of being alone made him want to talk with someone, reach out. He might even have asked Robert or Carl or Maria to stop by sometime.

The crowd at this hour, thirty minutes past his usual period of transit, was so much smaller, intensifying his sense of feeling alone, which reminded him of the feeling of dread, and he wondered if that was what the dream was about. Did he sense that he'd be detained and that he'd feel alone? If so, was that the first time that day that he knew what would happen in the future? The second time being when the police arrived? Perhaps he dismissed the coincidence too easily.

As the sense of dread returned, sweeping through his body once again, he feared that someone was watching him. He moved away from the dome center and turned to go to work. No one appeared to be following him, but the sense of something being wrong lingered. It could be another precognition. A third.

Keith scurried toward the elevator and was the last to enter. The doors closed and the compartment dropped thirty-two floors before it stopped, the doors opening onto a large shopping plaza. Storefronts were bursting with items for sale. Large, sometimes flashing, signs announced electronics, clothing, accessories. Several people exited the elevator. No one got on. Before the doors closed, Keith noticed a few children with their parents and wondered about his own family. Why had he forgotten them? Were they in Newcity? He could make an inquiry but didn't feel compelled to do so. He vaguely remembered being transferred to Newcity. Was that possible? Could he have been transferred away from his family?

Down another twelve floors and the doors opened to a courtyard of tables and imitation foliage. Hallways peeled off in many directions from the space. Bland, windowless office doors lined each hall. Keith left the elevator and stepped into the courtyard as the elevator doors closed behind him. He traveled down a hall that led deeper into the maze of offices. He turned to the right and walked to the end of that hall as well. Along the way were emergency-exit doors, closets, and other offices. A man he didn't know came out of one office and said, "Good morning." Keith automatically the greeting, and continued on his way until he came to the Office of Goods and Services, his work area.

Satisfied that he no longer felt a feeling of dread and that he would soon satiate his sense of being alone, Keith opened the door to the offices. Maria sat behind a high counter in front of him. Framed abstract artwork spread in a variety of sizes behind her and along the wide wall. Two sofas and several chairs rested along the walls. Maria had dark hair and large eyes. She was pleasantly dressed in a beige blouse with decorative stitching along the collar and down the row of buttons. He couldn't see her skirt, but knew that it would be perfectly matched to her blouse. Maria always dressed handsomely.

"You look very beautiful today," Keith said, settling into the start of his workday. Purpose was a wonderful emotion. It brought the realization that he was effective and necessary. Even though he recognized that his personality stepped into a new place when he was at work, it was okay with him. He suspected that there were actually several unique but complimentary personalities within him. The work personality was perhaps his most refined and familiar. No wonder, for he spent more hours at the Office of Goods and Services than he spent anywhere else in Newcity.

"Thank you," Maria said. "And you look dashing."

Keith nodded and placed his arms on the counter.

Maria handed him a stack of paper. "Hard copy reports from maintenance and shipping." She flipped down about half way. "The blue page starts the shipping reports. Could you deliver them downstairs before you start?"

"Of course." Keith always accepted a job where he got to go somewhere or deliver something. Although he enjoyed sitting in front of his terminal and shuffling through quality or maintenance reports, he rather liked the movement. He picked up the hard copies. The information would already be in the system, but they produced hard copies as backup, the Stack Printer ejecting neat bundles of reports all day. The reports would then be distributed by hand and eventually stored in filing cabinets in their individual offices.

Maintenance offices were one floor down and Shipping was two floors below that. Keith decided to walk. After observing himself in the mirror that morning, he figured he could use the exercise.

He left the offices and strolled down the hall, shoved on a large metal door and entered the lighted metallic stairwell. There was no carpeting on the floor, and ribbed metal strips ran across each step. The landing was long and wide, and several doors were set back from the open space just as the doorway he now occupied. He stood there for a moment, secure in the small, closed-in space around him. He took two steps and the landing opened before him.

He walked down the stairs and stopped on the next landing. He took his time. A small sign announced the maintenance offices. Keith wandered across the landing and stood in the alcove for a brief moment before pulling the door open. The halls were empty. For having so many people in Newcity, there were a lot of places that appeared empty.

Newcity, he knew, was at full capacity. Everyone understood that another building was going up somewhere. But most of those who lived in Newcity would never see the next residence. Perhaps some of the children he had seen would be transferred there.

He delivered the paperwork to the receptionist in Maintenance without noticing or focusing on her or the offices. He had been there before and was rather businesslike in his communications. Back into the hall, through the door to the stairs, and he entered the next alcove. It felt good to stand in the small space, but he quickly made his way down to the next level. Just as he turned to go down the stairs toward shipping he stopped and glanced over his shoulder. A small, darkly dressed figure—a child?—hunched down into the corner of one of the alcoves.

Keith's heart beat a little faster and the feeling of dread returned. He scurried down the stairs, while simultaneously turning his thoughts to something pleasant, the possible meeting with the woman from the Companion site that evening. It appeared to work. His nervousness subsided. At least he hoped that he had felt nervous. That emotion would not register as a threat. Yes, nervous. He had not expected to see anyone in the stairwell, especially a child. It wasn't dread, then. There was a difference.

As with Maintenance, Keith quickly delivered the reports to Shipping. This time, instead of using the stairs, he traveled the long hallway to another courtyard—similar to the courtyard near his offices—and into the elevator. By the time he arrived in front of Maria again, he felt calm and satisfied that he had avoided another meeting with the Newcity Police.

Chapter 2

The apartment didn't feel the same when he returned home that evening. Nothing had been moved or disrupted, but the day had been long and the strange events had made him anxious and tired. He possessed a slight unease that the Police would soon arrive again, but quickly shifted his thoughts to prepare for the arrival of the Companion he had requested. Or he could cancel the rendezvous. He'd first double-check the system to be sure someone had responded to his request. If it wasn't too late, he could cancel or reschedule.

He opened the terminal next to his bedroom door and passed his finger over the morning's selections. Using voice commands, he entered the Companion site and saw that someone named Nellie would arrive in twenty minutes. Because of his anxious feelings, he checked to see if there was time to cancel, but there wasn't. Well, that gave him, he looked at his watch, nineteen minutes to prepare for her arrival.

He imagined that she had already left her apartment and strolled slowly toward an elevator. She would be a little nervous, but eager as well. Nineteen minutes, though, meant that she must be traveling from clear across Newcity. Out of curiosity, Keith entered the site to retrieve her stats.

A photo of a dark-haired woman with a broad mouth and full lips appeared. He asked for a full view. He read that she was five foot six inches tall and weighed one hundred and twenty-eight pounds. She had a pleasant shape, and shoulder-length curly hair that fell near her high cheekbones. Her complexion was dark and her eyes brown. He cocked his head when he realized that she was of African descent. That was not so unusual in itself, but the fact that she bore the appearance of an old race was unusual. He couldn't remember the last time he noticed a person bearing hereditary features. Few Newcity residents exhibited the appearance of any particular nationality at all. Over the years, the merging had eliminated such a separation. The world had become one people.

He had fifteen minutes to prepare.

Would she have eaten? Probably not, so he shuffled through the terminal to find suitable nourishment for the two of them. Instead of preparing something, he ordered rice and vegetables along with two sauces, a beef byproduct and a chicken-flavored tofu. That should take care of it. He closed the terminal and side-stepped into the bathroom. Now that he couldn't cancel, he was getting into the mood. It would be nice to have someone to talk with. He brushed his hair and wrestled with a clean shirt. He changed into shorts, then changed back into slacks.

Five minutes.

Stepping into slippers, he wandered toward the mirror and looked at his teeth. He grabbed a sonic and pushed the toothpaste button for a split second. Running the brush through his mouth quickly would freshen his breath and put a fast shine on his teeth. He rinsed just as a light knock came to the door. The food?

Unless his watch had de-synched it shouldn't be Nellie. He had two more minutes.

Although the doors can't be locked, entrance was forbidden unless invited, even for the Police, who would only proceed to a forced entrance if a resident were potentially dangerous. Keith had only once, as long as he could remember, heard of such an event on the news.

In the living room, he said, "Come in," then quickly turned to the kitchen counter where he expected to receive the dinner he had ordered. He stopped when the door only cracked open.

Through the opening, Nellie shyly poked her head. "It's me," she announced in the softest voice that Keith had ever heard. She was perfect. Not too noisy, pleasant to look at, and apparently respectful of his space. The only downside was that she came by early instead of on or slightly after his requested time, nonpunctual.

"Welcome," he said. "I ordered a light dinner. I hope you haven't eaten."

"I haven't." Nellie stepped around the door as though sneaking into his apartment. She carried a small overnight bag, and lifted it to show him. "In case," she said. "You may not want me to stay."

"You may not decide to," he said politely.

"True."

Nervous feelings returned, but that was part of the experience. A stranger, for all practical purposes, was a stranger. Yes, everyone in Newcity was documented and chipped for erroneous emotions, and that provided relative safety, but he and Nellie knew nothing about one another and had never worked together, so...

"I'm Nellie," she said as she advanced with her hand out.

There was something aggressive about her, even though she acted shy. The way she approached him while looking into his eyes belied her initial shyness about entering the room. Perhaps it was confidence, which was rather exciting to Keith. He took her hand and pulled her close to give her a quick hug. She smelled nice, but different, fresh in some way. Her odor reminded him of real plants you could get on one of the shopping levels. Flowery, but also moist. Her shoulders were firm and her body athletic. He hoped she wasn't displeased with his body's softness.

She pulled away and lowered her head, giving their eye contact a rest.

Another knock came to the door.

"That's the food," he said.

"I'll get it for you," Nellie said. Right away she turned and took the few steps to the door and opened it. "I'll take that."

After the door was closed she brought the sack to the counter and set it down.

"You didn't have to open the door," Keith said.

"Habit," she said. "Where I'm from, you don't let people just walk in."

"You don't? Where are you from? What level?"

She squeezed her lips together and squinted her eyes. "Five," she said.

"Five? I've never been ... ah, there, before."

"Not very many people go that far down, but there are humans there. You work in the Office of Goods and Services, you must know that almost everything in Newcity comes from the outside." She raised her eyes and stared into his.

He looked away, hesitated, then began to pull the food out of the sack. "Not everything. Manufacturing is done inside. Do you work in manufacturing?"

She laughed, "No. But let's talk about you and your job."

"Why?" he asked. "And how do you know where I work? It's not on my profile."

"I have friends who repair the computer systems. I had one look you up." She accepted a plate of rice and pointed to the meat sauce.

Keith poured sauce over her rice and selected the chicken tofu for himself. He motioned for them to sit down. As they wandered toward the couch, he said, "Why would you want to know where I work?"

"Discussion topics," she replied.

They sat near one another without touching.

"Well, then. My job is rather interesting. I document and organize everything that enters Newcity, everything that is manufactured here, and all the service needs. I'm not the only one working there, of course. The work is split up. My particular job focuses on the services. For instance, when plumbing or electrical work is needed, I document what work was completed and what materials were used. I pass that information along to ordering – also part of the Office of Goods and Services – and follow up to be sure that we are stocked for the next service need. It's fascinating work, sometimes. Interesting to see what's going on 'on the inside,' as they say." He was glad she asked about his work. Talking about work allowed him to feel important and accomplished.

"Do you ever get service information about security issues, like the entrances or exits from Newcity?" she asked while focusing on her food.

Keith sensed a planned direction in their conversation and hesitated.

Nellie looked up at him and smiled. "I'm just interested in the breadth of your responsibilities. It sounds as though you're an important man." She cocked her head with intrigue.

He remained silent, pushing rice with chicken tofu sauce into his mouth. She had asked an odd question. Security concerning entering and exiting Newcity was a sensitive subject. Only a few of those in his office had access to those records. He happened to be one of those few.

Keith had viewed a movie one time that involved an undercover policeman who pried a criminal for information then arrested him. His earlier precognitions had led him to the thought that the police would arrive yet again. Was she a member of the police? Should he lie and say that he has nothing to do with the services pertaining to security, or just tell her that they are restricted areas of conversation? As an undercover policewoman, did she have the authority to arrest him for lying? Regardless, she probably knew the answer to her own question already.

"You don't need to answer that question," Nellie said. "I can see that it bothers you."

"I am restricted from talking about some areas of my work," he said.

She waved her hand and shrugged her shoulders. "No matter. I was just curious." She shifted so that her leg touched his. She leaned in. "You belong to any groups?"

Keith put his plate on the side table. "I used to. A movie group. We'd sit together and watch movies twice a month and then talk about them, their meanings, the symbols of violence, the difference between what we watched and where we live now."

"Older movies, then?"

He shook his head. "Who knows when they were produced? Most took place in Newcity, but a few were from the outside. They were scary. No violence control."

"Those people aren't chipped," she said.

"How do you know?"

"I've seen them."

"How? What do you do that you'd have contact with people outside Newcity?" He leaned forward and turned toward her. He met her eyes again and saw a glint of excitement in them. "Come-on, tell me." He smelled the fresh scent again and imagined it to be from the outside, a wild place, one he had never seen.

She laughed. "You don't want to hear about what I do. It's nothing. Not important like your job. I could easily be replaced and no one would know."

"I would know," Keith said before thinking about it. His eagerness turned to fear for a second. He tried to cover up what he'd said. "I meant that, if we were to become friends or wish to see each other again, I'd know if you were gone."

"That's sweet," she said, and leaned in to kiss him.

He kissed her as well and lost touch with his fear. It turned into excitement.

Nellie stretched over him and set her plate on the side table with his. From that position, she moved very slowly and brushed against Keith as she settled back into her seat. Her hand rested on his side and her body pressed against him. She kissed him again.

Wrapping his arms around her, Keith bent to kiss the softness at the base of her neck. Her quiet voice entered his ear as she said, "Shall we move into the bedroom or would you like to finish dinner?"

Keith recoiled a bit. "Let's talk a little more."

"That's right, you wanted a shy woman."

He gave her a questioning look.

"My friend," she said. She placed both hands on his thigh and moved in close to him. "What would you like to talk about?"

"You never said what your job was on the fifth floor."

"I don't work on the fifth floor, I live there."

"Then?"

It felt to Keith as though she tucked her shoulders in just a bit before answering. "I'm a plant handler." She became still, apparently waiting for his reaction.

"Oh, my… You go outside," he said. "That's dangerous."

"Not like you might think," she said. "Most of the time, I help with the selection of items. It depends on freshness. How long they'll last."

"Flowers?" Keith said, breathing in her scent, which made more sense to him now.

Nellie smiled and shook her head at him. Her chin pushed up. "That is the best part," she said.

He pulled away so that he could see her face. It glowed with a sense of happiness or satisfaction. He couldn't decide which it was. "I bet it is," Keith said. He relaxed and found that he smiled with her. He reached toward her. She was not an undercover policewoman after all. He had nothing to be concerned about. He touched her cheek with is palm and drew her near. "Maybe we should go into the bedroom," he said.

He knew that she allowed him to lead her into the bedroom, but it didn't matter at the moment. He liked her confidence, and very much liked the way she smelled. There was something wild about it, free. He imagined her working outside amongst the non-chipped laborers, their emotions unchecked and un-monitored. Perhaps that was why she was so fit.

He watched as she removed her blouse and bra and got excited seeing her firm shoulders and breasts. It made him self-conscious as he slipped from his clothes and ducked under the sheets.

Nellie turned away – ah, the shyness revealed – as she finished undressing. Her body had a sheen to it that appeared to ripple and flow like water as she moved. She was not awkward at all; every movement appeared to be controlled. Even her hair appeared to do what she wanted, slipping over her cheeks as she bent to pull back the sheet, sliding slowly over her bare shoulder. On her forearm was her only blemish, a tiny scar he had not noticed before.

She reached for him a few moments after she entered the bed. That was the first awkward movement she had made, as though her shyness caused her to hesitate, like she had not fully decided to be with him. A certain sense of reluctance fell over the situation and he asked her outright, "Are you sure?"

He knew that if she felt coerced at all, if she felt afraid that he might hurt her if she didn't go along with his request, her chip would set off an alarm and the police would be there in a moment. His precognitive feelings returned. He waited for her to answer.

"I'm not used to this," she said.

"You don't have to."

"It's okay. I'm fine. Just, could we turn off the lights?"

"You can't turn them off," he said.

"I forgot. Then can you lower them?"

Keith requested that the lights lower, and the room became darker.

She lay down and nuzzled close to him. She threw one arm over him and pressed her breasts to his chest. She brought a leg up between his, slowly moving her thigh along his until she made the slightest contact.

Keith stopped thinking so much and fell into the senses of the body, the pleasures of their closeness.

When they finished, Nellie held onto him instead of rising to clean up and get dressed as usually happened when he had a companion over. In fact, she placed her head on his chest, pinning him down from rising out of bed. What should he do?

"Are you ever curious why you don't remember your dreams?" she asked.

He stiffened. "How do you know that I don't? I sometimes do."

"Seldom," she said.

"What are you saying?"

"Nothing. I was just drowsy and dosing off a bit." She ran her fingers down his stomach and back up again.

Keith relaxed. He liked her, the fact that she stayed close to him as though their encounter meant more than just being a companion for the night. He let his arm rest over her back and squeezed her closer to him. She pressed into his chest in return.

"I never remember the bad dreams." He thought back and realized that wasn't all. "Sometimes I wake up so excited about a dream, so happy, but I can't remember those either."

"Dream space," she said.

"What do you mean?"

"Dream space is where all the best things occur," she said.

"And the worst. The nightmares."

"How do you know they aren't the most exciting ones? Like the movies that scare you. Don't you like that? Aren't you excited after seeing them?"

"But they aren't real."

"So, you believe that your dreams are real?" She lifted her head enough to look at him.

"I didn't say that," he said. He bent down and kissed her forehead. "Is that what you're saying?"

"Indians, long ago, thought that our dreams were just another part of living. They knew that they were real. They knew it. Are we so smart?"

"But dreams aren't real. This is real." He tapped her back with his hand. "This place, this room. You. You're real."

"Oh," she said.

"Nellie? What are you trying to say? Where did you hear that dreams were real?"

"Dream space. How do we know that it's not just another place? Another life we get to live? I was just wondering."

"I know when things are going to happen sometimes," Keith said. "I don't know how I know, I just do. I think it has something to do with my dreams. Do you think that's possible?"

Nellie's breathing deepened as she slipped toward sleep, and she mumbled something.

Keith rubbed her back. "What did you say?"

She stirred. "What do you think?"

Keith stared at the ceiling and thought about the question. He wasn't sure what he thought. The answer could go either way. And what he thought had nothing to do with what was true. Truth lay outside thought, outside believing. He really wanted to know what was true. He shook her. "What do you think?"

"Dream space is real," she said.

The idea scared him. As she lay across him and slept, he felt nervous about the possibility. He also wondered why, if dream space was real, he couldn't remember it.

Chapter 3

DAY 2

An unusual and exciting night had ended and Nellie dressed quickly before leaving Keith's apartment. She did not talk in the morning, which he was grateful for. He got up with her even though it was long before his scheduled wake-up. He dressed in pajamas and waited for her, watched her.

"Enjoying yourself?" she said while bending at the waist and slipping on her bra.

He turned away. "Would you..." he started reluctantly. He imagined her looking up at him, directly into his eyes.

"Would I what?" she said.

"Agree to see me again?" He closed his eyes and put his hands together, rubbing them.

Nellie shoved him from behind and he almost fell over. "Hey." He turned around. "Why'd you do that?"

She straightened her shoulders. "What do you mean, why?" she said. "Does it bother you?" She darted toward him and pushed again. "There," she said.

His back slammed against the wall. His arms went up to protect his face. He had to control his emotions. After such a pleasant night, why would she attack him? What did she want?

She advanced again, only this time her hands were out. When she got close, she began to tickle him. Her fingers wriggling over his sides and stomach, her face laughing up at him, close to his face.

Frightening and funny. "Come on," she said. "I'm just playing. Haven't you ever played before?"

Confusion ran through him. His raging senses were on overload. What kind of signal would his chip be emitting? "Stop," he cried out. "Don't. Please. They'll come back. Please."

Nellie slid her hands up to his cheeks and kissed him. While doing so, she made a humming sound and then a loud smack when she pulled away. "Fun, isn't it?"

Keith breathed heavily. There were tears in his eyes. Got to calm down, got to calm down, he thought. He shook his head. He was afraid to say anything, afraid she might start again.

Nellie squared off with him. She walked over and slipped her arms around his waist.

Keith leaned against the wall and raised his hands, giving in to whatever she chose to do.

"You like me?" she said.

"It's not that so much," he said.

"Oh," she said coyly.

Keith laughed.

"Come on," she said shaking him.

"You know this is highly unusual. Companions are meant for just that."

"A night's work," she said.

She was back to normal, but he was on guard. "No. I didn't mean it that way. I meant until one feels the need to become a parent, one doesn't look for a mate, only a companion. That is how the system works. I shouldn't feel as though we could stay together." He reached around her shoulders and pulled her close so that she couldn't look into his face and see his embarrassment.

"Until one. Who might that one be?" she chided.

"You should go," he said. He had never requested that a friend, let alone a companion, come back the next day. Even if he enjoyed someone's company, two days in a row was too much for him. He usually waited until much later, after he had time alone.

She walked out of the bedroom with him following. At the door, she swung around. "Did you remember any of your dreams?"

The question caught him off guard. He thought for a moment. "No, why?"

"Pay closer attention." She opened the door and passed through the opening as though floating. She poked her head back around and looked at Keith seriously. "I'll be back tonight. But only if you request it. It's up to you." She disappeared behind the door, which closed with a click.

He stared at the closed door. "Only if he requested," she had said. So, now he had a second chance. He didn't have to make the request. He took a deep breath and smelled her scent. The room hummed from where she had been, as though she were still there. An energy had been left behind. Keith shook but there was no chill in the air. He checked the clock and found that he had almost two hours before his wake-up.

In the kitchen, he got a drink of water and turned to look at the door again, as though she could come back in, unannounced, crouched into a playful stance, wriggling her fingers at him. He laughed out loud. She had really scared him, yet the police didn't come by. He thought about his fear and what could have been different about it that it didn't alert the authorities.

Did he ever feel as though she'd really harm him? He searched his feelings, his thoughts. She had exhibited both shy and aggressive traits, but never appeared to be dangerous. Maybe that was it. He knew that she wouldn't hurt him. But how could he know? Well, no one had ever hurt him. The system was nearly flawless in that sense. Of course, that was the reason. She couldn't be dangerous in any way or the system would have detected it and dealt with it. So, he decided, the fear was excitement. She was an exciting person…in a dark sort of way.

Keith placed his cup on the counter to use later in the morning. Going back into his bedroom, he kept an eye on the door. She could still sneak in. That's something she might do.

He lay down but it was impossible to sleep. Nellie had stirred his blood to being fully awake. There was a ringing in his ears. He rolled over, then curled into a fetal position. He pushed his face into his pillow. Finally, he just lay on his back and closed his eyes. He thought about the day before and all the things that happened. More went on that day than any day he could remember. It all appeared to have a purpose, but he had no idea why he thought so.

Here's how he put the pieces together: the dream had alerted the police so that they could detain him. When he got to work, he had to make the morning deliveries, which he only did occasionally. Then he saw the boy in the stairwell. Then Nellie, who was nothing like what he had ordered through the Companion site, but was much more interesting, more fun, and more frightening in the end. Now what?

As he thought back through the day, he relaxed, and soon, even though he wasn't asleep, images played out in his mind. Ideas, people, actions whimsically and quickly flashed before him. He couldn't catch most of them fully enough to know what was going on, if anything was going on at all. But he became curious, an unusual feeling in itself. What he wanted was to know more about the boy curled up in the alcove in the stairwell.

He dozed off for a moment and the boy's image came alive, but only long enough to stir in the shadows inside the alcove, then lift his face and look into Keith's, blinking from the harsh light.

When the clock spoke his name, Keith took a deep breath and opened his eyes. He remembered the boy blinking up at him. The shadows blurred the edges of the boy's clothing so that he couldn't tell how large or small the boy was. Keith remembered only the face, the blinking. He closed his eyes and the image didn't return as he had hoped.

The ceiling's pale white color stared back at Keith while he lay on his back. The alarm spoke again, soothing the air in the room, reminding him how peaceful most of his life has been. He rolled to one side and placed his feet on the warm carpet, then reached over and pushed the alarm off. For some reason, he didn't want to hear the voice again. Every time it spoke, it brought him closer to the present and he had more trouble remembering the image. He couldn't really call it a dream, for it wasn't that. It was merely an image, a small movement, and a feeling.

Recalling the feeling, he noticed that it was not as dreadful as it had been yesterday, but something more curious that reminded him of Nellie. But it wasn't her exactly. It was how she made him feel. Wary? Apprehensive? Anxious without the knowledge of what he was anxious about. So, he had traded dread for apprehension.

He shook his head and stood. His saliva was pasty. And he felt more fatigued than usual.

He went through his bathroom routine hardly noticing the room or the items he used. His thoughts shifted back and forth between the boy in the stairwell and Nellie. The emotions attached to each appeared to be opposites, yet similar. He couldn't be sure which intrigued him more, or which was the most pleasant.

Time pushed together in such a way that Keith unconsciously went through his morning without noticing many details until he found that he stood in front of the terminal flipping through the Companion site. His fingers perched over the keyboard when panic hit. What if it was illegal to ask for a companion two days in a row? He did not know the rules, but he did know that everything was monitored. Such an unusual event would surely be noted. It would prove that he was not like others in Newcity. Is that what he wanted to happen? He already felt watched, monitored.

Keith stepped back from the terminal, his eyes wide. He rubbed the back of his neck, then turned away and walked into the living room. It was almost time to leave, but he sat on the sofa for just a moment. Closing his eyes, he drew in a deep breath and blew it out slowly and long, almost to the point where he felt dizzy. Afterwards, he stood to go.

In the hall, as he turned right toward the elevators, he spotted the police. As they rushed toward him, his reaction was to run. But where could he go? He turned down another hallway and collided with someone. The physical contact sent shock waves through his body. The man's head had hit Keith's head hard and they both teetered for a moment, the physical contact sending shock waves through Keith's body. The man stumbled backward. Dressed casually in a gray and white dress shirt and tan slacks, the man looked as though he wasn't going to work at all. Keith glanced around. The police were still advancing, so he turned toward a doorway.

"Wait a minute. Where do you think you're going? You ran into me."

The man yelled much too loudly for Keith, who held up a hand to stop the angry onslaught, to stop the man from drawing attention to them. But it was too late. Two of the five police coming down the hall peeled off and headed directly for them. The others were rushing past. So he didn't have to be concerned? Keith felt stupid for trying to get away. He'd never done such a thing before. And now he'd actually caused them to advance. His ears were ringing, and he felt a burst of adrenaline as though it were injected into his neck. The police. Two days in a row. What would this mean in the system?

The yelling man, too, was coming at him. Keith just backed farther into the doorway until his back bumped flat against the door.

"Come in," he heard inside the apartment. Keith reached back for the doorknob.

"I'm talking to you, Mister," the yelling man said, as he stepped up to Keith and pushed a finger into his chest. Again, unrequested physical contact.

Then, abruptly, the police were on the yelling man, one at each arm, pulling him back and away from Keith. "We are very sorry for the interruption, sir." They addressed Keith, but he didn't know how to answer. He had expected the officers to take both of them. What was happening?

The policeman to Keith's right said, "You may carry on."

Keith stared at him.

"Sir," the policeman asserted, "you may go to work now. There is nothing here that you need to be concerned about. We'll handle it." He was smiling at Keith the whole time he talked to him.

The yelling man tried to pull loose. "It's him," the man said. "He attacked me. I did nothing wrong."

Keith saw one of the policemen reach for his gun.

He drew his hands over his eyes and turned away. The policeman spoke to Keith sternly, "Please sir, we have this under control. Move along." No one else in the hall had even stopped to see what was going on.

Keith rushed from the three of them, passing other people as he darted away, practically falling into a jog. When the noise behind him seemed to subside, Keith slowed. He was the last to enter an elevator. A breeze of air came from the outside as the doors closed. He realized how heavily he was sweating when the air brushed the sweat across his forehead, momentarily chilling his scalp. What had just happened? Were they coming for him and then the angry man drew them away? Confused their sensors? He hadn't seen where the other police were headed and whether or not they went to his apartment, but he could imagine that happening. He had lived through such an unusual evening and night and then morning, that he would not have been surprised if they were headed for his apartment.

The doors opened and Keith stepped out and began to walk away, until he realized he was on the wrong floor. Many of them looked so similar and he had been wrapped in thought, not thinking about where he was going, not focused on getting to work. He looked around and turned back just as the doors were closing again. A burst of nervousness helped him to thrust his arm into the small gap between the closing doors. They hit his arm and bounced open. "Sorry," he said as he stepped back inside.

He focused this time and when the doors opened on his floor, he strolled out as though nothing had happened, although his body tingled with the morning's events.

He stepped into the offices and went up to Maria's desk. "I'd like to deliver the reports again today, if you don't mind." He had no idea why he suggested it, but just as he did, he could visualize the boy in the stairwell. He had to see if that boy looked like the boy in his dream image. And if he did, then Keith wanted to get the image clearly embedded into his memory in case the dream occurred again. For reasons he couldn't put a finger on, he thought that another encounter would help him receive more images, and perhaps even provide an entire dream.

"Of course you can. I'll call when they are ready," Maria said.

Keith did not compliment her on her attire today, but instead walked around her counter and down the hall directly to his office. Sitting in front of the terminal, he didn't move. He wanted to know what was happening in his life. Why were things so different than just a few days before? Was this still part of his feelings of dread? And if so, how could he stop it from happening?

His terminal booted as he sat down and said, "Good morning, Keith." He nodded and sighed. Perhaps a solid day of work would relax him. He lifted his hands toward the terminal and began to run through the day's reports. Everything looked fairly normal until he saw several security reports in a row. Normally, he would have scanned through them, made sure that the materials had passed through the right channels, that the items used were reordered, that the job had been completed and properly notated. But this time he stopped to read the reports.

He didn't get far when Maria buzzed in. "Delivery time," she said in a pleasant voice.

"Be right there." Keith got up from his desk and went out to deliver the reports. Something inside him shifted, a sense of urgency, a compelling drive, and took over. He rushed toward the stairwell as though he were going to miss something. He was suddenly aware of the cameras staring at him. He could see them through his peripheral vision. The shifted focus caused him to walk funny, at least for it to feel different while he walked, and he wondered if the cameras could pick up on such a thing and record it. He closed his eyes just before shoving against the metal door to enter the stairwell.

He entered and stopped.

The door closed behind him. After he heard the clunk of the latch, Keith backed into the alcove. A slight shadow shaded his eyes. A sense of security washed over him, and a moment later he became fearful of what he might find. Hiking the reports under his arm, he stepped onto the broad expanse of the landing and trudged over to the stairs. He descended with purpose and care. At the second landing, he saw the boy tucked into a ball near the back of the alcove to the right. Over the doorway, it said EXIT. But Keith knew there was no real exit unless you were on one of the ground floors where he had never ventured in his life, and had no plans to.

Although his blood ran hot and his nerves tingled with excitement, Keith advanced. His internal monolog was that he was curious, eager to find out why the boy was there. Was he sleeping, resting, hiding?

"Hello," Keith said while standing a few feet away.

Just as in the encounter earlier that day, the boy stirred in slow motion and turned his head toward Keith, whose eyes widened as the boy moved. What he saw took a moment to register, but when it did, Keith jumped back and stumbled onto the floor. The reports fell, but remained fairly organized. "What happened? What's that?" he pointed to a round dot of blood on the boy's forehead. And as Keith's eyes adjusted to the darker space, it looked to him as though the blood seeped from a hole as big around as his little finger.

It was as though the boy let Keith stare and become uncomfortable before he spoke. "Have you ever wanted to leave here?" The boy's voice was a whisper, fragile, like he was too weak to have the energy to speak louder.

"Newcity?"

The boy glanced up at the EXIT sign. He nodded. "I know how to get in and I know how to get out," the boy said.

"No. I don't think so," Keith said, his voice edging into the hysterical. He continued to stare at the wound in the boy's forehead.

"A bullet hole," the boy whispered. "You know."

Panic shot through Keith. "I don't know. I don't know anything about it. I don't even know who you are. What are you saying? Why are you saying that?" Keith scrambled to his feet, grappling with the reports, which now hung unevenly from their folders. "Go away," he said.

And with that, the boy with the bullet hole in his forehead stood and opened the door, with some effort, just far enough to slip out.

A strange smell swirled into the stairwell.

Keith bit his lower lip. He was almost in tears. He had never seen anything like that before. How could the boy be alive with a bullet hole in his forehead? Keith was scared, then worried that the Newcity system would detect his widely swinging emotions. How horrible. What he had seen wasn't possible.

The face—was it the one from the image?—He couldn't remember. The bullet hole had taken all his attention. He could see it clearly, could imagine putting his little finger in the hole and rubbing against the blood-damp sides. As Keith's memory reviewed and magnified details of the image, black crust grew in places along the edges of the hole, clotted into a scab. But the wound seeped still.

Bile climbed into Keith's throat and he forced his thoughts in another direction.

He had to calm down. He breathed evenly. He tried to relax his shoulders where the stress had settled, as he walked down the steps. But his movements were jerky and unsure, as when he shifted into peripheral vision earlier. His body didn't belong to him anymore. It wasn't totally in his control. Leaving the stairwell to make his first delivery, Keith noticed that he was sweating again. He decided to take the elevator.

When he returned to his office, Carl, his supervisor was leaning over Keith's desk.

"Carl, can I help you?" Keith said, almost strangling on the words that squeezed through his throat.

The man was built like Keith but had light brown hair and lighter colored eyes. He wore a blue shirt with cuff links that matched his wrist-phone. His pants were nicely creased down the front, and barely touched his shoe-tops, causing the slightest wrinkle.

"Why did you stop on this page? Is there something wrong with the report?" Carl asked.

"I don't know," Keith said. "Let me look." As he stepped next to Carl and leaned in, he noticed first off that the security report was for the EXIT door where the boy with the bullet hole in his head had been sleeping. He hesitated, trying to think what to say, wanting to scream out about the boy. But he swallowed and said, "Nothing specific. I was just running through reports when Maria buzzed me to make deliveries."

"You asked to make deliveries today," Carl said.

"I needed the exercise."

Carl studied Keith, which made him feel uncomfortable. "You were late, but credited, for work yesterday. Is there something you need to tell me?"

Keith knew that he could be credited for work for any number of reasons, and that Carl would not have access to police records unless it had to be entered into Goods and Services. He had no idea what

Carl suspected, but wasn't about to tell him the truth, which might spawn another emotional shift. But it wasn't like that hadn't happened several times already today. The police would probably be lounging at his apartment now, just waiting for the workday to end in several more hours.

"Keith?"

"Sorry, Carl. There's nothing you need to know."

"Are you sure?"

Keith looked away from his supervisor. "I'm sure." He squeezed by and sat in his chair. "I have a lot more reports to go through," he said.

Carl tapped the top of Keith's desk and put his hand in his pocket. "Carry on," he said before he left the office.

Keith took a moment and read through the report still on-screen before he moved on. There were notes of several door latch replacements in that particular place in the last month. Flipping through other security reports, Keith noticed that other doors were prone to damage as well. He didn't know what it meant, but he figured that security was monitoring the situation. It would be fine.

He carried on for the rest of the day. The boy with the bullet hole in his forehead remained on his mind, though, and he couldn't help but worry that the police would either rush into his office and take him away or be waiting for him when he got home. Either way, he wasn't in for a pleasant evening.

Chapter 4

After work, Keith went shopping before going home. The police never showed up at the Offices of Goods and Services, but Keith didn't want to rush home just to find them waiting there. Instead, he took his time wandering through clothing racks, and then stopped by to pick up a few snack drinks for his refrigerator. He finally milled around the food court and ordered a hamburger as dinner. He sat alone and watched people wander by. Everyone was pleasant, talking quietly to one another, some holding hands, all looked peaceful. The few children scurried to a play area and rode electromechanical animals, animals that Keith had never seen in real life, only on television and very seldom.

He looked at the hamburger meat sticking out the side between the buns and wondered what it would be like to actually touch a cow. Was the burger real or synthetic? Any other time in his life it wouldn't matter, but lately he felt like he was missing something. The boy with the bullet hole in his head had mentioned going outside. Or was it just into the exit space? No, it was outside. And the smell from the stairwell, was that the smell of the outside air?

Keith ate at a slow pace. Nellie had shoved him against the wall, but that was exciting. When he had a similar exchange with the man in the hall, it felt abusive. It didn't matter that the encounter was an accident. What was the difference? Why was her roughness so easily accepted? Newcity residents were not allowed to be rough with one another. That's what led to violence. The man in the hall, yelling. Keith knew how close he'd come to having the man push him, or even hit him. It's a good thing the police were in the area.

The police. Yes. Where were they going earlier that day, anyway?

Keith finished his sandwich and wiped his fingers over a napkin, then tossed the napkin into the trash receptacle in the center of the table. It was time to go home.

The police were not at his apartment when he arrived. Keith didn't know why they had not noticed the emotional swings throughout his day, but he tried not to be concerned about it. He removed his dress shirt and put on something more casual. Then he removed his dress pants and replaced them with pajama bottoms. He considered watching a movie, but decided on flipping through television channels instead. He stopped at the Newcity News channel.

"Several frightening events went on today: a pregnant woman was taken to the clinic because she was having her baby before her scheduled cesarean; a man was yelled at in the halls of the Office Workers section of Newcity; and another man is missing from the system. These stories and a Meat and Produce report after these messages."

Keith muted the news and waited. He knew that he would be the man yelled at and wanted to see if they mentioned where the police were headed.

The news came back on and the pregnant woman was the lead story, and the longest. Not only did they mention the early delivery, but they had a scientist talk about how it used to be that "the human body would begin the birth automatically when it was time for the baby to arrive." But now, with the aid of scientific auto-body controls mounted inside each Newcity resident's chip, "the body's automatic system should be squelched." Apparently, something was wrong with her chip and there was some concern over that because there were several million of those in operation.

Keith wondered how many other bodily functions the chip squelched. Was that why he couldn't recall his dreams? Only dimly remembered his childhood? His parents? He thought about what he'd heard. Didn't anyone else consider such things?

The next segment was, as he had guessed, about the man yelling at him. The video showed the police heading straight for them as though they knew what was going to happen. The video focused on the two policemen, who separated from the group and came to investigate Keith and the yelling man. It did not focus on the other three policemen who had peeled off and continued down the hall. Again, the problem all stemmed around the failure of the chip, but this time it was because the man – Keith didn't catch his name – had overridden the circuitry due to an enzyme in the brain that actually deleted a whole sequence of signals from the chip. "Scientists feel that evolutionary occurrences are the root cause of these enzymes and that they expect to be able to control them with the next generation chip. In the mean time, a standard vaccine is under test and is hoped to be available within the year." The announcer went on, but Keith muted the television again.

He watched the announcer speak, but kept the set on mute. When he tried to concentrate on the idea of having his emotions shut down, for any reason, his mind became muddled and slow. Perhaps he was tired. Perhaps it didn't matter. He had a good life, and enjoyed his work. In fact, the purpose of Newcity was to provide a safe and comfortable place to live, and things were going well for Keith for the most part.

He stood up to get one of the snack drinks he had brought home when he heard a knock at the door. The sound was quiet and he almost doubted that he heard it. He expected no one. The police? He waited as the doorknob turned and Nellie sneaked in as though she were being followed.

"What? I didn't request..."

"I know," she said. "But you should have. You wanted to," she said. She had a navy blue fabric pack with her and threw it onto the sofa. "You asked me to come by."

"But you aren't allowed to unless I request it through the Companion site. I thought there were rules against us getting too, too..."

"Too involved. I know, without it going through the Family system. It doesn't matter anyway. We're not that involved. We just like each other's company. Right?" She stood near him now. Her face leaned close to his, too close. "Right?" she said.

"Okay. But look, I had a rough day. I can't be with anyone, so please."

"The boy with the bullet hole in his forehead?" she said, shaking her head at him.

Keith whirled around and stepped away from her. "What are you talking about? What are you saying? You…"

Nellie grabbed his arm and, with a force he never expected, swung him back toward her. She grasped his triceps, dragged him to the sofa, and shoved him down. "Look, I know about it and you've got to stay away from him. There's nothing there for you. You want to be here. I'm here. You want to stay inside."

"I have no intention…"

She leaned back and pointed toward the door. "I've been outside. You know that. You don't want to go."

"I thought you said it wasn't so bad," he said.

"For me. I have a job out there and they leave me alone, but you couldn't handle it. Chippies are too weak," she said. Her eyes widened and her movements stilled. "I'm sorry," she said. "I didn't mean that. I shouldn't have said that." She knelt down in front of him and placed her arms across his thighs, her hands on his waist. "That's not how I think of you. Forgive me."

Keith reached out and rubbed her back with both his hands.

She pressed her head into his stomach. "I'm sorry. I didn't mean to call you that."

"It's all right. I've never heard anyone say that before. It means nothing to me, except…"

"Except what?"

"Now I know what that scar is from. The one on your arm."

Nellie sat up and rolled the scar on her forearm into view. "You noticed."

For reasons he couldn't quite understand, Keith wasn't scared. He was intrigued. "How is it that you're in Newcity if you're not chipped?"

"We live here. Work here. We just don't belong here."

"We?"

"I don't know how many. I only know that there are a lot more than me," she said.

"Your computer system friend?"

"Yes."

"Why are you here with me? What do you really want from me, and why can't your friends get any information they want?"

Closing her eyes, Nellie took a deep breath. "If I tell you, can you stay calm?"

Already Keith's heart pounded. "I think so."

"We want out. We want to go free." She stared at him, waited.

"How does the boy with the bullet hole in his forehead get inside?" Keith said.

"We don't know."

"How does he live like that?"

Nellie bit down and her jaw tightened. "We've only seen him on the monitors once in a while. It's as though he just appears. But he must get inside somehow. There must be a security breech. If we can find it."

"Then you can escape Newcity." Keith had no understanding of freedom or of the outside world. He only knew that, lately, his life felt different to him. Things were happening that had never happened before. After watching the news, he figured it was a crazy evolutionary enzyme, whatever that meant. His brain must have started to secrete a new fluid that was affecting his chip. That was the trend, or so it seemed.

He reached out and touched her face. "Why don't I feel the need to leave Newcity like you appear to?"

"You won't understand. I don't understand. But it has something to do with this," she touched her scar.

"The chip. You call us Chippies."

"It's like you're asleep. Like your emotions can't produce any extremes at all," she said.

"What about last night?" Keith asked.

"Sex? What is it without passion?"

He felt hurt, but that didn't stop him from thinking about what she was saying. It didn't stop him from trying to find a space inside him where he could sense her words, feel them. But she was right. He even felt dulled in some way that he couldn't put his finger on. He felt—what was the word?—muted. Yes, it was like he was acting out without sound. Only in this case, he just didn't feel the need to have more. In fact, at that very moment, he was perfectly happy to be just who he was. "I'm okay here," he said.

"I know." Nellie began to get up from the floor. "But I'm not." She brushed her hair back from her face.

"The boy?" Keith said.

"We're not even sure he's real."

"How can you mean that?"

"It's what one of my friends said. I don't know. He thinks the system could be creating the image. But you saw him. Physically. And at the same time that he showed up in the system." She shrugged her shoulders. "Either you actually saw him or you're so connected to the system that you registered the illusion."

"Why would the system create an illusion like that?"

"We don't know. We may never know. But you don't have to know everything about a situation in order to make the decision that it's not for you."

She was right. He made decisions every day, even thought they were small ones: what to eat, what to wear, what to watch. Sometimes, like ending his association with the movie group, he just knew it wasn't for him. He didn't have to know why.

He liked Nellie. Her strange behavior and emotional swings brought variety into his life that he didn't understand, but enjoyed all the same. He couldn't explain how he felt about her or about what she'd told him, but he knew one thing he could do.

"I'll help," he said.

She pulled him from the sofa and held him. "Thank you. I don't know where this will lead, but thank you." She stepped back and held his shoulders, gripped them firmly. "But you can't go outside. It's not for you. They'll take advantage of you because you're, you're…"

"Asleep?"

"We've waited a long time for you. You're chipped, but you have a slightly broader frequency of emotion than anyone else in your office. Plus, your chip doesn't kick in at the same amplitude. We think you may be an anomaly. But you're still chipped. You're still part of Newcity. We need you to stay that way."

Keith nodded.

She hugged him again.

He rubbed her back. Even though she appeared to be happy about his helping her, a sadness came over him. He understood that he couldn't feel the same emotions that she could. He sensed that there was a missing part to his life, to his body chemistry. No passion, he thought. What would sex be like if performed with passion? How different was passion from excitement?

When Nellie separated from him, he thought that she was going to leave, but instead she pulled a map out of her pack. He had never seen a printed map before.

She unfolded it onto one of the side tables. "Here's the complex."

"The Newcity system, you mean," he said.

"Yes. It's really just a huge building, a complex of multiple building types according to my friends," she said.

"You never mention their names. Why?"

"The least you know, the better."

"You're taking a great risk."

She smiled at him. Then she smoothed the map and pointed. "Many of the exits only go to another part of the complex. Like little escape routes from one section to another. Each can be closed off if something goes wrong."

"What could go wrong?"

"A fire. A collapse. Like what happened to your..." She stopped.

"Nellie? What happened?" Keith felt his face flush. "What are you saying?"

"Don't get upset. Please. We don't need things to end here. Forget it. Trust me." She turned back to the map.

"You've got to tell me," he said.

"Next time I'm here. I promise." She looked sincere.

He knew what she was going to say anyway. So, he'd wait until she had more time, when she could get into the details. Besides, by now he knew that he couldn't force her to speak to him. She was strong willed. He didn't even want to try to force her to talk. He leaned over the map. "What else do you want to show me?"

"There are several exits that lead outside, but we've never been able to break through the security at those points. The only way we can get in and out is through service doors and they are heavily guarded." She pointed to where the boy had been curled up. "Here is where you saw the boy." She traced the map to the edge, pressed the corner and the image changed. She followed that page and pressed the button again. She glanced up. "You can see where I'm going." She pressed the corner repeatedly then stopped at the bottom floors. "There are several outside exits on the opposite side of the building from where I work. There are many others that are used as service entrances, as you can see. There are parts deliveries, meat and eggs, produce, everything you can imagine that isn't manufactured inside. Most things are manufactured inside."

"So what do you need?"

"I need to know which of these doors the boy is coming through. That door will be the least secure," she said.

"If he can get in, you can get out."

"Exactly."

"What about me? Will you take me with you?" he said.

"I told you…"

"But you can protect me. Maybe you can remove my chip."

She folded the map. "I can't. If the system found you gone and followed you, which they can do through your chip, we'd all be doomed."

Keith didn't like the sounds of that. "And if they found us together? Now?"

She stuffed the map inside her pack. "Please," she said with an air of urgency in her voice, "help us break free of this place."

He touched the scar on her forearm. "Will you tell me what it's like? What the difference is? Will you tell me why your chip was removed?"

She closed her eyes. "It was an accident. Several years ago, in a restaurant there was an outbreak. Someone got angry enough to override the chip. You know what I mean. You've seen the news."

"Like this morning."

She shook her head. "This morning? What happened to you this morning?"

"I bumped into a man and he screamed at me. It was horrible."

"I don't like this. Too many events are happening to you." She turned her head and whispered. "It's got to be a system test of some kind."

"What do you mean?" he said.

"There's a lot of activity around you. Maybe too much. What if the system knows that we contacted you and is trying to trap us?"

"I'm not sure I understand."

She looked into his eyes. "I'm not surprised. Perhaps you're not able to understand."

"Your arm," he said. "Let's get back to the story."

Nellie shook her head as though she understood something that he didn't. "Yes, the story," she said. "Well, the man had a steak knife in his hand. When the waiters came to calm him down he threw the knife. I raised my arm to protect my face. Miraculously, the knife killed the chip. Million-in-one shot." She shook her head. "You'll never understand what happened. The strange tingling. The rush of pain, of emotion. It was the most horrible thing to ever happen to me. And the most wonderful."

Keith stroked her hair.

She leaned in and kissed him.

"Can you stay the night?"

"No. If I get caught here…"

"How do I contact you if I find the security breach?"

"I'll come by, or I'll see you in the hall. I'll find you," she said.

"You can't let anyone see you entering the apartment. They stop unwanted visitors."

"I'll take that chance."

Chapter 5

DAY 3

The next day, Keith awakened with the sound of his alarm speaking softly to him. How pleasant to hear the familiar voice. A normal day could easily ensue from such a beginning. He only briefly remembered Nellie's unrequested visit the night before. He had promised to help her, them, with their escape route. Normally, he would feel nervous about such a thing, but this morning he felt only calm and peace. He decided to take the project on as he would any other work situation, as a request for information that he was very capable and highly qualified to provide.

And with that thought, his daily routine began. He rolled onto his side and swung his legs from the bed and onto the floor. The warm carpet welcomed his feet. As his weight shifted and he stood, the light in the sterile white room brightened. He stretched his arms over his head and bent at the waist. His back cracked as he stood straight again.

He felt the tug of curiosity as he made his way to the bathroom. His new project felt as though it was a game, a puzzle. Could he find the route that the boy with the bullet hole in his head used to get in and out of Newcity? Of course he could. He already knew the answer to that question.

The bigger mystery was whether he could find the route without being caught – by Carl or by the system. He ran through his morning routine preoccupied with trying to create a plan that would limit suspicion from Carl. He settled on reorganizing his day, by segmenting how he went through the reports. He'd upload only one type of report first, then all of another type. One set at a time. This way he could review all the security reports consecutively, which would allow him to concentrate on how they might be connected.

But he didn't have the map. He brushed his teeth thinking about how he'd remember the route if he couldn't recall the map; how would he follow the path through the maze of floors and sections? Especially if the boy came all the way from the far end of the building? The time it took him to traverse that distance alone would mean that the boy would have had to enter Newcity – Keith checked the time on his wrist terminal – from before his alarm had woken him that morning. Good for tracing the boy's steps, at least.

Keith had an egg and cheese sandwich for breakfast and flipped on the television. The news seldom interested him because nothing really went on unless you wanted to know what sales were happening or what groups had started up that you could join. He did want to see whether the missing man had been found. He had missed much of the story the day before. He turned up the volume as the announcer began to speak of the man.

"...and according to Newcity central, Ronald was not so lost after all." Another announcer took over the conversation. "No, Jane, he was merely walking the halls a little dazed." Back to Jane. "It appears as though his chip had malfunctioned and sent a memory inhibitor spike into his brain, causing him to temporarily forget where he resided. All is back to normal now, and Ronald has been reassigned for the duration of his stay."

Keith turned the set off. Reassignments were fairly normal, but what did they mean by "the duration of his stay?" He would have to ask Nellie about that. Perhaps she knew.

He stopped for a moment and thought about Nellie. She acted so different than anyone else he knew. She was unpredictable, aggressive one moment and shy the next. Her emotions, he knew, must swing so much further in every direction than his.

He rubbed his thumb over the space where the chip was located. Only a slight bump could be discerned. Installed at a very young age, the chip did nothing more than monitor and adjust his emotions to eliminate violent outbursts. They could be over-ridden through extreme chemical shifts, better explained as imbalances, but were not meant to change any personality traits in doing so. Such was the official version drummed into everyone who wore the chip.

How could that be? He never examined the idea before, but how could a person's personality remain within the limits of what was acceptable by Newcity laws and still not be changed or altered? The two were mutually exclusive. Yet, he couldn't put his finger on why that was true. In a moment, he lost concentration and shifted his thoughts to a more pressing issue: getting to work.

He double-checked his clothes by straightening his collar and tucking his shirt into his pants. He dropped the remains of his breakfast into the waste receptacle and the cup from his morning coffee into the cleaning receptacle. Ready for work, he opened the door and entered the halls filled with residents either going to work or returning from work.

For the third day in a row, Keith saw police in the halls. On this day they wandered slowly, as though ready for something to happen. Looking around, he noticed the area fill with more people as they left their apartments to enter the fray. Many of the people were of a similar age, which made him wonder if there could have been a run of bad chips, all implanted during the same few days, and now they were failing one by one. But that wasn't the issue for him. His greatest concern was whether or not the system could control images in his brain. Could the boy be a system image?

But that wasn't it either. What was that about? Nellie suggested that the system had control of some sort, of him, of his chip. But that couldn't be true. He never felt as though he was being controlled. Someone made a turn in front of him and he almost ran into him. Keith shook his head. He didn't want a repeat of the day before.

He was thinking way too much that morning. He needed to keep focused on the project at hand. He had promised to help Nellie with the puzzle of the boy's entrance and exit. He could do that.

When he reached the office that morning he found that Maria was not there. She had been replaced. Another woman sat behind the counter as Keith entered. The girl was similar in build to Maria, but had wispy blonde hair and bright, blue eyes. Her smile appeared pleasant and her demeanor gracious and friendly. "Would you like to deliver the reports today?" she asked when Keith approached her.

"How did you know?"

She pointed to her terminal. "I have a note here on your profile. It came up when you walked in."

"I hadn't planned on it, but I suppose I could," he said. "I could use the exercise."

"I'll buzz you when they're ready," she said.

Keith began to step away, then turned and went back to the counter. "What happened to Maria?"

"Nothing that I know of. Reassigned, I would think. How long was she here?"

"I don't know. About as long as I have been," he said.

"Are you staying?"

He tapped the counter with his hand and walked away. The conversation didn't feel real. Something strange appeared to be going on, but he had no idea why he felt that way.

He poked his head into Carl's office on his way back to his own. "Good morning," he said.

Carl turned around from his terminal. "Good to see you. Ready for a long day? I see that a lot has gone on the last few hours," he said while pointing at his terminal.

"I'm ready," Keith said. When he darted back into the hall, a strange sensation came over him. What was it? Was there something different about Carl's office? He stepped into his office and switched on his terminal before sitting down. He closed his eyes for a moment to recall his short time with Carl and realized what bothered him. Carl's terminal had displayed a security report. Was he checking up on Keith?

It didn't matter. Not now.

Keith rushed through a handful of maintenance reports, standard ones, plumbing and electrical. A number of the electrical reports were from the same area, which usually meant that a section would have to be evacuated so that a rewiring could be done. The whole idea had him wondering how old Newcity was. The complex, as Nellie called it, could have been named Newcity many years ago. Were there other complexes? Newer ones?

Keith shook his head. He worked slowly, reading the reports more closely as he passed from one to another. He wasn't even halfway through the electrical service reports when he switched to the security reports. His hand shook as he read through the first two. Hours ago, long before his alarm woke him, an exit three-quarters of the way across the complex went down. It was near the place where the electrical system was failing. He went back several reports. The electrical problems actually started near the exit and moved vertically several stories, then stopped being an issue.

He rolled through more security reports until he found one near where the electrical reports had quit showing up. This time, it was a mechanical problem with one of the doors. No wonder it was hard to figure out how the boy got in.

Keith checked the time each occurrence was reported and felt that he could tell how fast the boy moved through the maze. What he didn't know was why the boy came into the complex at all. What purpose could he possibly have for hiding in an alcove?

Reading the reports more closely caused time to slow for Keith. Like a dream, time appeared to wait until he was ready for it to go forward. The differences between the times the reports were entered and the real time it was in his office began to shorten. Keith read and watched. He could imagine the boy with the bullet hole in his forehead as he moved through the maze of stairwells and hallways – how could he be among people and not be recognized? The entire process shifted his sense of reality until finally, and without expecting it, a fresh report came through for the door connected to the alcove that he had seen the boy sitting in just yesterday, and as soon as he recognized the location, he was buzzed.

Keith jumped.

"The reports are ready," the new girl said.

"I...I...ah, okay. I'll be right out." This time Keith flipped through a few more reports, glancing to be sure that they were standard service requests. He let the terminal stand at a waste receptacle problem somewhere across the complex. He got up and headed toward the front for the reports, knowing what he would find when he reached the stairwell.

He grabbed the folders without even looking at the new girl. "Thank you," he said while pivoting on his heels and stepping through the front doors. In the hall he wondered what Carl would think if he really was checking Keith's work. After planning to check reports in groups, he had actually checked them in what might appear as a random pattern, as he followed the boy's progress. Would his work appear erratic? Would it garner suspicion?

Keith, just like the day before, shoved the metal door open and stepped into the stairwell. Letting the door close, he put his back against it and closed his eyes, waiting for his breathing to lengthen and relax. The boy would be waiting for him on the next level down. He had no doubts.

Keith stepped into the open. He headed toward the stairs and took them one at a time, one hand on the railing and the other holding the reports tightly under his arm. At the next landing, he looked into the alcove. This time, the boy was standing. He looked to be about ten years old, wearing clean, but rumpled, clothes, well worn but not yet tattered. His pants hung from his waist, a dark green color matched by the boy's shirt, like a uniform of some kind.

Keith kept his distance. "I know how you got in."

"Have you ever wanted to leave here?" the boy whispered.

That was exactly what he said before. Keith closed his eyes and let the boy's voice sink in. He shook his head. "I don't think so," he said.

"I do think so," the boy whispered. He had a wee, small voice that was hardly audible.

Keith leaned toward him and opened his eyes. He bent down slightly. "What? How would you know what I want?"

The boy smiled. He turned toward the door and pried it open using his fingers instead of the handle. "We have to go now," he said.

"I don't," Keith said. "Wait. Just tell me what you're doing here?"

"You let me in," the boy said. "You listened."

Keith turned around to leave, then turned back.

By now the boy had the door open and held it that way, apparently with some effort. "Now. I won't come back," he said in a tone that should not have been audible. Then his foot stepped out, into the darkness.

Keith dropped the reports and dived for the door, his fingers barely catching it before it closed. He didn't know what he was doing. He didn't know how he'd ever return. But he yanked on the door enough for him to slip through and follow the boy beyond the exit. He slid into a dimly lit area he hadn't known existed until recently.

His first thought was to wonder about Nellie. He had dropped the reports and had disappeared. There was no way he could return to his office if he followed the boy. They'd be waiting for him if he came back using the same route. How could he help Nellie find the way out if he couldn't return? He recalled her dark skin and her erratic nature. She would not like his decision any more than Carl, the police, the system.

The boy appeared to float as much as walk and advanced much faster than Keith would have thought possible. Before long, there was a ladder made of a black gnarled material that hurt Keith's hands as he descended.

He had to continue moving to keep up, but had time to notice that the farther along they got, the poorer the condition of the space. At one point, water dripped from the ceiling and along the walls, which were stained with a green-colored slime he had never seen before. A black sludge had settled in the corners.

He kept his hands close to his body, not wanting to touch anything. He didn't want to get his clothes dirty, either.

The narrow chasm twisted and turned. Keith could imagine the path through the reports he'd gone through that morning. They reentered the complex several times, and at one point Keith found that they were in the halls of a section he had never visited. Again, the condition of the section was dingy and run down. Even the people they passed in that section appeared to dress in grayer colors. And it was like being invisible. Neither he nor the boy was noticed. The people walked slower than what he expected, blank and drone-like. He followed the boy in and out of small groups of the walking dead without effect. Then, it was into another stairwell, through another exit door, and down another ladder.

Keith had to follow closely so as not to get left behind, which meant that he didn't have time to become concerned about how he felt. And when he saw a rat, his heart skipped a beat with fear, then returned to the task at hand, rushing through the next doorway, down the next passage.

As Keith became tired, the boy slowed, but only until Keith could catch his breath and speed up again. The emotional connection between them seemed to get stronger as they maneuvered through the complex. And the deeper they went, the more run-down and shabby the space became, the darker the areas they traveled through.

Keith had never been in the dark before, so when the overhead lights were out or so dirty that they hardly lighted the area, his nervousness increased. His eyes adjusted slowly. The boy became a dark shadow in front of him. He was happiest when they'd turn a corner and the ceiling lights would be bright.

After a while, he realized that he didn't know where they were. He had stopped following the reports in his head. There had been too many turns, too many trips up and down ladders. As he tried to think back, it occurred to him that the boy most likely took a different path on his return. Why not? That made sense.

Keith glanced at his watch. They had been traveling for over two hours. "Where are you taking me? How much farther are we going?"

The boy said nothing. He continued forward.

Keith reached out and grabbed the boy's shoulder and instantly regretted it. The boy felt frail and weak, cold to the touch. When turned, Keith saw that blood had run down the boy's face from the wound in his forehead, and had smeared.

The boy wiped a hand across his forehead and the blood stopped momentarily, then a bead began to form.

Keith snatched his hand away and stumbled backward. He caught himself before he fell by reaching out and letting his hand slide along one wall. The rough material hurt his grasping fingers, but he was able to stop from falling. He wiped his hand on his pants.

The boy turned back around and continued on, walking faster than they had been traveling.

Keith stepped into longer strides. He had begun to cry and wiped a hand across his face. He looked at the back of his hand, half expecting to see blood, but there were only tears. He couldn't remember the last time he cried. Had he ever?

They climbed down a long ladder, longer than any so far, as though these floors were three times the height of the rest of the floors. During the descent, the odor changed. Keith recognized it as dirt, just like what he'd smelled at the flower shop. Was that the outside? It must be. He jumped down from the ladder and landed beside the boy.

They went through a doorway and into some sort of storage area where crates sat one on top of another, high into the air.

The boy crouched as he walked and Keith followed suit. They came to a door. The boy turned around, pointed, and spoke. "You first."

Chapter 6

Keith stood in front of a heavy metal door, his face so close to the metal he could smell it; his hands perched chest high, ready to shove. He hesitated. He had only a moment to consider what he had done.

Before he could change his mind, he heard voices approaching from a few rows of crates over. He glanced over his shoulder at the boy.

The boy appeared nervous and leaned toward him. "Go." It was an urgent whisper.

Keith shoved, but the door didn't move. He put his shoulder into it and there was a crunch and a squeak. The door opened a crack, barely large enough to squeeze through.

"Hey, what's that?" he heard one of the men yell. Then there were footsteps coming toward them.

The boy with the bullet hole in his forehead scurried through the opening. While doing so, he reached out and tugged on Keith's shirt.

Keith rolled across the door, through the gap, and let it close behind him. The area they stepped into was dimly lit, and Keith felt water hitting him from above. Ground water sloshed over his shoes as he followed the boy toward a group of crates.

Then the boy rushed beyond the crates into an area where machines had been parked.

Keith followed.

Before long, they ran down an alley and around a corner. Suddenly, Keith halted. The boy, as though he knew Keith's every move, slowed to a near stop without even looking around.

People wandered the streets in the rain. The sky stood over towering buildings. A slight glow pushed through clouds, but the rain was heavy. And there was noise. People yelled, cars splashed by, and other noises came from horns or buzzers. Keith had only seen cars and streets in movies. He knew only the horror of the outside world, which had obviously been toned down from what was really here.

He didn't know what to expect and froze in place. Nellie said that they'd take advantage of him. What did she mean by that?

The boy motioned for Keith to follow. When Keith wouldn't budge, the boy came back and took his hand.

Tears streamed down Keith's face, but no one would notice with all the rain. He felt his hair plastered across his head and water drip down his cheeks and the front of his face. As rain ran down his neck it entered his already soaked shirt. "I can't," he said. "This is horrible. I'm afraid."

The boy tugged for Keith to follow him, but Keith stood still until he saw a man rushing toward him. "Hey, buddy. Hold on a second."

Keith's hesitation ended as the man got closer.

Keith followed the boy down the street and among the crowd of people. He made eye contact with no one. His head stayed angled down as he rushed along, watching only the boy as they scrambled through the streets, making turns and going through alleys. Finally, they came to a rusted and slightly bent door. The boy stopped and pointed. "Go inside. I'll be back."

"No!" Keith yelled as the boy rushed away, but it was too late. The small figure disappeared into the crowd.

Keith waited and stared at the door. Should he knock? Yes, he decided, so he knocked. The rain pelted his back as he waited. He knocked again. Still nothing. The boy had said to go inside. Perhaps it was the boy's apartment. It would be all right to enter, then. The boy had said so.

Keith reached up and grabbed the handle and pulled on the door. It opened easily, despite its appearance. He stepped inside.

The walls had been painted a greenish-blue color. The furniture looked as though it had been dragged in from a variety of places. None of it matched the look of the rest of the room. The baseboard was orange; the lighting fixtures hung down from the ceiling or stuck out from the wall. The sofa was square, the chair rounded.

Alone, Keith realized how tired he was and sat in the stuffed chair, the cushion holding him in its soft embrace. He relaxed and let his eyes close. He wondered when the boy would return, if he would return. The strangeness of the room didn't stop him from leaning his head back to rest. He raised his arm to look at the time on his wrist terminal.

"You won't need that any longer," a voice said from behind him.

Keith craned his neck to see who was talking. An old man approached from an open doorway that Keith had not noticed when he arrived.

"You can be followed, you know?" The man approached the side of the chair and reached to take Keith's hand. He slid a pair of scissors from his pocket and in one swift, smooth motion cut the terminal loose. He pulled it away, and held it before his face, studying the device briefly. Then he let it drop to the ground and crushed it under his boot.

"What are you doing?" Keith asked in a careful tone. He didn't want to upset the stranger.

"Come with me, young man." The old man bent down enough to grasp Keith's forearm. "Let's get this done."

"Who are you? Where are we going?" Keith protested with questions only. He stepped ahead of the man, knowing that he was going through the open door into another room.

The man's grip was firm, but not rough. He had a few days growth of beard on his cheeks and chin and hair growing from his ears. His bushy eyebrows twitched every now and then. His clothes were all white, even his boots. "I'm the doctor," he said. The man pulled a towel from a hook beside the door and placed it onto Keith's shoulder. "You can dry off a little with this," he said.

"I don't need a doctor," Keith said. He rubbed the towel over his arms and head, then laid it across his shoulders, letting it hang over his chest.

"Nobody needs a doctor, but they all want one when there's something wrong."

"There is nothing wrong with me," Keith said.

The man stopped Keith in front of what looked like a dental chair. He removed the towel and set it on the floor. "Nothing that you know of," he said. "Now, sit down."

Keith obeyed.

"So, who are you?" the doctor said.

"Keith."

"Keith who?"

"You mean my residence number?"

"Never mind. So, what do you do?" the doctor said as he moved a tray of instruments into place. He sat on a stool and slid it so close to Keith that his leg touched Keith's hip.

"You can't touch me unless I ask," Keith said.

The doctor laughed. "Things are different out here, Keith. Very different." He pulled a bucket next to the chair. "You may need this. So, what did you say you did?"

Keith was afraid of the man, yet didn't have the power to resist him. He thought of the boy with the bullet hole in his forehead, and how he was delivered here. There must be a reason. "I work in the Offices of Goods and Services," Keith said.

The doctor reached out and rubbed his thumb over Keith's arm right where the chip was located. "Goods and Services," he said absently. He swung the chair's armrest around and placed Keith's arm on the cold plastic. In one smooth movement the doctor slipped a strap across Keith's wrist and one around his elbow.

"Wait. I can't get loose."

The doctor smiled again. "That's the idea. But you can lean over your arm if you need to vomit."

"Vomit? No. You can't do this."

The doctor picked up an instrument from the stand. It looked sharp—a blade, though not quite a scalpel. He also grabbed a device that looked like tiny pliers. He stopped and stared into Keith's eyes. "This will hurt, but then you'll feel a surge of energy like you've never felt before. If you close your eyes—and sometimes if you don't—you'll imagine all sorts of things, images will appear, feelings will rise and fall. You'll get the sensation that you're spinning or falling. Some people vomit." He pointed to the bucket. "Which is what that's for. But ultimately, when it's all over, you'll be fine. More than fine."

And with the last word he bent down and said, "Hold still."

Keith closed his eyes just as he saw the blade touch his skin. The pain was like nothing he'd ever felt before, but he couldn't keep his eyes closed. He had the strongest sensation that he needed to watch. He began to moan at first. He clenched his teeth.

The doctor had already slid the blade across Keith's arm, and now reached in with the pliers and tugged an oblong component from the arm. The pink device was still connected through vein-like appendages. The doctor replaced the blade in the stand, picked up a pair of small scissors, and snipped each of the appendages to free the chip.

With each cut, Keith felt a rush of unbelievable energy crash through his nervous system. Images of people burst before his eyes. He recognized his parents, siblings he realized he had not seen for years, and other people he didn't know. Images of hospitals came too. And then the pain. His arm could not move, either of them. His head ached like never before. He felt nauseous, but didn't vomit. Instead, when the bile rose into his throat, he swallowed, then screamed. As his mouth opened and the sound came out, it hurt his ears. He felt embarrassed. He felt angry. He hated the doctor for removing the chip. He hated the boy, too, until the image of the boy appeared before him and then he screamed from fear, the horrible image of the seeping hole, the blood, the utter impossibility of the boy's existence.

Keith began to scream, "No!" over and over again. Then he stopped. Something heavy crushed against his chest. His headache intensified, as though his skull had been split open. His tightly closed eyes burned. He let them crack open just enough to see what happened next.

The doctor tied off a few stitches, and snipped the thread. "That wasn't as bad as some I've seen." He patted Keith's hand and removed the straps.

Keith just sat there breathing heavily. He closed his eyes again then opened them. The room was lighted by a strip of bulbs that stretched across one of the walls. An overhead lamp had been turned off, but still held its position above the chair. His face felt flushed, beads of sweat cooled at the edges of his hairline, and his heart beat uncontrollably.

"You'll want to rest. You can lie down on the couch in the other room if you like." The doctor rose from the stool.

"The images?" Keith said with a scratchy, dry voice.

"Memories, most likely," the doctor said. "You can ask questions about that later. For now, you rest, let your emotions level out and readjust."

Keith climbed from the chair and found an unstable stance. He reached to take hold of the back of the chair until his legs regained balance. The stitched area of his arm itched, but he didn't touch it.

"Need help?" the doctor said.

Keith shook his head. "I can do it."

With a shrug, the doctor reached down and picked up the towel, walked it over to a hamper, and dropped it inside. "You've got to get some dry clothes. I'll have someone drop them off while you sleep."

"I'm not going to sleep." Keith straightened and walked through the door and into the waiting area where he sat in the cushioned chair. He plopped down and put his head back. Chilled, he wrapped his arms around his chest.

It sounded as though the doctor was cleaning the instruments from the tray. He rustled around in the other room for a few minutes before Keith heard a door open and close. Then there was only silence.

He stared at the ceiling, which was speckled with dark spots over white paint that had faded to yellow. The corners of the room appeared dirty and the walls, he realized, were not originally blue-green, but had turned that color from age. The longer he sat, the more the chair felt grimy and the more uncomfortable he became. That was until he began to pay attention to his senses, which slowly drew him to a variety of things he had not noticed. Already, what he looked at had adjusted and changed. Next came what he heard. It was not so silent in the room after all. A buzzing came from one of the walls. He could hear the people talking and yelling from outside. Occasionally a horn would blast. The rain increased and decreased in intensity. At times he thought he heard people talking beyond the walls, but inside the building. He was sure of it.

Keith licked his lips, and even that motion brought something new to his senses. He could taste the room. It tasted like it smelled, which was musty and damp. A certain sharpness to the flavor alerted him to what he could only describe as disinfectant.

While his senses played, he thought back to the images he'd seen. First, his parents and siblings. Why had he not remembered them while living in Newcity? He knew why. Anger rose inside him and his muscles tensed. He pounded a fist against the chair arm. They had no right to do that, to take the memories away.

His headache returned and he closed his eyes. His body began to twitch, and he couldn't stop it. He let out a long moan, wishing that the doctor would come back into the room to see what was the matter. He had questions.

He reached up and rubbed the back of his neck to try to ease the pain that had spread from his head down along his neck and into his shoulders. If he rubbed too hard, the arm hurt where the doctor had removed the chip. It felt as though the stitches would burst apart. He imagined blood and the vein-like strings moving around as though they were alive. He rolled his head back and forth in pain. He gripped the chair arms. The sensation of the dirty cloth, once plush, rubbed against his palms. The smell of disinfectant rose to nauseating levels and bile pushed into his throat again. This time when he swallowed his stomach collapsed into a chasm of hunger. He had not eaten lunch and the lack of food let his stomach build acid. But he would not allow himself to vomit.

He cried out, but no one came to his aid. The cold bore down on him and he curled his legs into the chair. He tucked his head into his arms and squeezed his eyes closed as tightly as he possibly could.

When he discovered, after a time, that his headache had gone, he also knew that he had slept. His clothes had partially dried. His shirt felt clammy on his back. He shivered.

He uncoiled from the chair and saw that someone had placed a change of clothes on the sofa. Keith reached out and lifted the clean shirt. It felt synthetic, but soft. It was a light blue color. The pants were a darker blue, a rougher material. And there was a pair of black boots. As he unfolded the shirt, underwear and socks slipped onto the floor.

He looked around the room and quickly changed, noticing how the clothing slid over his skin. Every nerve appeared to be heightened.

Curiosity broke through as he stood there in his new clothes. He felt completely different, if that was possible. Returning memories crowded his mind for space. He was curious and cautious at the same time, afraid and anxious.

He glanced at his wrist, but there was no terminal. He looked at the floor. Someone had cleaned that up too. How long had he been sleeping? Not long enough to dry his clothes. His hunger returned, too.

The room felt smaller as he walked around exploring pictures on the wall, certificates, mirrors. There was something different about his appearance too, he thought. He looked stronger, or more confident. He squared his shoulders and cocked his head. Then he shook his head and lowered his eyes. He wasn't stronger, just rested. Now he needed food. Glancing at the door where he'd come in, fear set in. He couldn't go outside. He didn't know what to expect. Without his chip or his terminal, he had no credits, couldn't buy food or transport. Where would he go?

That meant that he couldn't care for himself. He looked around in panic. The door to the room where the doctor had removed his chip was closed. There must be someone in there or through another door. He had to find someone. He had to find out what was happening to him, what was next and how he could survive. And where was the boy with the bullet hole in his forehead?

Keith rushed to the door and opened it. The chair was empty, the room sparsely furnished. Another door stood to his left. He went over to it and grabbed the doorknob. He waited long enough to take a deep breath, then turned the knob and opened the door. The next room was lined with shelves and cabinets. Medical utensils and packages lined the shelves. There was no doorway out of that room.

Keith swung around and went back into the surgery area. There was another door, hidden somewhat by the lack of a frame, behind the chair. That's where the doctor must have exited.

Again, he hesitated, took a deep breath, and entered the next room. Inside that room stood a table surrounded by wooden chairs like none Keith had ever seen. They were old, smooth, and decorated, carved with swirl decorations. And seated around the table in the chairs were the doctor, the boy with the bullet hole in his forehead, and a beautiful young girl with dark sunken eyes, a pale complexion, and deep black hair. Her cheeks were shaped perfectly and her lips slightly parted, full, and turned up at the corners.

Keith stopped where he had entered. His eyes widened.

The doctor held a pen poised above a pad of paper. He glanced up at Keith. "Tell me, son, what do you see here?" The other two did not move.

Chapter 7

He didn't understand the question, so he stared at the doctor. His eyes averted once toward the others, then back to the doctor again.

"Well?" the man repeated, "what do you see?"

Keith said, "What do you mean? I see you, all of you."

"All of us? And how many are there?" He appeared ready to write down what Keith said.

"Why are you taking notes?"

"Why are you avoiding the question?"

Keith closed the door behind him. He stood in a kitchen area. Cabinets protruded from the wall around the sink, refrigerator, and stove. He recognized the stove, even though his apartment didn't have one. To his left, the kitchen opened into a living space where there was a sofa and chair similar to the ones in the waiting room where he had come from.

When he looked back at the table, neither the boy nor the girl had moved. "You're kidding, right?"

"You are still hallucinating." The doctor glanced at a clock on the wall. "It's been three hours. The images should have abated somewhat by now."

"Hallucinating?"

"Like an afterimage. You know, when you stare at something then turn away. The image remains for a short while."

Keith squinted and tried to understand the connection.

"What do you see, Keith? Tell me what you see." He swept his arm around the table and beyond it, to include the living area. "Everything."

Keith rubbed his eyes. This couldn't be true. Tears came quickly and without warning. "What have you done? What's happening to me?"

The doctor slammed his pen down on the table. "Answer me, God dammit!"

Keith shouted in defiance, "I don't have to. Not until you tell me what's going on."

The old man shook his head. "Well, at least that's working." He got up from the table and reached a hand out to Keith as he walked over. "Come in. Maybe you should lie down a little longer. Let me tell you a little more about this." Holding Keith's hand, the doctor gently guided him to the living area. "Others have left Newcity, always following the same illusion. We don't know where it's coming from. We're trying to figure out..."

Keith glanced over his shoulder.

"He won't go anywhere," the doctor said. "At least I don't think so. He should begin to fade. But I need to know as much as possible about him. Then you can tell me how this started. What brought you to this point?"

"What about her?"

"Sit here so you can still see them." The doctor lowered Keith onto the sofa in such a way that he could raise his feet and be facing in the direction of the kitchen and table. "There, there, now. So, son, there are more than one?"

Keith raised his arm and put a finger on the stitches. "He wasn't real?" Tears rushed down his cheek.

The doctor closed his eyes. "I know about the boy with the bullet hole in his forehead. Dressed in dark green most often, but not always. But who's this other person? A woman, you say? I'm not familiar with her." He waited.

The boy, after staying still for a long time, turned to the girl and said something. His lips moved, but Keith only heard what could have been the sound of a breeze blowing through the room. The boy got out of his chair.

"Where are you going?" Keith asked.

"I'm not going anywhere," the doctor said.

"I mean him," Keith pointed.

The doctor shot up as though he were going to stop the boy, but grabbed his pad and pen instead. He began to jot something down while standing at the table. "He moved? Is he still here?"

"Next to you."

"And who else is here?"

"A girl. Not a woman. Maybe a little younger than me." Keith felt a combination of worry and pride.

"What's she look like?"

"Dark hair, pale skin. Beautiful in a way I can't describe. There's something about her." It was odd talking about the girl while she was in the room.

"Okay, okay." The doctor wrote more notes on the pad. "The boy still here?"

With that question, the boy shook his head as though telling Keith to say no. "We have to go now," the boy said in his wispy voice.

Keith didn't know what to say. As he waited to decide, the girl got up from the table as well. She stood over the boy. She wore a tan blouse and black knee-length skirt, which made her legs appear very white. Keith turned his head to follow their movements.

"Is he here? What are they doing?" the doctor said.

"They're both standing now," Keith said.

The boy shook his head again, this time more assertively. The girl turned to leave and Keith noticed a large bulge in the back of her blouse that ran from her shoulder to her waist. The protrusion stood out on the left side only. He turned his head away. Was she deformed too? He felt weak and tired and confused. He let his arms rest on his thighs and his head hang down.

The doctor ran back to the couch, sat again at Keith's side, and placed a hand on his shoulder. "You've got to talk with me while you can. Explain everything."

"Why?"

"We need to learn what's happening in there." The doctor gave Keith a warm smile. "And you can help."

"Let's go now," the girl said. She spoke louder than the boy, but still had a soft, gauzy voice, as though she were talking from behind a closed door.

Keith jumped when she spoke. He hadn't expected it.

"What?" the doctor said. He put a hand on Keith's hand.

Looking down at the man's arm, Keith noticed that there was no scar. The doctor was either chipped or had never been chipped.

When Keith's gaze met the boy's again, there was a smile on his face. "You see?" the boy said.

Keith slid from the sofa. The doctor stepped back.

"You can't leave," the doctor said.

"I just need to get up for a minute," Keith said, walking around the sofa.

The boy and girl pulled open the door, went through, and let it begin to close.

Keith knew he only had a moment. He swung around and shoved the doctor backwards then rushed to grab the doorknob at the last moment before it shut. He yanked hard, slamming the door against the wall. As Keith ran through the medical room toward the waiting area, he saw the boy and girl already going outside. He heard the doctor screaming for him to stop. A buzzer went off.

"Get him!" the doctor yelled.

But it was too late. Keith flew out the door and into the street.

The rain had stopped, but the streets had remained puddled and skinned over with water. The sky had darkened. The boy and girl were a distance ahead of him. He watched as they turned a corner up ahead. He ran faster, to catch up, but as he turned the corner, he saw them farther ahead crossing an alley into another street. He kept them in view as well as he could, but a few minutes later lost sight of them. He found himself standing in a deserted alley far from where the doctor was. He had escaped, but why, and to where?

The walls of buildings in the alley were wet, and litter tumbled through the deep shadows. As Keith looked in either direction, the streets outside the alley were brighter, but there were a lot of people and noise as well. Leaned against a building made his shirt wet. His back could feel the roughness of the stone. The chill air smelled different than anything he could remember. Rainwater continued to plunk and plop, dripping off the buildings or trickling down their sides into puddles. Had the hallucinations stopped? Were the boy and girl gone now?

He lowered onto his haunches and rested his arms out over his knees. Overwhelmed, he cried again, for what, the third time that day? Only that morning he was in his apartment, at work. What had he done? Followed an illusion. Nellie was right. It was the system that created the boy. But why?

Waves of unfamiliar feelings flowed through Keith while he rested. With the feelings came images he hardly recognized. Rooms he didn't remember being inside of. Toys that someone who felt like him played with. And a field of tall grass, a creek. He didn't understand how he felt about the images. Even though they appeared visually as new, they felt personal and familiar. At one point, people he knew to be his parents and siblings were sitting around a table saying goodbye to him.

He shook his head and looked up toward the thin strip of sky between the buildings. How had he come to be there? He glanced down at his hands, turning them, looking at them. He was not the same person he was only an hour ago. An hour. How could that be?

He pushed up from his crouched position and rubbed some of the chill out of his arms. There wasn't anything to do but to enter this new world where he found himself and see where it led. His resolve to go back into the streets came from a place he didn't recognize. The Keith who lived in Newcity would not have stepped into the change so easily – or would he? After all, he had followed the boy into the dark interior of the building, the complex. He had let Nellie stay with him, even though she was not what he'd asked for in a companion. Had he been breaking down for some time now? The last time he had had a feeling of dread, was that the first time? Why couldn't he remember what happened?

He advanced toward the street, hands in his pockets. Beyond him stood a world that filled him with a feeling of dread. So there it was. It stared back at him in defiance of what he'd awakened from, of what he'd done, his escape into his own fear. That's all it could be. He had been afraid of noise and people if they were around too much, and now he was forced into it. He wasn't escaping anything; he was facing something.

He glanced at his wrist, but there was no terminal. Time was irrelevant anyway. What order was there now? Where did he have to be?

He entered the motion of the streets, heard the noises of the machines, the voices of the people. His heart longed for understanding, but his mind went deeper into question. Keith found that the strange new place was not as frightening as he once thought it would be. That was as long as the people ignored him. In that way it was like Newcity.

He was careful not to bump into anyone, start no confrontation. Instead, he became extremely vigilant in his awareness. He noticed police among the people, who were mostly men and a few women, even fewer children. Stores lined the streets and often had their goods spilling onto the sidewalk under awnings low enough to hit his head if he didn't duck. Even in the rain, products sat on dirty shelves waiting to be sold.

Keith walked for a long time, aimlessly. He became colder as the light from the sky dimmed and the vendors began to pull their goods back into the hollow eyes of the buildings. One by one, the stores closed and the traffic decreased, both foot traffic and machine traffic, cars, trucks, police vehicles.

Hunger gripped him with arms of steel. He began to look for another alley to sleep in that night, somewhere closed in, secure from the wind and possibly the rain if it came again, which it looked like it might.

As the last of the stores locked down, the pedestrians remaining in the streets looked shabbier than ealier. Those with homes departed to them, and those without homes, like Keith, roamed the streets looking for a place to sleep. Many of the alleys were already occupied.

When he stepped into an alley that looked empty he heard someone shout, "Get out of here." He bolted away and decided that he could sleep in a doorway of one of the stores if he had to. He'd be more exposed, but it would be out of the rain if he were on the right side of the street.

As despair set in, Keith continued to lower his standards. Even the doorways were being taken over. He could curl around a parked car or a lamppost.

Searching the area for the right place to spend the night, he glimpsed what looked like the boy and girl. Amazed that after all this time he could still see them, he ran toward the images. He didn't care if they were an illusion or not, if they could lead him out of his present dilemma, he'd follow them to the edge of the world.

They weren't looking in his direction, so he advanced as inconspicuously as possible. They scurried across the street up ahead and he jogged along his side of the street until he could cross safely. The girl stood a few feet over the boy's head and reduced her stride to keep pace with the boy. The lump on her back bounced with buoyancy, which caused Keith to wonder what it was. He imagined a fleshy breast-like mound, loose, unrestrained. His face wrinkled at the thought. He could understand why the doctor would be curious about the illusions and how they were being produced inside the Newcity complex. Keith wondered about his two as well. But more importantly, why had they not faded? Why were there two of them?

Thinking pulled his attention from the issue at hand and he lost sight of them. Stopping, he turned completely around. The sensation of fire shot through his nervous system. He ran a few feet in one direction, then turned and ran a few more feet in another. He focused the best he could, then ran back to where he last recalled seeing them. Rushing around a small group of men, Keith traversed the sidewalk and swiveled around a corner on the balls of his feet. He stopped abruptly. The sky opened into a larger view. Buildings squatted shorter and looked more similar, one after another. He turned back. The change in scenery was abrupt.

The wider sky made him feel exposed. But he only had a moment to let it affect him, for he saw the boy with the bullet hole in his forehead walk behind a parked car. The girl was there too. Her lips moved and she raised her head to look at Keith.

He ran toward them. "Wait. Please. I need your help."

They stayed where they were. He was shocked that they didn't run ahead, instead feeling relieved and satisfied. When he reached them, his legs were tired. He bent down and panted, "Thank you. Thank you so much. I don't know what to do, where to go. I'm hungry. Tired."

When Keith looked up, the boy stood in front of him. Hair hung down over the boy's forehead covering the hole. He looked familiar. For the first time, there was something about the boy that made Keith want to vomit. "What is this? Why are you doing this?" He fell to his knees. The rough road surface stabbed at his skin, running pain up his legs. He reached, but the boy stepped out of the way.

It was like looking into the face of his younger self. The illusion had taken on the appearance of him as a child. Keith whimpered until he felt a hand on his shoulder.

He rubbed his face with the back of his hand and then pushed the heels of his palms into his eye sockets as if trying to wipe the images away. "This can't be true," he said while looking up at the girl who stood over him, expecting her to look like him as well, or Nellie, someone familiar. But she didn't take on any of those appearances. She had her own look. But he had been mistaken about her age. Her face was strong and experienced. There were traces of wrinkles around her eyes. It was her small frame that had him believing that she was younger than he was.

"We need to go," she said.

Keith's mind filled with questions, worries, anger at what was happening, but he kept it all inside, and closed it off like lowering the lid of a box. "Who are you?" Keith demanded an answer.

The girl looked at the boy with the bullet hole in his forehead.

The boy's mouth opened and the whisper was barely audible. "She's your angel."

Chapter 8

The girl slid her fingers down Keith's arm and took his hand. She waited for the boy to lead. Pulling Keith along behind her, the angel went next.

He allowed himself to be dragged along. His breathing was labored and his legs became heavy. His eyes closed every few steps. He wanted to stop and rest. Thankfully, the three of them moved slowly now, letting him clomp along behind them, splashing through puddles, the bottoms of his pants legs becoming soaked as they progressed.

The soft grip of the angel's hand barely made his senses aware that it was even there. The slightest pressure held to him, as though she were just letting go. But it held, it held in that place of not holding. He found that his thoughts went quickly to the two of them, the angel and the boy, as illusions, and how unphysical they were. The physical senses were there, but like memories, they weren't real, and they were flighty.

They didn't walk far before they turned up a sidewalk toward one of the houses. "They won't find us here," the angel said.

Keith gave her a slight grin. "Who's looking for us?"

"For you. You know," she said.

"Newcity." He let the word slip out, fall over his lips and into the air.

The three of them entered the house. The walls and ceiling were painted white, like his apartment in Newcity. Furniture had been strategically placed into a semicircle pointing toward a television. There was something ordinary and familiar about the house. Any anxiety he held had been dispersed through his exhaustion and the comfort he felt standing there.

"Lie down," the boy whispered.

He didn't have to tell Keith a second time. Although he wondered who lived in the house and what would the people think when they saw him sleeping there, his exhaustion permitted him to shelve those thoughts and to lie down as he was told. He pulled a loose cushion from the back of the sofa and placed it under his head.

Keith's entire body felt as though it had been sucked into the sofa. He had the sensation of falling. His hands and feet felt heavy and tingling. His breathing stretched to uncomfortable lengths then became easier, then easier, then — sleep.

As he slowly became conscious, he heard someone moving around in the room, a muffled sound of clothes rubbing, the chair adjusting to weight. How long had he been asleep? He didn't stir even though his limbs ached with disuse. His wrists and ankles would crack if he rotated them. And he wanted to, but he didn't move a bit. He hoped that the person making the noise would say something or do something. He hoped that it was someone other than the boy with the bullet hole in his forehead or the angel. He hoped the illusions were gone, that everything had run its course and he was back to normal — as normal as he could be.

Keith heard breathing and wondered if the illusions breathed. He had not noticed before. He heard motion, as though the person was shifting his legs, crossing one way to another. He sensed that whoever it was, was sitting in a chair adjacent to him at the foot of the sofa, perhaps watching him, or keeping an eye on him so that he didn't go anywhere.

He remembered, just prior to nodding off, what the boy had said about being safe in the house. He didn't understand why Newcity would want him back, why they'd be after him unless it was to ask more questions, to learn more about the boy and girl. And with those thoughts came the logical concern of, what *was* happening with Newcity?

"I know you're awake." It was a man's voice, and not a whisper. The voice had a strength to it, like it was being pushed out a physical mouth and not through a wall or whispered with your head turned away.

"Why are you watching me?" Keith said. He didn't open his eyes, but did move his arms and legs. His wrists and ankles cracked as he had expected. He began to lift from the sofa and his back snapped as well. He recognized all the stiffness as being there because he'd slept so deeply. He swung his legs over the sofa's edge and placed his feet on the carpet. He hunched over, his back rounded, his face looking at the floor. Then he opened his eyes and took in the legs and feet of the person sitting in the chair. Tan pants, brown shoes.

Keith raised his gaze and looked directly into the face of his father. His chest tightened. He knew that man. Not just his features and appearance, but the way he felt, breathed, his presence. More than a physical being, there was an aura of authenticity about him.

"There, that wasn't so bad was it?" the man said.

Keith shook his head in disbelief. He didn't know what emotions he was supposed to have, but a sadness ran through his veins like he had never known before. The loss of a loved one was his first thought about the feeling. And it was true. His second thought was a memory of being told that his father had died. With that thought, the room fell into a new space, that of despair and loss.

"I don't understand," Keith said.

His father laughed. "I'm not surprised. How could you understand? You've just recently arrived."

"Are you an illusion too?"

"Too?"

"Like the boy with the bullet hole in his forehead and the angel?" Keith meant to be specific. He stared. His father struck him to be real. There was a few days' stubble on his face and his gray eyes appeared moist, like someone living. The man's hair was graying along the sides, short, but full and thick. His hands rested on the armrests of the chair and his legs were placed squarely in front of him.

"I'd rather be called a spirit, or at worst an apparition," his father said.

Keith fingered where the chip had been in his arm. The area around the stitches bulged red and itched. "Shouldn't I be through with the illusions?" The thought brought back feelings of fatigue, then disbelief. He looked down. His pants had dried. His shoes felt stiff and his feet clammy. "Am I still in Newcity? Did I go crazy? The more I think about it..."

"Just listen," his father interrupted.

Keith stopped. He started to stand.

"Stay where you are."

"All right, but you've got to tell me what's going on." Keith tried on his firmest voice, his most assertive look, but his father didn't flinch.

The man leaned forward. "I don't know what's going on with you. But, I do know that somehow you can see me and hear me. Son," the man's voice softened, "I died nearly thirty years ago. Things are different for me now. It's something I can't explain, so I won't try. It's ineffable. Think of it as an ineffable goodness. I'm here to warn you to be careful. It's going to be difficult for you to know who to trust."

"I don't understand any of this. If it's so good for you now, why do I feel such sadness being here with you?"

"You feel sadness, I don't. But listen, things are about to change. They're coming for you."

Keith's eyes widened and he began to rise again.

His father held out his hand and motioned for him to stay seated. "Not Newcity, but the people who live out here. They know when someone goes free. But rest assured there are always those who are happy to go inside." He shook his head in disbelief. "Just like there are those who would rather sleep than be in the world. Even in this world, most have remained asleep to what's truly here, the beauty, the multitude of senses."

Keith waited for his father to speak again, but a knock came to the door. The sound caused his father, the most physical of the three illusions, to waver and shift.

"When I'm needed, call me," he said as he disappeared.

Keith didn't know what to do, so he rose to his feet and started to walk around the sofa. But those who were behind the door opened it and rushed inside. Five men and women came at him and he cowered in fear, pulling his hands close to his chest and tucking his chin in. His first thought was to wonder how these people could find him when the Newcity police could not, but he didn't ask. He waited to find out what they wanted.

From behind the first few people came a familiar voice, a woman who broke through the others and wrapped her arms around him and held him. His mother's completely gray hair stopped at her shoulders. Her clothes were rumpled and old. Her eyes sagged. Her frame felt frail and weak.

Keith didn't know how to react. She didn't feel as familiar as his father, yet she was the most real. She *was* real. He checked himself, and there was no sense of sadness. "Then..." he looked around at the others.

His mother shook her head. "No, your brother and sister are in there," she pointed toward the outside city he had just left, but Keith knew what she meant — Newcity.

She reached for the closest man. "This is Roger." She pointed to the others one at a time. "William. And this is Sam." She switched to the other woman, "And Sandra." Everyone nodded as they were introduced. They all looked older than Keith by at least ten years, his mother by much more than that. But Keith had seen so few older people that he couldn't guess at her age, not that it mattered.

"Come with us," Roger said, "we'd better go. There's a lot to be done."

"Where are we going? Is there food?" Even in the excitement, Keith's hunger had returned as a burning, almost nauseating fact.

"Of course," William said. "And you can meet the others."

"The others?" Keith wasn't used to so many people gathered around him, touching him as though he had asked them to. As he was ushered outside into the night and down the sidewalk toward a large van, he felt himself get angry.

"Not many," William said. "Most of those who get out of the complex don't make it past the doctor before they're re-chipped and back in service."

"In service?" Keith questioned.

Roger opened the van door and Keith edged in between Sam and William. His mother rode in the front with Roger, and Sandra sat in a broad seat behind the three men.

"Could you not sit so close?" Keith asked.

"Still doesn't want to be touched," Sandra said. "That'll change soon enough."

Keith didn't know what she meant, but the two men scooted away to give him more room. His anger abated and he relaxed for the ride. Since he had never been inside a motor vehicle before, he eased into the motion except when there was a jolt or bounce.

The sky had remained cloudy and there were few streetlights, so the darkness outside the windows encompassed his entire view. If he stretched his neck, he could see out the front where the van's headlights showed little more than the road. He did notice the air become cold and the smells to sharpen. The people inside the van remained relatively quiet.

Once again, Keith nodded off. The motion of the van and the sound the tires made against the road lulled him to sleep. By the time he awakened, there was light emerging from over a far hill. The view caught his breath. It gave him a start and he woke up completely. "Oh," he said.

DAY 4

"It's beautiful, isn't it?" Sandra said from behind him.

"More than that," Keith replied. "It's frightening." Feelings rose in him that he could not recall ever having. Complete awe was the one that overtook him. He could hardly believe the vista before him. Hills rolled on, changing their appearance as they got farther away. In the distance, the hills turned to blocks of bluish gauze, illusionary, looking as though they were about to fade into the background of sky.

The van's nose pitched down slightly as they traveled into a valley. Scenery sped past, and as he stared out the side window, the landscape blurred into a wash of color. The sun peaked a far hill to the right, throwing shadows across the road. They drove into and out of the shadows, the light inside the van getting dark, then light, then dark again.

Keith had seen all this on the television from time to time, when he watched movies with the others, but had never been exposed to it in reality. There were no words for how this experience made him feel, no words for the sensations, the emotions, all coming at him simultaneously as the van of people bounced and thrummed over the hard surface of the road. He didn't want to blink his eyes for fear of missing something. He wished they had awakened him earlier so that he could have seen this as they approached. He took a deep breath and shivered, not so much from the chill in the air, but from the staggering view.

About a third of the distance down the hill, Roger made a right turn onto a side road. The sun glared through the front window and Keith had to squint and put his hand over his eyes. He turned his head and saw that they were traversing down a narrow roadway, tall grass and bushes rushing past. The van slowed, and it wasn't long before they turned onto a dirt road, which bounced the van around as they progressed. The bushes turned into trees, and soon the sun didn't glare through the window so forcefully. A canopy of green shaded them.

When the van stopped, dozens of people approached from a cleared area near the road. Roger had his window down and the air felt much colder. "Stay back, you guys. He's still a little anxious about being touched. Don't close him in."

An older man approached Keith's mother's door. "You must be so happy," he said.

She reached through the window and took the man's face into her hands and kissed him. Keith felt a surge of anger run through him, but didn't connect to where it came from.

"Come on," William said as he exited the van. "You can stick with me for a while."

"This one special or something?" a man about Keith's age asked as they passed. The man didn't look happy about it, and Keith sensed an instant dislike from the person. The feeling was mutual.

He followed closely behind William. Sam followed, his arms out to his sides producing an invisible barrier to ward off the people from getting too close to Keith.

Long tables had been set up under canvas canopies to keep the sun or rain out. The tabletops were lined with platters of food. Many of the people, Keith finally noticed, had plates of food in their hands. Eggs and fruit, bread and muffins; he smelled sausage. Where had it come from and how could he get some?

He slowed and turned toward the table, but Sam shoved him forward. "Keep going. We'll get food for you in a moment."

Up ahead stood a tall square shaped tent. William ducked down and entered in front of Keith. Inside sat a thin-legged table with electronic equipment on it, a desk with a terminal and some other gear, and an older man who had the same broad face and raised cheekbones as his father.

The man got up and reached his hand out. "I'm your uncle Bradley."

Keith reluctantly took the man's hand. The thick palm roughed Keith's soft hand with a scratchy earthiness he had never experienced before.

Bradley excused William and Sam and told them to get Keith some breakfast, then indicated for Keith to sit in a wooden chair.

"What is this place?" Keith asked.

"A temporary outpost, you might say."

"Are the Newcity police looking for you?"

Bradley grinned and reached an arm to rest it on the table next to him. "It's complicated." He tapped a finger. "And somewhat controversial."

"How so?" Keith's curiosity vanished once Sam brought in a heaping plate of sausage and eggs and bread. "Oh, yes," Keith said taking the plate and fork. "Thank you so much. You are now my best friend," Keith said.

Sam laughed. "If that's all it takes…" he said before he left.

Keith shoved food into his mouth like he hadn't eaten for days, although as he recollected, it had actually only been one day. One day. He slowed with the thought, and looked around as he chewed. The tan tent glowed with the backdrop of sunlight coming through. The air felt warm inside. The equipment hummed and the people outside the tent were talking and laughing. The noise would have been unbearable had he been inside Newcity, but out here it all felt rather normal. He could have had less noise, but he was getting used to blocking it out while he was busy concentrating on other things.

He nodded while he thought.

"What is it?" Bradley asked.

"I'm finding that I can concentrate for longer periods of time," Keith said, automatically answering the question.

"Glad you noticed. The truth is, you can focus now, where inside Newcity everything is scheduled and arranged so that you don't have to. In fact, it's not so much that you can't focus, as that you can't focus whenever you have a strong emotion along with it. That's how the chips work, little logic circuits you might say: one input and one output, two inputs and no output. Well, a nulling signal."

"That's how they work?"

"You trade a life of security — food, shelter, peace — for a life where your emotions can run wild, where violence happens every day, where you often have to suffer for proper food and shelter. You trade a complicated life for a simple one, some say. I don't tend to agree." Bradley closed his eyes for a moment. "Essentially, why build robots when you can program humans? Well, not really program, but coerce, convince, call it what you will."

"So do people volunteer to go inside?" Keith said.

"You did."

Chapter 9

Keith held up his diminishing plate of food. "An hour ago, I would have done it again."

"Some have. So now we provide some of the essentials—peace, security, and food—just like you'd have inside. Show you the contrast so that you can make a different decision."

"Will I?" Keith liked Bradley, felt that he was being honest for the most part. Experience was the element Keith was missing. But maybe he was a little confused, too, concerning his dead father and a certain boy with a bullet hole in his head and an angel. He thought of her again and it dawned on him that the lump might be a single wing. For a moment his mind wandered to what might have happened to the other one. He swallowed a mouthful of food and found that his thoughts had shifted, but he was able to go back to his original stream and pick up where he had left off. Fascinating. It could be that his mind would be the most interesting part of his outside experience Newcity.

"You're smiling," Bradley said.

Called back from his thoughts, Keith saw Bradley leaning forward in his chair. A moment ago there wasn't anything in view except his thoughts. Could he have been that deep inside his mind that it blocked out sight? He shook his head. "I'm just amused, I guess. How I can dive into thought so deeply that I can follow several paths in different directions. It's odd."

Bradley nodded approval. "Now we're getting somewhere." He cocked his head. "More breakfast?"

Keith saw that his plate had been cleaned. "You know, I think I would like more."

"Sammy!"

Sam poked his head in right away.

"Another plate of food?"

"Right away," Sam said while rushing in to take Keith's plate. He handed the fork back to Keith. "You can hold onto this."

Keith sat with the fork in his lap and stared back at Bradley.

"How are you feeling?" Bradley said after a few moments.

"That's a good question. I don't really know. I go from complete external awareness where I am almost intimate with the sounds and odors that are right here." He stomped his foot on the ground. "Then I'm off in my own head wondering about the boy and angel, about Dad. I go back and forth. Both feel more real than my life inside Newcity that's only behind me by a day. It's strange." He paused only a second before he said, "And when I think back, that person doesn't even feel like me anymore…or I don't feel like I did then. So, to answer the question, I'm not sure how I'm feeling."

Bradley shook his head. Sam brought another plate of food and a glass of juice. "I thought you might want to wash this down with something."

Keith looked into Sam's eyes and recognized a softness of gaze coming from a frame of tanned skin and a few wrinkles, a roughness of structure. "You are being so kind," he said. "Thank you."

Sam gave Bradley a strange look and then departed.

"You were going to say something, weren't you?" Keith said to his uncle. He began to eat again, but slower this time. After putting a forkful of eggs into his mouth, he pointed to the pile on his plate and said, "These are really good."

"I was just thinking that this might take longer than usual. I have a lot of questions for you," Bradley said.

"About?"

"This angel you mentioned? Your father? This is new. I haven't encountered anything like it before."

"Only the boy with the bullet hole in his head," Keith said, "like the doctor."

"Like the doctor? Does he know about your dad and the angel?"

"Only the angel. Dad was in the last house." He looked up, "You know, where Mom picked me up?

Keith pointed at Bradley with his fork, a slice of sausage stuck on the end. "I've been thinking about that doctor," he continued, and instantly knew that he had not been thinking about the doctor at all, but that something had just occurred to him. From where? "If others have escaped, why didn't he have guards in the room, or locked the doors? Didn't he sort-of allow people to escape?"

Bradley made a toothy smile that almost looked evil to Keith. The man nodded with his head and shoulders, a great affirmative. "Yes, we have wondered the same thing. I am glad that you noticed. We'd also like to know why there is an apparent pattern to which particular house escapees are brought to. Although you are the first to see what we might call an apparition."

"That's what Dad said, that he'd rather be called an apparition."

"I must ask: does your mother know about this?"

"I slept most of the way here," Keith said in way of an answer.

"Then let's keep this to ourselves for now. I wouldn't want her to become upset in any way. You know, she's carried on with her life, and if she felt for a moment that Dan was still, shall we say available, then it may change things for her." Bradley tapped his fingers on his knee as though getting impatient.

Keith's heart leaped into his throat. "I don't know if I can do that. I'm used to answering questions when I'm asked and it feels uncomfortable holding things back. Lying is difficult; it takes a lot of concentration."

"Yet, you were able to lie – even if it was just a little – in order to get out of Newcity." Bradley set his jaw. "Look, Keith, this is important. I'm not kidding here. Before we can talk about this openly with the rest of these people, especially your mother in this case, I have to know more of the details. I have to figure this out." He began to stand, then sat back down. "Something is happening inside Newcity that can, and will, affect us all." He looked away. A breeze rippled the canvas behind him, generating a murmuring sound as it did so. His eyes closed slowly, then opened again before looking back at Keith. "You are the link to that understanding. I'm sure of it. Even more sure now that I've talked with you."

Keith sensed the feeling, the urgency, the commitment behind Bradley's words, and it scared him. If he was the link to anything, wouldn't that put him in danger, wouldn't that make him vulnerable? "I don't know if I like this. It might be easier to just go back inside." His stomach wrenched as he said the words. The sensation was so unexpected that he dropped his fork on the ground and clutched at the pain. Emotions rushed through him, several at a time, anger and euphoria, excitement and anguish. He wanted to cry, to run out screaming, but someone else, someone other than the Keith he had been a day ago, held him back. It was unbelievable to him that he could sense the strength inside, that he could notice the difference between the two people named Keith: one in the past and one sitting inside him at that very moment.

"I didn't mean that," he said. He looked around and set his plate, with the remainder of food, on a stand near where he sat. He bent down, picked up the fork, and laid it on the plate. "What now?" he said.

"Yes, indeed." Bradley slapped his knees with his palms. He was obviously focused on his next move, but his anxiety showed through his body movements, visible as tiny jolts—the fact that he looked as though he was about to stand up one moment and then would lean back as though trying to get comfortable. "I don't want you to go out there until I can be sure that you'll only discuss your escapades with me and not with the others. This debriefing has already taken longer than usual. There'll be suspicion if it takes much longer." Bradley couldn't try to hide his tension any longer and stood up. "Please, promise me that we'll talk later, in private."

"It's your camp," Keith said. "I think I can do that whenever you want."

Bradley stepped closer to shake Keith's hand for the second time that morning.

While shaking hands a small voice he now recognized as his own said to Keith, "Find a quiet place." Keith looked around to where the voice came from.

"What is it?" Bradley said.

"The boy," Keith said.

Bradley cocked his head and said very slowly, as though not wishing to scare the boy away, "Is he here?"

Keith surveyed the area. "Not him, just his voice."

"Amazing. After all this time." Bradley patted Keith on the shoulder. "We will definitely talk about this later."

"What does it mean that I'm still hearing him?"

"Somehow, you are connected to the Newcity system beyond the chip's influence." He smiled broadly again, "Just my guess at this moment. We'll learn more about that connection later when we talk again, and I can promise that I'll figure it out. But for now, you've got to meet some of the others. You've got to appear as though your experiences are not unusual. I know you can do that for me, can't you?"

It was no use telling Bradley that holding everything in and lying to the others would be difficult for him. Keith had already expressed that concern. Now Bradley was stressing his hopes as much as his assertions. "Okay," Keith said, to appease the man's worries.

Bradley appeared to be satisfied with that. "Sammy!"

Again, Sam immediately pushed back the flap and entered the tent. Keith could imagine Sam listening to their entire conversation, and surmised that he must be a loyal member of the group, one who Bradley could trust.

"I think Keith may need some privacy. This has been a lot for one man to go through. Show him to his tent so that he can get settled and have some quiet time." Bradley squared off to Keith one last time. "That'll be your home for the next few days or so, at least."

Keith forced a grin. "Privacy sounds good," he said. And it was just what the boy had ordered. "But I'm not used to a tent. I've never slept in one and I need a shower." He rubbed his face, "And a shave."

"Sammy can help with that, too," Bradley said. "We'll talk later."

Keith turned away and followed Sam outside. The sun shot through the trees with arrows of light. The morning had already warmed and the long food table was being cleared by a group of the people. Others appeared to be doing chores here and there, collecting wood on a pile, cleaning the dishes by hand, moving chairs around. Everything was done by hand, no mechanisms of any kind. He didn't see a TV anywhere, nor did he hear music. The whole place was primitive to the point of ridiculous. In a world where practically everything was automated, or could be automated, they used none of it that he could tell.

Sam nudged him when he stopped for too long. "Come on, some of the others who escaped will want to meet you."

Keith's stomach felt like it slipped into his throat. This would be where the lying would begin. The others would know about the boy intimately, except that the boy would look like them instead of Keith. And the angel wouldn't exist. His father, too, would not be part of the conversation. He thought about the lies he'd have to tell, or the information he'd have to hold back, as he followed Sam through a path in the woods.

Sam stopped at a side path marked with an orange ribbon and pointed. "Down there is where you'll find a place to shave and wash. Your tent is this way." He proceeded with Keith on his tail.

Beyond the compound stood six dark blue two- or three-man tents. About a dozen men and women — obviously from Newcity — noticed him coming into their smaller encampment. There was a soft look to their builds, and a reticence in their demeanor.

"Oh my god," one of them said, but Sam ignored it and showed Keith to his tent, which lay to the far left of the others. "You'll sleep alone for a while. Until you feel more comfortable with the closer contact you'll have here."

Keith opened the flap and saw a sleeping bag and a small pack of some kind. He wondered what was inside the pack, but didn't go into the tent to find out. He'd explore that later. When he turned back around, he noticed how some of the other escapees were touching one another, holding hands. One man had his hand on the shoulder of the man in front of him. Perhaps this is what Sandra had meant in the van when she said that he'd get used to the touching soon enough. But the group didn't advance on him. They stood back and gaped. He hoped it was out of respect for his privacy.

Sam reached down and took Keith's hand and shook it. "Well, look, I'll leave you to get acquainted here, and maybe later I'll come by and introduce you to the rest of the group." He nodded to the escapees and rushed off like he had other work to complete before the morning ended.

"It's unbelievable," a blonde woman said. She stepped forward, letting go of the man's hand she held.

Keith stood still, not knowing what to do.

The others slowly stepped around him, but continued to give him plenty of space. They looked him up and down and more words of amazement came from their mouths.

"What?" Keith said.

"Do you realize who you are?" the woman asked. "Do they?" She pointed into the woods where the other group was working away at their chores.

Keith glanced into the crowd before him without turning his head. His eyes shifted back and forth, his body still, waiting to see what they would do next. "I'm not sure what you mean," he said. "They know who I am. My mother is there."

The woman approached. "I'm Stacy. And you, my friend, are the boy with the bullet hole in his forehead." Her head twisted around to glance at the others, "Grown up, of course."

Keith couldn't answer. The idea was preposterous. How could it be? Tears worked their way to his eyes. Finally, he squeaked out one word. "Why?"

Unexpectedly, everyone moved in closer and reached out to him. He was sure they wanted to comfort him, but the overwhelming contact and closeness brought on more tears, which turned to sobbing. As though the entire experience came down on him at once, he couldn't hold back his anguish. But he couldn't stand the attention either. Finally, he lashed out with his arms, "Go away! Leave me alone!" He felt closed in.

Stacy opened her arms, but not to hold him. She backed away and with her outward reach created an invisible circle around Keith.

He fell to his knees. His nose ran and his mouth filled with saliva. He coughed then sucked in as much air as he could, suffocating from his own panting need for breath. He let out a long "Ohhhh," and continued to weep. He pleaded with his own thoughts to explain what was happening. He voiced it out loud, calling on the boy, the girl, "Please someone tell me why."

As his heaving subsided and he breathed in deep repeated sighs, Stacy approached slowly with her hand out. "It's okay. It's all right. Go ahead and let it out. I would have thought you'd known," she said.

Keith kept his head down. He said, "I did know, but not until late. It's just…"

"Just what?"

"I thought that the illusion would have looked like each of you. It sounds ridiculous now that I think about it. How could the boy look like a girl? But when I realized he was me, it made no sense that he would appear that way to everyone." He sighed again and let his shoulders rise so that he could look up at Stacy. Had Nellie known the boy was him?

Stacy sat down on the ground in front of him. "It's okay. We'll help you through this."

"It's an omen," one of the men behind her said. "It's coming for us. You didn't think you could escape that easily, did you?"

Stacy turned around and shushed him. "Ben, we can talk about this later. Right now, we've got to help Keith relax."

Ben pushed through the others. His build matched Keith's in many ways, even his height. "The Newcity system reaches farther than any of us could know. Even through him," Ben said.

Stacy gently raised Keith's arm. "Look, Ben, the chip has been removed. It's over. He's free." She turned to Keith. "You don't see or hear from the boy — yourself — any more, do you?"

"I've only heard his voice recently," Keith said.

Her shoulders dropped and she let go of his arm. "Still? After all this time?"

"Only once." He tried to recover.

"I'm telling you," Ben said.

Stacy turned to Ben. "There's got to be an explanation. Maybe the fact that it's his image the complex was using has him confused about whether it's the complex or him. He can't tell them apart yet."

"It could be that he's chipped in more than one place. He could be filled with the things. Or his brain chemistry has been altered. There are so many possibilities that we could never guess at. What I do know is that I don't like it. We need to be very careful here." Ben lowered onto his haunches near Stacy. "We've got to know more about him, and we have to be on the lookout for something to happen." He placed a hand onto her shoulder. "We need to tell Bradley about this. Let him know that Keith isn't just one of us. That he may, in fact, be one of them."

Stacy didn't look too sure about that idea.

Chapter 10

Keith retired to his tent as much by his own admission as to the suggestion of Stacy and the others. They needed to convene among themselves, he knew, and he welcomed the time to be alone. He had to think things through, as much as they did. His first concern was the connection between the main group where Bradley and his mother lived, and the escapees. Why were their living areas separated? Why didn't the escapees mingle freely with the others, the outsiders? Why hadn't his mother visited him? And the biggest question for him was why he had to keep his experiences from everyone?

Inside Newcity all residents were expected to be honest, for the most part. Deception brought on violence and caused emotional distress.

Keith tried to decide on a reason for being asked to lie, but couldn't come up with anything except that Bradley might want information the others don't have as a hierarchical power. And that wasn't a good thing in any society, as Keith understood it.

He sat up and crossed his legs. The pack lay in the rear corner of the tent, so he reached across and grabbed it. Opening each compartment, one at a time, he took a quick inventory of food, including some fresh fruit and a box of crackers. There was a separate packet containing a shaving kit, toothbrush, and soaps of several kinds. Two towels occupied another compartment. And there also a pen and notebook, which he seldom used in Newcity, but might be useful here. He remembered how to write, but the going was slow at first, even though he just wrote down a few things: meeting his mother and the others, the ride in the van, and his early breakfast. He tried to describe the sunrise, but could hardly grasp the words. "Amazing" and "beautiful" didn't capture his feelings.

After he put the notebook back into the pack, he left the tent with the bath supplies to get cleaned up. The other escapees watched him leave, but looked over at Stacy for directions. She held up her hand and they went back to whatever it was that they were doing.

Keith turned onto the side path with the orange guide ribbon and wandered downhill. The sound of the outdoors grabbed his attention right away. The rustling of leaves overhead from the breeze whispered, while the rustling of leaves under foot scratched and crackled. But it wasn't just those sounds—there was something about the quality that announced that they were outside in the open air. The sounds had depth.

The smells of morning refreshed him in ways he couldn't describe. Everything he neared had its own odor, some earthy, some sweet. A long vine climbed up a tree and hung down like a bushy flowering plant. its pink blossoms smelling like honey as he passed. He stopped for a moment to take it in. Then the dusty odor of rotting leaves kicked up while he walked. Even the air he breathed opened and closed with new odors as the surrounding vegetation closed in or opened to the morning sun. When he came to a level area where several makeshift showers and toilets had been erected, the odors suddenly turned sour or fresh, depending on what side he stood closer to.

Other people milled around the area. Keith felt watched, but went on as casually as possible under such circumstances. He entered one of the toilets first and when finished there stepped into one of the shower areas. It consisted of two very small chambers, the first with a seat and hook for his clothing and gear and the second contained the actual shower. He had no idea where the water came from but took a very pleasant shower, shaved using a mirror hung on the wall opposite the showerhead, and dried off using the small towel he had brought with him. When he stepped into the room where he had left his clothes, Sam was standing there. Keith pulled the towel in front of him. "What are you doing here?"

Sam smiled pleasantly. "Brought you a change of clothes." He pointed to the hooks. "I'll take these and have them cleaned and delivered to your tent." He continued to look at Keith.

"Is there something else?" A sense of awe came from Sam that Keith couldn't quite understand.

"You're different than the others," he said.

"How so?"

"I don't think I'm supposed to be talking with you until Bradley does." Sam turned to leave.

"But," Keith said reaching out to Sam, "I'm talking to you." He waited for Sam's reaction, but got nothing. "And you wouldn't want to be rude."

"No, I wouldn't," Sam said at last.

In a quiet tone, Keith asked Sam, "What's different about me?"

"While inside Newcity, from my understanding, your lives are controlled: how and what you eat, your activities, exercise. That's what has you all looking so similar, at least to us. Anyway, when the others came out, they stopped seeing and hearing things that the complex created, but remained rather passive. They're adjusting slowly to being outside. With you, it's almost as though you've been outside a long time. There is something about your, your, energy or something, that's stronger. Different. Plus, you are still seeing and hearing things. It makes me wonder."

"What? What's it make you wonder?"

"Well, it makes me wonder which world is prominent for you. And right now, I wonder how you're able to walk in both worlds." Sam glanced at Keith's chip arm. "Even though you aren't chipped anymore." Sam pivoted around to leave, then swung back. "I'm sure you know that I heard part of your conversation with Bradley. I don't know what to think about it all, but I do know that I'm not supposed to be talking with you about your experiences. Not until he has a chance to fully debrief you." He said the last sentence as though talking to himself. "Bradley wouldn't like it." He looked a little nervous.

"And I won't tell him," Keith said. "I'm already lying to the escapees about what's happened."

"That's another thing. Your focusing ability is way stronger than the others." He reached to open the door and leave.

"Can we talk again sometime?" Keith said.

"Maybe. I'd better go." And Sam left.

Keith held to the towel in front of him and thought about the conversation, but gained no more insight than a simple exchange between two people. Sam was trying to understand why Keith was different, and Keith was doing the same. The conversation only confirmed his feelings. It was as though he was searching for his true self among the pieces of this stranger who shared his name and body.

He dressed slowly, putting the clean clothes on and checking their fit. Then he rolled his shaving kit and soaps into the towel before he rose to open the door.

Bradley was standing outside. "Have a minute to talk?"

Keith's face became flush. He could feel the blood rush to his cheeks and hoped that Bradley didn't notice the sign of guilt Keith felt was pasted across his chest.

"Well?"

Keith shook his head. "Sure. Yes, this is a fine time." He held up the bundled towel. "I'll have to bring this with me."

"We'll drop it by your tent on the way."

Keith followed Bradley and answered questions concerning his routine inside Newcity. He knew that Bradley was merely making small talk while there was the possibility of others being around. He also noticed a small notebook stuffed in the man's back pocket.

As they entered the area where the escapees were located, the others appeared to be wary of Bradley. They kept their distance and clustered around one another, touching, holding hands. It was strange. Keith threw his bundle into the front of the tent and rushed to follow Bradley farther into the woods. When he caught up to his uncle, he said, "Are they afraid of you for a reason?"

Bradley laughed. "The change is traumatic. They have to have time to adjust. Later, you'll meet a few who have been integrated. They're different than these guys." He cocked his head toward Keith while they walked. "You may integrate early. You're not going through the same stages as the others. You've probably noticed that they're like a family of farm animals." He laughed at his own analogy. "Well, maybe you wouldn't notice," he said. "But here's what happens in a nutshell. At first they don't want to be touched, then they go through a short period of paranoia until they realize that no one is here to hurt them, then they crave comfort. That's where most of these guys are. There are a few who carry their paranoia through the touching, comfort stage, but their fear shifts to us. That's why we keep them a little separate at first. Give them time to adjust without the upheaval of dumping them into a totally new structure."

"A new structure. So, they're just going from one structure to another one?"

Bradley slowed. "That's all there is. Even complete freedom has its structure: you wake up hungry and forage for food, you create a shelter of some sort, find more food, take a mate, food again. Your body forces one type of structure and your mind another. If you have a need to think, then you find a structure that allows that. The Newcity structure is similar to the schools during the twentieth century. They were created to produce an army of factory workers, people who could be controlled easily, and who could do the same work day in and day out without complaining. Sound familiar?"

"Then what's the difference between being in Newcity and living out here?" Keith asked.

"Free will." Bradley stepped beyond a small grove of trees into an open space. The hill dropped off swiftly into a field of grass. Hills rolled on for a long time, and mountains stood in the distance. "On the far side those mountains is the ocean. It's beyond explanation. It's power."

Keith's body filled with the space and the wonder of the landscape that lay before him. There were a few clouds in the sky, and he saw how they created shadows along the ground, adjusting the shades of green and brown. The air rippled in the distance, and when Keith questioned the cause of the illusion, Bradley explained how the heat being generated by the sun rose through the air and created movement as it caught dust and pollen. Shaking his head as though disbelief was stronger than belief, Keith breathed as deeply as he possibly could, until he became light-headed. He wanted to smell the distance, hold to the inspiration.

"Let's sit," Bradley said. "You've been standing here a long time."

"It's a lot to look at."

"This view often frightens the newly freed. It's too grand. You appear as though you can't get enough." Bradley sat on the ground and motioned for Keith to join him.

Keith sat and instantly became aware of the texture of the grass and how the color changed as it moved down each blade. He saw insects, hundreds of them, different kinds and was fascinated. "Look at all these, these, bugs." He used the generic term.

"Free will," Bradley said, apparently to get them back to their conversation.

"I remember," Keith said. "The choice to live in there or out here. The choice to live in this compound, or in the city surrounding Newcity, or in the houses outside the inner city. I get it. And each one has its routine."

"Okay, so you understand that much," Bradley said.

"In Newcity my awareness was dulled. Why?"

"To produce utopia? To create an army of workers who *can't* complain? Create a place where there's no crime, no violence? I'm not really sure what it is anymore. At one time it seemed like a good idea. Maybe it still is. There are plenty of people willing to hang their choices and their emotional extremes on the rack to enter into an easier life. I've considered it myself." Bradley stared into the distance. "But I can't give this up." He reached over and patted Keith's knee. "Now, let's get to you. I want to know all about the boy, the girl, and your dad."

"There's not much to tell, really. Like I told you, my dad was an apparition. He said that he was there to warn me. He told me to be careful who I trust." Keith shrugged. "As soon as Mom and the others came to get me, he faded into thin air. I figured it was another illusion."

"He looked like your dad?"

"I don't remember my parents or my siblings. But it felt like my dad and he looked, well familiar, so I accepted my sense about it,"

Keith said. "My sense about Mom is different though. I feel no real emotional commitment to her."

"You look a little like your dad. Same hair color, same shape to your face," Bradley said.

"It was Dad."

"How about the girl? None of the others ever mentioned a girl either."

"She's beautiful. The boy told me that she was an angel, but…" Keith stopped to consider his words. "She… I don't know how to say this. Through her blouse, it appeared as though she had only one wing."

"An angel with one wing? What could be the meaning of that?"

"The meaning?"

"If everything is pointing in the direction we think it is, the Newcity system created the boy with the bullet hole in his forehead as a symbol of each person's inner self, the damaged part, the part that is either dead or dying; I can't tell which one because the boy isn't actually dead. It could be the part that wants to die."

"Then the angel?" Keith asked.

Bradley leaned back on his hands and took a breath. "What do you think it is?"

"If the boy is the damaged part, then the angel is the beautiful part," Keith said after reflecting for a moment. "But then why one wing?"

"Exactly." Bradley sat back up, rubbed his chin, then pulled the notebook from his pocket and jotted down a few notes. "What did she look like, specifically?"

"Dark hair, oval face. Her eyes were hazel or blue, something other than brown. I don't know if I really looked at her as closely as I did the boy. It's embarrassing to stare at someone so beautiful." He raised a finger. "Ah, except at first when I thought she had a hump on her back. That was before the boy told me she was an angel. At first, the protrusion was sort of horrifying. I thought she was malformed."

"Did she talk to you?"

"Very little. She told me to leave the doctor's home. Told me it would be all right."

Bradley wrote a few more things. "Huh, you followed your wounded self and were comforted by your angel. Amazing."

"It doesn't matter. I haven't seen them for a while. Or heard them." Keith glimpsed Bradley peripherally.

"You tell me if you do," he said.

"You think it'll happen again, don't you," Keith said.

Bradley grinned. "We'll see, won't we? Now, about the boy?"

A breeze swept over the ground causing the grass to sway in waves. The trees whispered. Keith weighed his knowledge and memory of the boy. When he spoke, he let his voice rise as though he was asking a question of Bradley. "The boy was me?" And he was asking a question. He wanted to know if Bradley suspected that he was the boy with the bullet hole in his forehead.

Bradley turned the page in the notebook. "Do the others know this?"

"The escapees? Yes. Why?"

"We may have to move your tent already. I'm not sure how they're going to react. In fact, that's probably why they acted so strange when I came by with you. I sensed something was going on." Then he shifted so that he was angled in Keith's direction. "So, all this time, the boy was you. It wasn't just a random image? That leads to more questions."

"Let me stay with the others for now," Keith said. "I'll be fine. Really. I'd like to be with them. They know what I've been through and I feel comfortable there. I don't feel threatened at all."

"Some of them are still going through their paranoid stage. I wouldn't want anything to happen."

"They're not dangerous. I'm sure you've never had anything go wrong," Keith said.

Bradley nodded. "I don't know if I like this, but because you asked we'll try it out. So, fine, you can stay there. But I'll have someone walk through every once in a while to be sure nothing is amiss. I need to have you here. This is a leap beyond what we're used to. It may lead us to what's going on in there, in Newcity." He held up his notebook. "I want to get more details. Our little talk here is only the beginning. I'll want to know when the boy first appeared and why you didn't recognize him in the first place. What route did you take to get out of Newcity? A lot of other things to cover."

"Why is all this so important?"

"There are millions of people in there." He swept his hand out in front of him. "This would be gone. Much of the country is farmland as it is, growing food for the Newcity drones. The Earth can't handle more people out here. We almost destroyed it once." Bradley stared into the distance. When he faced Keith again, his eyes were squinted, his jaw set and stern. "I won't let that happen again."

Keith felt a different energy come from Bradley, and was uncomfortable with it. The sensation reminded him of when he woke with the premonition of dread. The feeling was strong and had its own nuances. No matter how hard he tried, he couldn't pinpoint its origin. "Can we return to camp now?"

Bradley stood. "Can you keep this to yourself for a little while longer?"

"I think so," Keith said, although he hadn't truly decided how he was going to handle his newfound concern. He just sensed that he could assert his way through the Newcity escapees easier than he could the people in the main compound.

Bradley's face shifted into a smile too abruptly and quickly to be real. "I'll walk you back."

They approached the escapee tents from the path. Everyone there had separated into small groups of twos and threes, each group with a different pile of items in front of them: leaves, several kinds of wood, small sprigs from bushes or trees. Keith jerked his head in their direction, questioning Bradley.

"We encourage them to explore their surroundings, to take notes in their notebooks, to get to know how amazing the outside world can be," Bradley explained. "It's sort of a learning process, but it also keeps them occupied as they're going through the different stages of integration. In fact, that's what our conversation was supposed to be about, you studying the area. I forgot to tell you." He stopped for a moment and put his hand on Keith's forearm to hold him back a moment. "Their nature keeps them from mingling with the main group. Like children going through stages, they'll only wander so far before they want to come back. It's hard on them when we move the compound to another location. Unless they're ready to integrate, they have to get used to the new surroundings."

"Why do you have to relocate?"

"I'm sure you can guess," Bradley said. "And from what you just told me, it might get worse. We may have to act sooner than I thought."

Keith wanted to ask what he meant by act, but decided that was for another time. He'd probably find out soon enough.

They walked the short distance past the tents, each group shying from Bradley as they maneuvered by. At the main path, Bradley shook Keith's hand. "Go ahead and explore the area, see what nature has to offer. We'll send someone with a food table for lunch, so you don't have to worry about that. Just spend some time getting used to the place, and to your neighbors."

Keith agreed, then turned back to the escapees. Their attention spans didn't appear to be so short to him until the groups rotated through, changing which pile of items they surrounded.

After Bradley was far enough down the path, Keith headed for his tent. Inside, he took a moment to spread his towel out to dry and place his bath items inside the pack again. He was almost through when a scratching came to his tent flap and Stacy's voice asking, "May I come inside?"

Chapter 11

K eith slid up into a cross-legged position on the tent floor and told Stacy that she could enter. The flap pushed in. Stacy's pale arm was the first thing Keith saw. She crawled into the tent and sat opposite Keith with her legs together and tucked to the side. "I won't get too close," she said, "but we do have to keep our voices down so they don't carry. I wouldn't want any of the outsiders to hear us."

"The outsiders or the other escapees?" he said, thinking particularly of Ben.

"Ben knows I'm here, if that's what you mean."

Keith waited. She had come to talk with him. Fine, he'd give her space to talk. There was nothing more he needed to say to her until he knew what this was about.

Stacy looked as though she were in deep thought, her lips pressed together and twitching. She peered over her shoulder suspiciously at the tent flap before addressing him. "Okay. Here it is. We think you were sent here to save us."

Keith kept his feelings of surprise to himself by not showing any reaction. His breathing became shallow, but he doubted she'd notice that.

Stacy took a deep breath. "Well, not all of us," she nodded to herself, "but most."

"What are you trying to say exactly?" Keith said.

"Ben and one or two others seem to think that the system is still controlling you and that you're here as a beacon and that they're coming to kill us."

"I thought you said he knew you were here."

"He does," she said.

"So, why would the system want to kill you?"

Her eyes looked down at a spot between them. "So we don't kill it."

Keith shook his head and scrunched his face in question.

"That's what Bradley is planning," she said.

"How would you know that?

"Tonight, I'll come for you and show you."

"And the rest of you," he asked, "how do you think I'm going to save you?"

"We believe that millions of lives are at stake. Not just ours." Stacy placed her hand on Keith's knee. "We need to warn them. I don't think they want to kill us. They want to stop Bradley and the others from killing them. We'll just get in the way. You are our savior; perhaps you're theirs as well. Some of us believe that a few at a time will escape until we're all free. But we're not free until we're away from Bradley."

"How many of you came out together? A few at a time, or one?"

"Half of us. Five or six at a time," she said. "Always, someone would have to sacrifice getting caught so that the rest of us could make it. But, you came out alone."

"Bradley never mentioned that."

"He wouldn't."

Keith didn't want to be anyone's savior. The whole idea felt wrong to him. But there was no reason to tell Stacy that, not yet. He needed to understand more about what was going on before he could act at all. "Why doesn't he kill escapees a few at a time as they come out? He appears to know where they'll be taken. Wouldn't that be easier than trying to destroy Newcity?"

"Two reasons," she said. "First, he believes others might be escaping through other parts of the building and that eventually everyone will leave at once. He's fearful of what would happen if Newcity poured that many paranoid schizophrenics into the world. And second, he needs our help. They're a small band of dissidents. What can they do alone?"

Keith listened quietly while Stacy explained how she and the others escaped by following the boy with the bullet hole in his forehead. How he wound them through the complex, often running into maintenance crews completing minor repairs. Because they were traveling in a group, the Newcity Police became suspicious and eventually attempted to arrest them. That's when one or two of the others fell back and were apprehended. "So that we could escape," she said.

It didn't take much thought at all for Keith to guess that the system's illusion, the boy, had followed paths that he must have laid while running through his morning reports. He wanted to reject the idea, but it was so clear to him at that moment. "No," he said.

"What is it?" Stacy sat upright and looked around even though there was nothing to see but the inside of the tent.

"You've got to go now," Keith said.

"Are you all right?"

"I have to be alone, that's all."

Stacy's passivity wouldn't allow her to resist his wishes and he knew it. She made her way out of the tent in a rush, the flap sending a breeze over him as she exited.

The system had used him to find a way out for the others. It also used him to create an escape route for himself. His consciousness, or subconsciousness, as it would seem, linked directly with that of the Newcity system. If he was still hearing the boy with the bullet hole in his forehead, that meant that he was still connected to the system. He must be. In which case, Ben was more likely to be right than Stacy. Newcity would know where he was as long as there was contact. But he hadn't seen nor heard the boy or the angel for a few hours now. Perhaps the connection had finally broken off.

Keith took out his notebook and jotted down some of the possibilities of what might be going on. He didn't outright reject what Stacy had told him, but did recognize that she probably wasn't thinking very clearly, that the escapees would keep to a simple conclusion. Since he looked like the boy with the bullet hole in his forehead, she automatically saw him as their leader. He led them out of Newcity after all, so why not lead them away from here as well? It made sense.

Bradley, on the other hand, appeared open and trustworthy one second and mysteriously vague the next. There was nothing simple about him. Keith had sensed an anxious anger under the surface of the man's outward congeniality and didn't know what to think of it. Then there was Sam and how frightened he appeared to be, yet curious about Keith's difference. Had Sam been an escapee at one time? Had he been integrated?

Keith jotted down the questions so that he could go over them later as he got more clues as to the truth. It could be, he wrote, that Stacy, like the rest of the escapees, was merely exercising her paranoia. Ben mistrusted Keith, where she mistrusted Bradley. The simplest possibility, clearly, was that Bradley was telling the truth and that he was helping the escapees to integrate. His uneasiness at times could be from all the responsibility he was forced to handle. As Stacy had put it, the outside world couldn't handle an inrush of millions of paranoid schizophrenics.

It wasn't long before people from the main group brought tables and set them up for lunch. Sam retrieved Keith from his tent, by standing outside and softly requesting him to come out and join the others.

Keith put his notebook and pen into his pocket and crawled out. His body felt sore from lying on the mat. He noticed each ache separately: the tightness in his hip and shoulder, a crick in his neck from leaning on his side while holding his head straight. The air temperature, as soon as he got outside the tent, dropped ten degrees, and he rubbed his hands over his arms.

"I'll have someone bring a jacket or sweater for you," Sam said. "I'm sorry I didn't think of it earlier."

"Thank you," Keith said.

The others had lined up and were placing fruit and bread onto plates. There were a pot of soup and what looked like cornbread as well.

"You should get something to eat," Sam said. He stood close to Keith and his voice was low.

Keith turned to him and asked, "Were you an escapee?"

Sam smiled and lowered his eyes. "No. But I appreciate your thinking so. I'm just more passive than the others. When you're born out here, it's a choice. This is what I choose. Bradley always tells me how lucky I am to be able to choose what others are forced to experience."

"Would it matter if you didn't know the difference?" Keith whispered.

"Yes. It does to me now. Maybe if I were in Newcity I wouldn't be able to concentrate enough to know the difference, but knowing what I know out here, it matters a lot."

"And the people in Newcity don't have a choice," Keith added.

"Originally they do. Only a few are born inside. Although some choose a placid life over a complicated and potentially dangerous one, others are sold into Newcity."

"Sold?"

Sam abruptly ended the conversation by announcing in a loud voice, "You should grab something now before it's gone."

Sam was obviously uncomfortable talking about such subjects. But Keith wanted a response to one last question. He turned to Sam and looked in his eyes, something he would never have done in Newcity, something that came from a place so deep inside him that it frightened him, even as he did it. He asked, "Do you think that in some way, the escapees are changing their minds? That it's possible that they're making a different choice?"

Sam walked away in a hurry and stood near some of the other members of Bradley's group.

Keith thought he may have hit on something and planned to consider it later, when it was quiet and he had the time to think. Right now, the noise of escapees talking and piling food onto plates wasn't the time to think. He got in line behind one of the others. He had never been introduced to any of them except Stacy, who had introduced herself.

As Keith stepped in line, the man in front of him backed away. "Please go on," he said.

"I'm in no hurry," Keith said.

Then several more in line backed away as well. "Please go," a woman who stood several people down the line said. "Or we could get it for you? You could wait in your tent, or find a place to sit? Whatever you want." She lowered her head.

One of the men from the main group must have been troubled by what was going on and charged in to break it up. "He's able to

get his own food. Just finish up here. We've got other things to do."
He pointed for them to get back to the table and closed in behind the
escapees, forcing them to step back into line.

The escapees shot into place, outwardly nervous about what had
happened. Two stopped filling their plates altogether and walked
away.

Keith stepped up to the table and ladled out two large portions
of soup. A few steps farther down he grabbed two pieces of
cornbread in one hand. He left the group and sat behind his tent.

Stacy joined him a few minutes later. "See what I mean?" she
said, standing over him. "We'll do whatever you ask."

"I'm not here to save anyone," Keith said. "I'll be lucky if I can
figure out what's going on at all. And then I doubt there's anything I
can do about it. Besides, what do you need to be saved from? You
have food and shelter and nothing to do all day."

"Until we're integrated. Then everything changes. I don't know
for sure, but I've heard stories and it's not good." She leaned against
a tree trunk.

Keith sat on the ground and ate, looking up at her every once in
a while. "Maybe the system needed someone to fashion the boy's
image out of and I won the lottery. And you can tell Ben and the
others that I haven't heard from the boy for a long time now. The
connection has been cut. I'm not a beacon."

She looked disappointed. "I'll tell him," she said. A few more
short moments went by as she stared at him as though trying to
figure something out, then she left without another word.

Keith felt a tinge of guilt about how he handled their
conversation, but rationalized his response based on how
uncomfortable he was with the way things were progressing. His
frustration easily grew to anger. And the truth was that she expected
something from him that he wasn't ready or willing to provide.

Sam came by for Keith's bowl well after he had finished eating.
The bowl sat on the ground next to him, a small stream of ants
already finding their way up its side. He had been watching them for
a while when Sam rounded the corner of the tent and swung down
and grabbed the bowl. "What was that about? Earlier?"

"Being nice to the new guy? Overly polite?" Keith said.

"No, there was something else. I saw how they looked at you."

Keith turned his head away. "I don't know what you mean. I just got here. I don't even know their names." Keith started to get up when several of Bradley's group came around the tent and grabbed his arms.

Sam stood back to let them through. When Keith shot him a confused look he said, "I'm sorry, but this is for your own good."

"So what are you going to do with me?"

"Bring you along," Sam said. "Something isn't right here and I have to let Bradley know. I didn't want to leave you with them after what I saw."

When they dragged Keith around the tent, half of the escapees stood in front of them so that they couldn't get by.

"It's all right," Keith said. "I'm just going to talk with Bradley."

"You don't have to go," said the woman who talked to him while they were in line at the food table.

"What are you going to do, hug us to death?" one of Bradley's men said through a large smile. He pulled on Keith's arm to move forward.

The escapees didn't move and Keith could feel the strength of their fear. He realized that they would push through their own terror to help him. They would stand firm until forced to move.

Keith raised his hands the best he could with the two thugs holding him. "Seriously," he said, glancing around until he saw Stacy. "Can you call them off? I'm fine. I can take care of this. He just wants to talk." He knew she'd listen.

"We'll have him back this afternoon," Sam said to the crowd. His words appeared to help the situation even though Keith knew that they weren't sincere. Sam had no idea what would happen.

The escapees turned to Stacy who nodded affirmatively. "Let them go."

The escapees parted enough for Keith and the others to pass through. Ben, surprisingly, had been one of those standing in the way and Keith wondered what might have changed his mind that he would want to help the others on Keith's behalf. That was unless Ben had other plans for Keith, plans his departure would foil.

On the way down the path Keith's abductors loosened their grips on his upper arms and allowed him to walk on his own. Where would he run to anyway? He had no idea where they were.

"Damned newbies," one of the men said.

Sam didn't say anything in way of a reprimand, which got Keith to thinking about the apprehension and how unusual it was that Sam appeared to be in charge of it. Yes, he was a trusted member of Bradley's group, but his personality wasn't that of a leader or decision maker. What would bring him to such action unless he was truly worried for Keith?

The men yanked Keith around a corner, which brought him back to the situation. He knew where they were going and should have been more aware. Now they held onto him more firmly, which was something he could have avoided.

When they arrived at Bradley's tent, one of the men put a hand on Keith's head to get him to bend down as he entered. Inside the tent he could stand again. "Sit down," the man who had called him a newbie said. Then he gave Sam a look of contention before leaving with the other man.

"Bradley will be here soon," Sam said.

Keith heard Bradley approaching from outside, swearing as he got closer.

Bradley crashed into the tent and stomped to a stop. "What the fuck is going on now?"

Sam looked scared. "When he was…"

"I'm not asking you, for Christ's sake, I'm asking him," Bradley stood close to Keith.

"I'm not sure," Keith said.

"I don't have all day here. You and I both know there's more to this than a simple act of politeness." He turned around. "I knew I shouldn't have put you with them. Especially after I found out you were the boy. Do they know about the girl? Your dad?" He snatched a chair and swung it around backwards and sat down with his arms crossed over its back. "Did you tell them?"

"No," Keith said.

"Then what is it?"

"They think I'm here to save them," Keith said.

"Save them from what? Me? The fucking nut cases. Listen to me, without the proper integration they'd just be a bunch of crazies on the loose. Half of them would have killed the other half by now." He puffed his cheeks and let out a long breath of air. "The system probably created the boy from your image as a random act, and they're reading into it."

"That's what I thought," Keith said. "But some of them think I'm some sort of beacon leading the Newcity police to you."

Bradley appeared to think that was funny. He laughed and looked over at Sam who smiled uncomfortably. "First of all, the Newcity police are worthless. They'd have to call on the guards who control the perimeter. They're, at least, used to dealing with outsiders." He leaned in toward Keith. "See, I know what the escapees call us." He sat back and said, "And second, I've tested every frequency possible and you're not a beacon. I guarantee it."

He stood up and lifted the chair out of the way. Bradley always acted anxious, as though he had a dozen other things to do and was late for every one of them. He tapped a finger to his chin. "You haven't had a visitation yet?"

"No," he said.

"It's like you're already integrated. You aren't like the others and I don't quite know why." He snapped his fingers. "You stay in our camp tonight. Sammy, get things ready."

"Yes, sir," Sam said.

"Can I see my mother?" Keith said.

Bradley said, "Maybe tomorrow. You're the first to come through who has family with us. I'm afraid that close contact could bring back too many childhood memories, which may cause you to exhibit other psychological symptoms. You understand, don't you?"

"I think so. But what could I remember that's so important? Did she sell me to Newcity?"

Bradley waited before he answered the question, and when he did answer he spoke slowly. "I'm not sure I know what you're talking about. My concern is that you've only been here a short while and I think it would be too much emotional stimulus for you to handle."

"But you said that I was integrating quickly," Keith said.

Bradley backhanded Keith and knocked him off the chair to the ground. "I said no."

The slap rang through Keith's head. He touched a hand to his jaw. Somehow, he had felt Bradley's anger as sure as he felt the man's hand across his face. Just as quickly as the anger came it subsided. The violence had drained Bradley's anger instantly.

The big man opened the tent flap to go. He turned to Sam and said softly, "Get him out of here. I'm too busy for this shit."

Chapter 12

I t took Sam a moment or two to gain his composure. When he did, he rushed over to Keith and helped him up.

"I'm all right," Keith said while taking his seat again.

"Are you sure?"

Keith looked into Sam's eyes and saw nothing but compassion. "It's not your fault." At times, Keith heard the words that came from his mouth but didn't recognized them as his own. This was one of those times. The slap had been some sort of wake-up call. He knew that now. The air had changed, the tent and its furnishings, even Sam, standing before him emitted a different energy. Keith rested and took in the area. He was sweating and ran a hand across his forehead. Feeling the dampness, he automatically checked for blood but there was only sweat smeared across his hand.

"You don't look right," Sam said.

"How do you mean?"

"I don't know. You should be enraged, but instead you appear meditative, like you detached from the situation." Sam stared in what looked like awe.

"Give me a minute," Keith said. His eyes jerked from one item to the next, taking in the contents of the tent. Everything he inspected took on a life of its own: the desk produced the sensation of firmness and solidity, electronic equipment chattered and hummed with motion, a lamp slept in place, and even the tent produced its own essence, its own vitality.

"You're making me nervous," Sam said. "What are you doing?"

"Taking it all in," Keith said. As he let the space settle into a flow of its own, a harmony of existence, the boy with the bullet hole in his forehead stepped from behind a stack of boxes. Keith stopped looking around and stared at the boy. He took a calming breath. He opened to how Sam felt: nervous.

"You must stay awake," the boy said.

Keith thought to ask what the boy meant, but decided against it while in the presence of nervous Sam. He closed his eyes for only a moment. When he opened them again, the boy was still there. Keith waited, but the boy said nothing more.

The boy with the bullet hole in his forehead, the boy who appeared to be a younger version of Keith, walked toward the entrance to the tent and passed through as though a breeze had parted the flap ahead of him.

Sam snapped out of his silence and reached for Keith, escorting him out of the tent and down the path behind the boy.

Keith couldn't understand what was happening.

A short distance in the opposite direction of the escapees' tents there was an opening in the forest. Keith's tent had been set up next to several others. The boy entered Keith's tent.

Sam stopped in front of the tent and turned to Keith.

"I'm staying here now?" Keith asked.

"My tent is next to yours," Sam trained his eye on the tent to the left. "There's a lot more activity around here, but you'll be safer."

"I was safe with the others," Keith said.

"Don't be so sure," Sam said before he left.

When Keith crawled into the tent, the boy was gone. "I had questions," he said to no one. "First of all, how did you get Sam to follow you when he couldn't see you?" Keith lay down on his back and closed his eyes.

As he relaxed in the warmth of the tent air, he heard the boy say, "It was you who showed him the way."

Keith jerked his eyes open and sat up. He was still alone in the tent. "Okay then," he said. He lay back down and whispered, "How could I lead Sam if I didn't know where to go?" The inner voice that was the boy didn't respond. Keith forced his relaxation and almost fell asleep, but there was no more contact. He removed the notebook from his pocket and jotted down what had happened. The boy had told him to stay awake, so he left the tent and took a short walk. Sam had been right; there were many more people from Bradley's group on that side of the camp. Most of them appeared to be going somewhere in a hurry, while others Keith ran into were sitting and talking.

The afternoon sped along as Keith attempted to sort out what had happened in Bradley's tent. His greatest question was whether or not Bradley knew what he had done in awakening Keith into contact with the boy with the bullet hole in his forehead. Was Bradley that aware?

Keith rejected the notion and decided that the boy had manipulated Bradley to open Keith's communications, and not the other way around. Either way, a lot of questions were still unanswered.

The rest of the afternoon, Keith paid more attention to the natural elements around him. He walked to the edge of the woods and stared at the hillside, taking in all the colors and textures of the grasses, the bushes, the trees. Birds and insects fascinated him. At one point, he glimpsed an animal running through the field, its short body partially hidden in the tall grass. The creature's dark color scurried like a deep shadow along the ground. The world was enormous in size and varied in its things, both living and nonliving. Keith found it difficult to take it all in through his senses. Surely, he couldn't see, smell, listen, and feel all at the same time. His sight became a fuzzy background image whenever he concentrated fully on listening. And when he noticed details in the images before him, the sound of insects would fade. It was like all his senses were being tested at once, but he could only read them one or two at a time.

That evening Keith ate alone. Sam brought him a plate of chicken and rice and another bottle of water. They talked briefly before Sam announced that he had to go help the others. Keith's wanderings during the day had tired him out, but he wandered a little ways away until the trees opened to the sky, which had taken on an orange glow. Keith could not describe the feeling he received from just looking at the sky. He pulled the notebook from his pocket and wrote down the colors, the random shapes, and the fact that the clouds were layered, but the words meant nothing without the image. He put the notebook back into his pocket and stood in silence. In less than a half hour the colors brightened, streaks of white luminescence lined one of the layers before fading into night. With a glimmer of light pushing through, and little color other than gray and blue, Keith made his way back to his tent.

He had only been outside of Newcity a few days and already so much had happened to and around him. He needed a good night's sleep.

Keith saw that his dinner plate, which he had set on the ground outside his tent, had been collected for cleaning. The others were very attentive and efficient in the camp, almost as efficient as Newcity.

He crawled inside the tent, still a little hungry, and ate a few of the crackers from his pack. He thought to take notes, but rejected the idea in favor of sleep. The darkness inside the canvas would have made it difficult to see anyway.

He slipped out of his shoes and socks, pants and shirt and climbed into the sleeping bag. As the light from outside dimmed into complete darkness, noises became more noticeable: a scraping sound, buzzing, occasionally something moving through the fallen leaves. Keith listened for a long while, trying to imagine what each sound belonged to. He had heard many of the sounds before, in movies, but had never been in nature as long as he could remember, although he knew that he had been on the outside as a young man, perhaps until he was the age of the boy with the bullet hole in his forehead. Even when he glimpsed a memory of his family, they were always inside a house or apartment, but the general feeling was that they were somewhere other than inside Newcity.

Before allowing himself to nod off, Keith asked the boy how long he was supposed to stay awake, but there was no answer. He asked the angel with one wing the same question, but received more silence. Finally, he asked for help from his father. "What must I do now?" Again, there was no answer. The tent closed in on him then and he slept dreamlessly.

DAY 5

It wasn't morning when he was roused from sleep by a hand over his mouth and a voice in his ear saying, "Be still; it's me, Stacy."

Keith rose to a sitting position and let his head clear.

A small amount of light sifted into the tent, allowing him to see her brown eyes and blonde hair close to his face. Shadow highlighted the roundness of her cheeks. Her breath was stale.

She turned her face away from him and whispered for him to get dressed as fast as he could and to grab his pack.

He acknowledged her command, and tapped her back when he was ready. He followed her through the flap and into the misty night air. The light came from the sky, but Keith couldn't tell its source, and only guessed that it was the moon and not lights set up around the camp.

Stacy reached for his hand and tugged aggressively for him to follow. He stumbled only once as they traveled the paths at night. There were twists and turns into side paths that he could not have remembered. As they came to a halt he wondered if this was the reason the boy had asked him to stay awake. He wondered how long he had been asleep. Was it minutes or hours?

There was little time to consider those thoughts. A large truck stood before them. Stacy dragged Keith to the rear of the vehicle where it was open. Inside were crates. Some were marked EXPLOSIVES in large block letters. "Weapons," Stacy said. "Do you see?"

Before he could answer, she tugged on his arm and he followed her for a short distance farther until they reached a parked van. The van looked similar to the one that had brought him to camp the morning before. Even in the moon's light, Keith could see that this one was dirt-streaked along its sides, and the windows were darkened with a layer of dust. A door opened along the side and Stacy guided him into a seat in the rear next to a man who already occupied the bench. The rest of the van was filled with people he couldn't recognize in the dim light.

No sooner were they settled into their seats than the van pulled away slowly onto the dirt road. The farther they got from camp, the faster the van transported them, until it bounced like a rolled ball rolled over an embankment. Keith held to the seat cushion on either side of his legs, pulling upward to affix his butt to the seat. The rescue had happened so quickly that he didn't have time to consider what might be going on.

When they finally hit an asphalt road and the ride smoothed considerably, he turned to Stacy. "Where are you taking me?"

"To safety," she said.

"Or not," someone said in front of him. The man turned and Keith recognized him as one of the escapees. "What's going on?" Keith asked. They weren't stable enough to be on their own. He glanced around to locate Ben, but only recognized one other person, and that was Sam, who was driving the van. Keith could see his profile whenever he turned to listen to the conversation that had started. "Sam?"

"Yes," Stacy said. "We planned this to get you out of there. Sam convinced Bradley to relocate your tent, making it easier for us to get you to the van. We weren't totally ready, but they were going to integrate me and we knew that Ben would try to kill you."

"Kill me? But if he just came from Newcity..."

"Don't kid yourself," she said. "That is when we're most violent. I don't know why you haven't noticed it in yourself."

"Yes, you do," Sam yelled back.

Others from in front of Keith turned to look at him. He recognized several escapees, but didn't know others in the group. He did remember the man who sat next to him as the same man who had held hands with Stacy when he first met the cluster of them. Then he noticed another fact that surprised him—the group he rode with appeared to be paired off. There were two women and two men in front of him and a woman rode in the seat next to Sam. The feeling it brought on was one of separation, of loneliness. He lowered his eyes and reached inside for a reason why they'd pair up, as well as why they would kidnap him from the camp, from Bradley.

"When are you going to tell me what's going on? What's really going on?" he said forcefully, knowing that Stacy would break.

She leaned forward and smiled at her partner, then looked into Keith's eyes. "That never did work, you know. Didn't you hear me a moment ago? I just told you that they were going to integrate me, actually all of us. You would have been left in that camp with Ben and the crew that came through with him. He led them and they're going to follow his lead until they gain some sort of self-awareness— at least enough to question his authority."

"So, you're the leader here?"

Several of the people laughed. Stacy looked around and put a hand on the man's shoulder in front of her, "Hear that, Will?"

Will shook his head and said, "I hear it."

The man next to Keith said, "We were all going to be integrated. We're beyond that stage. Stacy's just our spokesperson, you might say. We've decided that it would be better if you were addressed by one of us rather than all of us. We had no idea what to expect when we heard you had come through alone. We expected that everyone in your group had been detained, or worse."

"Then we saw you and knew that only you could have come out alone," Stacy said. "We know that you are here for a reason."

Keith couldn't fully understand how they all must have felt when they saw him, but he did know that he wasn't any kind of savior. There was no reason. At this point in his departure from Newcity, he didn't know what was happening. His struggle was internal, to figure out whom this new person was who occupied Keith's Newcity body. He still identified with both of them; only the outside person had definitely taken over the majority of his actions. "What about Sam?" he said, "And the others?" He meant those he didn't recognize.

"Molly is with Sam, up front," Stacy said. "She came out with us. So did Will and Rebecca," she patted the man's shoulder in front of her once again. She leaned to look around Keith. "And Brent, of course," she added, and then pointed to the two remaining people in the van, sitting side by side in front of Brent and Keith. "Robert and Amanda came through several months ago."

Robert turned around and raised his hand. "Sam and I are good friends."

"So, Sam's the only non-Newcity person here?" Keith asked.

"Bradley used me to deal with the escapees because my personality is so attuned to yours," replied Sam. "At least through some of the stages. He didn't realize how much closer I feel to you than to them, even though I haven't gone through what you've all gone through." Sam kept his eyes on the road as he talked. "This is where I belong."

Stacy leaned close to Keith and said, "And he knows Bradley's plan."

"What's that?" Sam said.

"I told him that you know Bradley's plans," she said.

"You have no idea," Sam said shaking his head.

"Do you?" Keith said to Stacy.

"Not completely, but you saw the weapons, the explosives. Sam said he'd debrief us when we got back into the city."

Keith didn't like the sound of that. The last place he could imagine going to would be back into the city. "Wouldn't that be a little close to Newcity? Aren't you afraid you're going to get caught?"

"I told you, they're not after us," she said.

"We're going back to warn them?" Keith said, recalling their conversation earlier that day.

"You are. We're not sure how we come into this yet. But you'll tell us when it's time."

Chapter 13

It occurred to Keith that his companions could as easily be delusional as they could be coherent. He thought that Sam might be more logical about things, but he had not heard what Sam knew that the others didn't know in order to decide for sure. And the pairing off was one of the stages the escapees went through on their way to being normal – at least according to Bradley. If that were the case, it was difficult to imagine that they were going to be integrated unless integration was how they would eventually socialize and break their initial attachments.

They drove on for another hour or so before light began to ascend from behind the distant hills. Patches of fog settled in an area over the embankment and to the right of the road they traveled. The gray curled up from the ground in slow motion.

"Riverbed," Brent said. "It'll burn off early this morning."

Keith loved the way the fog meandered through the trees following the steady flow of the hidden river. He stared as the van rumbled along, the steady hum and vibration placing him in a sort of meditation. His head lolled and his mind wandered until he saw something out the corner of his eye. Rotated so that he could see into the rear of the van where supplies had been loaded, Keith's neck cracked from a settled stiffness. What he saw tucked into the corner was the boy with the bullet hole in his forehead. Keith still hadn't fully accepted that the boy was a younger him. In fact, he refused to think of the boy as himself with a bullet hole in his forehead. The whole idea felt too strange and unnatural.

He acted nonchalant about what he saw in the back area of the van because he knew that the others were unaware.

"We have enough supplies for a few days," Brent said. "It should be enough."

The boy pointed out the rear window.

Keith saw another van speeding toward them, still some distance off. "Someone's coming," Keith said.

Brent craned his neck to see. "It looks familiar," he said.

"Shit," Sam said. He speeded up.

The van bounced over the rough road, jostling its passengers as Sam attempted to keep it stable.

Keith straightened back around in his seat as though nothing was going on. But, he listened closely as the boy rustled behind him to get comfortable.

After only a few minutes, the boy said in a very clear whisper, "Turn left."

Keith leaned toward Stacy so that he could see out the front windshield past Sam. A crossroads lay up ahead. Keith's heart pounded and he became fidgety, but he didn't say anything.

Brent asked what was bothering him. "You're looking for something," he said.

Keith closed his eyes and shook his head.

The boy said, "Left."

"We need to turn left up here." Keith whispered at the same tone level as the boy.

Brent shouted to Sam, "Make a left, Sam." He glanced out the back window. "There's a rise in the road behind us. They've disappeared for a second. But hurry."

Sam didn't hesitate. He put on the brakes, shifting everyone forward faster than expected. Several of them reached to the seat in front of them for support. Both Brent and Stacy reached across Keith, holding him back in his seat as they leaned into the slowdown.

"Keep it coming," Brent said.

Keith stared forward, but could hear the boy in the back. "A right turn in about a mile," he said.

Keith clenched his lips together.

Brent reached around and put an arm over Keith's shoulder. "We know you're being guided. Please, for all our sakes, just accept it. What else do we need to do? It's okay."

"Make a right turn about a mile from here," Keith said.

"Did you catch that?" Brent called to Sam.

"No. Where're we going?" he asked.

"Right turn up ahead."

Sam made the turn onto a narrow macadam road. "Now where?"

Brent patted Keith's shoulder.

Keith turned in his seat to look into the back, but the boy was gone. He shrugged his shoulders. "I don't know."

"Keep driving until we get another sign," Brent said. "Did you see him? Before, I mean?"

"Yes, he was in the back, but he's gone now," Keith said.

"It's amazing," Amanda muttered to Robert, who sat next to her and in front of Brent.

"I'm not so sure," Keith responded. Then he laughed at his own comment. He watched out the window as they drove over the road.

The sun crested the hills, sending rays of light through the trees that flanked their travels. Splotches of sunlight strobed the road as they sped along.

"There's something up ahead," Sam said.

Keith leaned over to see what he was talking about and noticed an old barn to the right. Someone stood in the yard, and as soon as Keith recognized that it was the angel with one wing, he gasped.

"Slow down," Stacy ordered.

"Pull into the barn," Keith said, watching the angel motion them through the open barn door.

"I don't see a house anywhere," Sam said.

"It must be a storage barn of some sort," Brent said.

"Let me out first," Keith demanded.

Sam stopped the van and Stacy ducked as she exited the van. Keith stepped from the van and stood silently. Stacy remained beside him. "What is it?"

"The girl," Keith said.

Brent had a foot on the van's running board, but Stacy motioned for him to stay inside and said to Sam, "Get the van into the barn. Quickly. We'll be there in a moment."

The van crunched over a stone drive, popping and crunching its way into the barn. Once inside, the engine was shut down and the doors opened and closed with the sharp sound of air being displaced.

"You can go," Keith said, but Stacy didn't move.

"I didn't know there was a girl."

"Sam didn't tell you?" Keith said.

Stacy shook her head. "Who is she?"

The angel with one wing stood only ten feet from Keith. He could see the bulge from the wing lift slightly above the girl's shoulder. He wanted to see her wing, but didn't know why. He wanted to touch her, but knew that he shouldn't. He took a step forward and she took one backward. "Talk to me," he said.

She pointed for them to enter the barn. "Hide," she said. "Do it now."

"We're to hide inside," he said.

Stacy reached for his hand and they rushed off together. Although her hand felt soft her grip was firm. Keith could have done without them touching even though he longed for contact. He followed Stacy's lead and kept an eye on the angel as long as he could. Stumbling over a root or a rock made him momentarily lose his concentration, and the angel was gone. "Let's go," he said.

Once they were inside, Sam slid the barn door closed enough to hide the van's presence, the. The rollers squealed and the door shook as it moved. Dust floated in the air. Several stalls in the front of the barn were empty. The dirt floors had been brushed clean a long time ago. Two back stalls held bags of grain, and one stall was stuffed with bales of hay, but there were no signs of recent activity.

Seven of them poked around the barn's interior, while Will and Rebecca stood near the entrance. Keith meandered in the center of the space where he could watch the others.

"Sam?" Will whispered from the front of the barn.

Sam, Molly, and Robert inspected the grain in one of the back stalls. Sam pointed out that rats had eaten through most of the bags. After kicking one, dust rose into the air. The three of them left the pile and headed back toward the van. "What is it?"

"The van that was behind us just drove past," Will said. "It was one of ours."

Sam slapped Keith's back. "You saved us from getting caught. Now do you believe that you're here for a reason?"

Keith couldn't speak. His head was still swimming from the contact with the boy and girl. He wanted to be alone, to sit in a corner for a while. Crying might release the emotion he felt, but then again it might make it worse. He walked away from the group, entered one of the stalls and sat on the ground.

"What's wrong?" one of them said to Sam.

"Leave him alone for a while. This has got to be as strange to him as it is to us."

"I wanted to talk with you anyway," Stacy said. "I didn't know there was a girl."

"An angel," Sam told Stacy, as the two of them walked from Keith.

"Oh my God," she said.

"We had to get him out of there," was the last thing Keith heard from their conversation.

He slid deeper into a corner of the stall. The dirt floor felt cool and the wood wall roughed his back. There was security in being closed in. The barn had a natural feel to it, one that Keith accepted easier than the mechanical feel of the van. He allowed emotions to rise and fall inside him, to swell to near bursting and to wane so far that he felt he would disappear. In the time that he remained in the stall he smelled the dampness of age, heard the creaking of wood moving, and tasted the earth he sat on, the essence of it rising into his mouth and sliding along his tongue. With his eyes closed, Keith traveled throughout the barn, using his senses in ways he had never imagined. He felt that he had explored more of the barn while sitting in the stall than he would if he had wandered around and seen everything with only his eyes. Inside the stall, alone but protected by the other six, was the first time everything changed for Keith.

He became the barn.

He knew the rats and felt the wings of insects vibrate along his back. The dust that floated in the air was made of particles of hay and decomposed grain, not dirt. He swam in the air over the lofts; he floated into the wood and into the metal roof, sensing, tasting, becoming each part. By the time he finished exploring, he opened his eyes and was not surprised to see his father sitting on the ground in front of him, cross-legged and alert.

"Help me," Keith said while shaking his head back and forth. Nausea choked his voice. His mouth filled with saliva.

"Trust yourself," his father said. "These people are as lost as those inside Newcity. You know that."

"Where are they taking me?" Keith whispered, hoping that the others weren't outside the stall listening to him talking with himself.

"Where are you leading them?"

"They want me to save the others," Keith said.

"That can't be done. You can only let them out."

"Will you help?"

The man smiled. "I am helping."

Keith didn't understand any of the conversation. "You're not helping," he said.

His father shrugged his shoulders and said, "If that's what you think," then faded in a ripple of air.

"Who was that?" Sam stood in the stall doorway. His voice echoed along the walls.

"Does it matter?"

"The angel again?" Sam couldn't restrain a smile, as though he had won a prize.

"What are you going to do with me?" Keith said.

"We're following you," Sam said. "We started toward Newcity. You're the one who led us here. Not for long, I hope."

"I can't lead you anywhere. The images come and go. They're unreliable."

Sam stepped into the stall. "They are completely reliable." He swung his arm around and pointed toward the outside. He leaned toward Keith in earnest. "They would have caught us. Do you know what they would have done? Do you have any idea what Bradley is capable of?"

"How could I?"

"Hitting you was only a small part of his anger, Keith. You are the single biggest threat to his plans that has ever come along."

"Then why didn't he have me killed right away?"

Sam slumped from the weight of his understanding, but Keith couldn't reach in and take hold of any of it. As Sam kneeled in front of Keith he let out a long slow breath to relax. "He thought that you might have information that could make his plan easier. If he knew how you were able to escape on your own, he felt that you could lead us into Newcity through a totally unprotected area. Destroy it from the inside."

"But I just followed the boy. No different than the others."

"You are the boy. You know the way. Expand that thought for a moment and it takes on new meaning. Bradley saw that more was going on than what he could fully understand. He planned to find out as much as he could from you first." Sam reached toward Keith, but didn't actually touch him.

"First," Keith said the word and knew where it led.

"The angel, the ghost of your father, well, that expanded the idea of 'You know the way' by a measure of ten times. I think there's a part of Bradley that fears you."

"What do you make of it all?"

"I don't know. But I do know that you have been sent for a reason," Sam said.

"I wasn't sent. I followed. Out of curiosity, nothing more."

"You still don't understand fully, but you will. I'm sure everything will be revealed to you eventually. Until that time, we're going to follow you, or the boy, whoever is leading us." He acted sure of himself, as though he knew something that Keith didn't.

Stacy and the others crowded in behind Sam. The audience. "We all believe in you. You don't have to understand. It's the ineffable good that you bring to us."

"Ineffable?"

"Beyond explanation, beyond understanding," she explained.

"I know what it means, I just don't know how any of this can be called good. Isn't it possible that there is an ineffable evil as well?" Keith said.

The group of them fidgeted. They did believe in evil. He saw it in their eyes.

"Maybe it's Bradley, or his fears," Sam said.

"We can overcome that," Stacy added.

Keith felt frustrated talking with them. As much as they were ready for integration, none of them, including Sam, appeared to be open to possibilities beyond their first thoughts. Similar to their need to place their love into another's hands, they needed a person to place the idea of good and evil on. He had become good, while Bradley had commissioned the slot for evil.

Sam slapped his knee and pushed into a standing position. "You seem tired," he said. "Maybe we should all rest, get something to eat, and get back on the road. I suspect that we could backtrack and be on our way without worries. Since the others passed us by we should be safe." He turned around and asked if Will and Rebecca were still monitoring the road.

"Yes," came a reply.

"Good. We'll stay for an hour. If Bradley's men haven't returned by then, we'll assume they kept going."

A few nods of approval and the stall doorway emptied. Keith again sat alone inside the security of the wooden walls. He didn't understand any of it, so how could they? Sam was probably right. If he could stay in contact with the images he'd been seeing, they would lead him, and in doing so lead them all. To where, or why, he had no idea.

It wasn't long after they left that Stacy and Brent walked into the stall with bread and fruit for Keith.

"You need to keep up your strength," Brent said.

The two of them sat near Keith, who took the food willingly. He tore off a piece of bread and began to eat. He waited for them to begin the questions and it didn't take long.

"We're all pretty amazed about the angel and the ghost of your father," Stacy said. "Sam didn't know a lot of the details – he only caught parts of the conversation while waiting outside – but he heard enough to make us all curious."

"I'm curious too," Keith said. "Nothing has been explained to me. And trust me, I've asked."

Stacy broke out with the big question. "Why would all this be going on with you when you don't appear to be that much different than any of the rest of us?"

"I wish I knew."

"Do you think you'll find out? Will it be revealed to you, as Sam suggested?" Stacy said.

"I hope so. In fact, I hope that it stops altogether, so that I can have a normal life." He laughed and looked at the two people who sat with him. "I don't even know what normal is out here, but I'd like to find out."

"Don't wish for it to stop," Brent said. "Not yet. You are our only hope."

"Hope for what?" Keith didn't understand. "Look, weren't things better for you inside Newcity?"

"We had no freedom in there. You must see how the chips kept us passive, reduced us to sentient robots," Stacy pleaded. "Out here, we can feel." She balled her fists and raised them to her chest. Her mouth and cheeks tightened. Her eyes closed.

Brent automatically reached over and held her. She leaned into his shoulder. Their actions appeared staged.

Robert strolled into the stall behind where Brent and Stacy sat. "And then Bradley takes us and makes us work for him. He seems perfectly nice at the beginning."

Keith continued to eat while they talked. Then he looked at them. "So what's the difference between the two?" He wanted them to think, to explore the situation. "It doesn't matter if you're being controlled by Newcity or by Bradley, you're still not completely free."

"There is no freedom. No complete freedom. Fine," Stacy said, "we know that. But what we also know is that we'd rather have the ability to choose for ourselves. And the others, the ones left behind, they deserve the same freedom."

"Even if they didn't ask for it?" Keith asked.

"We'll liberate them," Brent said.

"It may not make it better for them. Especially those who never asked to be liberated. Not everyone believes what you believe," Keith said. "Not everyone believes what Bradley believes." He scanned the three of them, but their faces hardly changed. At that moment, they could have been chipped. The lack of reaction was disheartening. "Bradley is going to try to stop you."

"We're going to help them," Stacy said. "Even if we have to kill Bradley and those who believe in what he's doing."

Chapter 14

Stacy's words made Keith shiver. They considered killing Bradley, to stop him from killing those inside Newcity. It didn't make sense to Keith. And for some reason, none of it sounded wrong to either party. Bradley contained a boiling pot of anger that lashed out seldom, so far, but simmered under the surface at all times. His anger was so strong that Keith literally felt it when they were in the same space. Stacy, on the other hand, appeared calm, yet completely serious about what she said. Killing Bradley, or any of those who were with him, was just another thing to do, a way to stop him, a way that, from where Keith was sitting, appeared to be okay with her. In Newcity they'd all be taken away by the police, there'd be no killing, and the issue would be over.

Stacy and Brent got up to leave. Brent reached for Keith's plate.

"You coming?" Stacy said.

"In a few minutes." Keith didn't want to go with them. Why go back to the place he just escaped from?

"We shouldn't have bothered you," Brent said. "You need to be alone where you can focus on our next move."

Keith smiled as they left. He didn't have anything to say. There was no next move as far as he could tell. They already had their own idea for what was going on with him anyway. There wasn't much he could do to alter their thinking.

He contemplated Stacy's last comment for a moment. There was no need to kill anyone. The Newcity residents wouldn't fight. They couldn't. Stopping Bradley could be much easier than any of them realized. If they blew up his weapons, it would take months for him to prepare again. A short term fix, for sure, but a non-violent one. He felt as though he understood the situation better than either party, as odd as that sounded even to him. Could it be due to the removal of the chip? To his unrestricted mind?

He reveled in the clarity of thought he'd gained by having the chip removed. But the most recent clarity – intimacy with the essence that was the barn, personal sensations shared with the insects – bothered him. He held out his hands and stared at the wrinkles in his palms. Turning his hands over, the knuckles pushed against his skin; the nails, with their white moons, laughed at him. It would be an understatement to suggest that he was not the same, that everything had changed for him. Add to the strangeness of the shift in his perceptions the fact that he continued to see apparitions, people beyond who was already there, and Keith feared for his own sanity. Of course there was always the idea that Newcity still had a hold on him, and that as the seven of them approached the city the images would become stronger. So far, he had followed their lead. What if he didn't? What if he fought back?

For now, the issue to worry about was the pending violence, and although the violence was surely kicked up a few notches, all the talk of killing didn't have much of an effect on him. Perhaps that's what Stacy exhibited, a lack of full understanding about what killing meant. He rubbed his jaw, still somewhat sore where Bradley had backhanded him. The anger in the tent had hurt more than the physical contact.

He shifted his thoughts to the beauty of the sunrise that morning, to erase the deepening gloom settling into him from thoughts of killing. Closing his eyes, he shifted to images of the sunset from the night before, which he had watched intently as the colors folded from one into another throughout the sun's last moments. The process was slow, beautiful, and filled him with feelings he could not explain. Those feelings returned as he reviewed the memory.

The spread of available emotions was extensive and widening further every day, but the ones he actually experienced were more real. They could be called up in memory and re-experienced almost as clearly as they were during the event that created them.

So, again, when he turned his thoughts to killing, he had difficulty sensing what that entailed physically. He literally couldn't sense it. The closest thing he had to the idea of death was from the movies that he'd watched. Even as he recalled them, no large swing in emotion occurred. He had no point of reference.

It was less than an hour later that the others were prepared to get back on the road. Their narrow escape had turned into a roadside rest, a break in the monotony of driving. Yet Sam had requested that Will and Rebecca continue to monitor the road even as the rest of them piled into the van.

A breeze swept through the barn, the scent of morning slipping in to arouse everyone's spirits and hurry their movements. It appeared to Keith that only he noticed how nature was as much in charge of their activities as they were that morning. The natural need for nourishment, the cool breeze exciting them into action, and the heavy presence of the barn as it pressured them to move on, to go back into the world from where they came. The natural signs shifted and turned all around them without their knowledge. The escapees acted on those signs without knowing that they were doing so. Keith alone seemed to comprehend how it all came together like an orchestra of life. Regardless of their mission, the others appeared to be following a plan that the world had devised, except for a few nudges from the boy and angel.

Keith went along with the escapees even though he was certain the world was involved in their decisions. Nature stood out as a coarse control. And if that were true, then the apparitions were the fine controls. Again, he thought of going counter to the boy's lead, to the angel's words, but why choose to go contrary to the world's motion when staying in its flow was so much easier? The question continually at the forefront was whether the boy and angel were part of the world's plan or part of Newcity's?

Once Rebecca climbed into the van, Will slid the barn door open. He leaned into it and again the bearings squealed and the door jerked as he shoved. Once it was open, he jogged to the van and leaped into his seat. Sam backed out of the barn, swung the van around, and retraced their tracks.

They were driving along a short while when Robert asked, "What if they parked someone at the crossroads?"

"I only saw one vehicle," Brent said.

"Doesn't mean there wasn't another one," Robert said.

Brent turned to Keith. "Well?"

"I'm getting nothing. Keep going," he said.

"We'll go with that," Brent said.

It wasn't long and they came to the crossroads and turned left toward the city. "They probably thought we took another route in," Sam said. "There are multiple ways to get into the city." Nonetheless, Sam speeded along faster than Keith remembered him driving the first part of their trip. The tension of those inside the vehicle rose in the air, even though there was little talking. Keith felt an array of emotions, including uncomfortable, worried, and then fearful. He listened and watched for signs, for the boy and angel, but received nothing he could interpret into a change in what they were already doing. Stay the course was what the non-message said.

As the road lulled some of them to sleep, Keith planned his escape. He wanted nothing to do with killing anyone. He figured that they would have to stop somewhere to regroup. They couldn't drive up to Newcity and announce why they were there, although that might be what Sam and the others expected him to do. But it was not something he was prepared to engage in. He'd wait until they were in the city before he ran off. Not that he'd be safer there, but with knowledge of more places to hide, escape would be easier. He had no idea what he would do after that.

They passed through farmlands where Keith saw people on tractors in fields of green and gold. Sam drove up and over hills, trees on either side of the road, wires strung on poles and placed near the road. As they crested one hill the scene opened to a hundred squat buildings as a small town opened in the distance before them. More cars had entered the road, increasing in number as they approached the town. Maysville, a sign said.

The tallest building, as they came into town, stood five stories high. The rest were shorter, most two-story or single-story homes. He must have passed through some of these same towns two days earlier on his way from the city, but he had slept then. Now, before him was the world he had missed. Traffic lights forced them to stop and go, as Sam maneuvered the van through crowded streets. The people on the sidewalks, young and old, dressed in suits as well as casual clothes, all appeared to be on task, rushing to unknown destinations to perform unknown jobs. Storefronts displayed clothing, tools, flower arrangements.

"Lock the doors," Stacy said.

A loud clunking dropped into the interior of the van.

"What is it?" Sam asked while glancing into the rearview mirror.

"They're staring. It's our clothes. We're all dressed the same," she said.

Keith looked out the window in the direction Stacy indicated with her own stare. A small group of young men huddled around a corner. Each dressed in jeans and a t-shirt. The shirts had writing on them and were different colors. They watched as the van crept along in the congestive traffic of Maysville. One man pointed and the others nodded. They didn't appear to be dangerous or fearful of danger, as far as Keith could tell. "Maybe they're curious," he said.

Stacy stirred and took a deep breath. She glanced around. "I don't know."

"Sam," Keith said, "have you ever lived out here? In one of these towns? Is there anything for us to worry about?"

"I have. I grew up on a small government-owned farm. The locals can be suspicious of people they don't know. A full van of strangers might make them nervous. We'll get out of town as soon as we can."

"What did you do where you grew up?" Keith asked.

"Farm work. Then I got tired of slaving in the fields and put in for a reassignment." He glanced into the rearview mirror as he talked to Keith. "I worked at the sewage plant for several years – which was even more labor intensive – until I met Bradley. I'd never go back," he said. There was a pause before he added, "But I don't agree with Bradley either."

"Didn't machines do a lot of the work for you?" Keith said, recalling how he lived inside Newcity.

Sam scoffed. "Technological advances stopped dead once Newcity and places like it went up. In fact, the outside world went backwards in time for all practical purposes. Originally, people out here were the ones who rejected the way technology was leading us. All those advances, and others I suspect, are inside there now. It was supposed to be nirvana, you know: no worries, jobs for everyone, comfortable living space, no disease, no violence. A cathedral of dreams you might say. That's what it was supposed to be. That's how they advertised it. But ask any of these guys and they'll tell you that even with the advances in technology, when you're stripped of your most important right as a human being, emotions, it's a living hell."

"It doesn't sound much better out here. Government farming, sewage plants. I mean, I don't want to go back into Newcity, but what is there here?"

"Nothing right now. But with the people from Newcity, we could share the labor and begin to live normal lives again. My dad used to tell me that there were enough people to work that they got days off sometimes." Sam turned in his seat to face fully forward. They were at the edge of town and he passed through the last traffic light and speeded up considerably. "Most of the people you see here are working to keep Newcity going. Most of the food produced goes there, the sewage plants all over this area are filled with Newcity shit, and the clothing, the furniture, you name it, come from out here. We work for you. And the more of you there are the more you work for you as well. It's a growing blemish on the surface of the earth. All it does is feed itself and rob us of our lives."

Molly, who Keith had never heard a word from since they began their trip, reached out and took Sam's hand. "It was terrible in there, but I didn't know it until I got out."

Ultimately, Keith agreed with her. Since he'd been outside, the world had assaulted him with heights of emotion he had never felt before. The clarity of thought was enough to make him want to stay, even if he worked in a sewage plant. "She's right," Keith said. "We worked every day. We were allowed time in the evenings, but always felt slow now that I look back. The monotony couldn't have been handled without the chips." He contemplated the differences. They had terminals in each residence and television and meals, yet there was nothing really to say to anyone. Television offered a world so unlike how he lived that it was nothing more than an abstract escape, and the food had become nothing but nourishment. That's how he remembered it now.

Outside of town, Sam pulled into a gas station. He asked if anyone needed to use the bathrooms and there were several takers. "Hurry," he said. "We need to be on our way."

Keith, Robert, and Will entered the bathroom, which protruded from the side of the building like an afterthought. The urinals were filthy and damp, and the floor sticky with what appeared to be dried piss. Keith almost threw up from the odor alone. "I don't know if I can do this," he said.

"This isn't the worst I've seen," Robert said. "Try not to breathe."

Keith obeyed the suggestion and washed his hands thoroughly afterwards. Robert held the door for him as they left. Shivers ran down his spine when he smelled the clean outside air. The air felt warmer in the sun than it did inside the van. A slight breeze took some loose leaves for a walk across the parking lot. A flag at the front of the gas station flopped and fluttered in the wind. The sound of cars shushed past, riding the same air they stirred into excitement.

The girls were still missing, so the men stood and waited for Sam to fill up the gas tank. After replacing the nozzle, he pulled a wallet from his pocket and removed some bills.

"Hold on," Keith said. "I've never seen money."

Sam handed him the cash. "We can't use terminals out here. Especially us. They're traceable. Like I told you, people went backward in time out here, by choice. But that was a long time ago. My great-grand parents returned to using cash."

The girls walked out from the side of the building, and Keith handed the cash back to Sam who walked toward the cashier's window.

"In the car," Stacy said in a nervous tone. "Come on, it's them. Sam!"

She was right. Three of the men they'd seen grouped in town had pulled into the station and parked near the building. They jumped from the car and were headed toward the van.

Sam shoved the cash toward the cashier and rushed back to the driver's side door of the van.

One of the three men stopped in front of the van to prevent Sam from pulling away. The other two men approached the sliding door. "Not from around here?" one of them said.

"Passing through," Brent said while ushering Stacy into the van first. Only he and Keith were outside.

Keith read the t-shirt of the man closest to him. It said Morning Light under a picture of the sun rising over a hill. He had seen that image before and recognized it immediately. "You provide produce to Newcity," he said.

Brent reached for Keith's shoulder. "Get in."

The young man with the Morning Light shirt knocked Brent's hand away and grabbed Keith's wrist. He pulled Keith's arm forward and turned it. The stitches puffed above the normal smoothness of his skin. "You're newly escaped," he said with a mixture of question and answer in his voice. "What are you doing heading toward Newcity?"

Until that moment, Keith had sensed no danger whatsoever. Now, the tension spiked in an instant and he didn't know what to do, so he searched the parking lot and station's drive-through for the boy with the bullet hole in his forehead.

"What the fuck you looking for?" the Morning Light man said. "Harry, get the jeep." His cohort took off for their vehicle in a slow jog.

Brent's energy changed too as he ripped Keith's arm from the man and swung Keith toward the van door. "In the van," Brent ordered. Then he swung around and stepped closer to the Morning Light man, who had been left standing alone, with one of his crew in front of the van and the other one retrieving their jeep.

Morning Light snatched Brent's wrist before Brent could pull away. "Another one? The whole van is filled with ex-Newcityers," he yelled to the man in front of the van. "You're going the wrong way," he said to the van's passengers. "You'll get caught."

While Brent and Morning Light exchanged shoves and tugs, the man in front of the van opened Sam's door and slammed him into the space between the front seats. "Get out of the way."

Keith sat next to Stacy, but poised himself so that he could rush out at any moment. The anger he felt blinded other sensations, yet it wasn't him in danger at the moment.

Morning Light reached up and gripped Brent by the neck. The man from the jeep leaped out, a knife in his hand. "You're coming with us," he said, and the two of them dragged Brent toward the jeep and forced him inside. "Let's go," Morning Light said as he dragged the van door closed. Then he jumped into the driver's side of the jeep and drove onto the road.

The new driver of the van yelled back to everyone, "Try anything and I run this van off the fucking road and most of you are dead meat. Got it?"

Some of them nodded. Keith steamed at the arrival of emotion, not understanding where it had come from and why it escalated so quickly.

They followed the jeep off to the right and down a few side streets where there were fewer and fewer houses. The road became bumpy and they bounced in the back as they sped along, turning sharply without warning. When they came to a two-story farmhouse they pulled close to the porch. Several other men and women exited the house and stood on the porch. Two of the men had rifles.

"What's going on?" Keith said.

"Shut up," the driver said. He jumped from the van.

Several men came to the side of the vehicle and slid the door wide. "Out," Morning Light said, Harry standing next to him, the knife pulled and ready. Brent stood between tow other men, his arms pinned to his sides.

The men who came from the house were older than the three young men who had apprehended the van and the escapees. One of them looked at Sam once everyone was out of the van and cracked him in the jaw with the butt of the rifle. Sam went down hard, sliding over the gravel of the drive, his hand and arm out to break the fall. "You thought you'd get away with this?" The man looked at the others. "Get 'em into the house."

Chapter 15

Sam's mouth bled down his shirt as he stood next to Keith. Molly tried to attend to him, but one of the women pulled her away and shoved her onto a couch with the other girls. Robert, Brent, and Will were told to sit on the floor with their backs together. One of the rifles had been handed over to the man who had driven the van, and he sat in a chair and pointed the gun at them.

Keith's emotions swirled like a tornado, angry and natural at the same time. The men and women in the room pulsed fear and fury, aggravation and angst at levels that practically produced pain for Keith.

The man who appeared to be the leader acted surprised that Sam would be with the escapees. They stood face to face. "Sam," he said.

"John," Sam said, mocking the other man's delivery.

"You are no longer needed, you know," John said.

"This is almost over," Sam said.

John's eyes narrowed and Keith experienced a foreboding feeling creep inside him. To break the confrontation, he said, "What are you going to do with us?"

John turned to Keith and drove his face even closer than he had with Sam. "You don't look so special to me."

John's breath smelled thick with rotted food and stale air. Keith turned from the words. But the man didn't appear to know why. He scoffed and stepped away.

The room was large and filled with odd pieces of furniture, including the couch where the four girls had been forced to sit; three chairs, one occupied by Robert, Brent, and Will's guard; and several hard-backed wooden chairs that looked as though they'd been dragged in from somewhere else. Some of the other men and women sat on those chairs. Then there were side tables near the couch, desks pushed against the walls, chests of drawers. None of the furniture matched. In the corner of the room, one of the desks held electronic equipment similar to the equipment Keith had seen in Bradley's tent.

"Anybody hungry?" A woman's voice came from behind John.

When John turned to answer, Keith saw around him. It was his mother. "My god," he said. "You're here? Mom?"

"Your mother's dead," Sam said. "That woman's a fake meant to lure you…" But he didn't get to finish his sentence before John backhanded him to the floor.

Molly sucked in a breath and began to get up. One of the women standing behind her slapped her shoulders and Molly collapsed into the cushions.

"Kill him," John said.

"No," Molly attempted to get up again, but this time the woman grabbed her hair to drag her back into the seat. Molly let out a screech and reached for her head.

Sam scrambled to get up as one of the bigger men lumbered over and grabbed him by the arm and lifted. He half dragged, half carried Sam outside, shoving him through the doorway. Keith heard Sam fall onto the floor of the porch, then the sound of rustling feet and footsteps on gravel.

John was just turning back to look into Keith's eyes when a shot was heard.

Molly began to cry.

Stacy and Rebecca turned toward her, both of them with tears in their eyes. Amanda sat petrified, staring at nothing.

"Anyone else want to get smart with us?" John said.

The man watching the other three men shook the barrel of his gun at them. "How about you guys?" All three of the escapees lowered their heads in answer.

Keith felt pain in his neck and shoulders. His muscles stretched like rubber bands near the breaking point. His head swam and his stomach churned. He liked Sam, even if he didn't agree with their plan. And now Sam was gone. But he didn't feel gone, only changed, as though Sam had not died, but shifted his energy into something else. Keith looked over at the woman he had thought was his mom, knowing that Sam was right about her. That was the reason he had felt no closeness to her when they first met. He should have paid attention to his feelings.

She shrugged her shoulders to dismiss Keith's glare. "Well, anyone hungry?" she asked again, as though nothing had happened.

No one spoke up. Not even their captors. So the woman left the room.

John wandered to the equipment in the corner and picked up a microphone. "Bradley, come in." A crackling sound came through the speakers and a voice that was too low to hear. "Got your loner. What you want me to do with him?" Bradley responded. Another muffled sound came through. "Roger." John dropped the microphone and turned back around. "I don't know why we need any of you. Least of all you." He pointed a dirty finger at Keith and strolled back into the center of the group. "Link or no link. I say we do the job and get this shit over with. We're ready." He strolled the length of the couch, offering each of the others a look of authority and satisfaction.

Keith closed his eyes and tried to calm his emotions, the torrent that ripped through his veins, the undecipherable currents. If he could relax, the boy with the bullet hole in his forehead would return, the angel with one wing would tell him what to do, or the spirit of his father would help somehow. But there was too much going on. A man had been killed. The presence of violence lay thick in the air. Even the furniture provided a place for hatred and futility to collect.

A jerk came to Keith's chest as someone shoved him. He stumbled backward onto the floor and fell on his elbow, cracking it against the hardwood.

"Didn't want you to fall asleep standing up," Morning Light said from above Keith.

The urge to strike back arrived without much fanfare at first. It was just a thought that concerned rolling to his side and kicking Morning Light's knee. Then, not a moment later he realized that Bradley must have told John not to harm them, which led to his decision and the impulse to go through with the attack. He rolled to place both hands flat against the floor so that he could push to his hands and knees. He leaned back, lifted his leg, and smoothly shot it toward Morning Light's knee. It hit squarely.

The knee cracked. The contact produced a terrible sensation that Keith felt as it transferred from his foot to his leg. Something inside Morning Light's knee not only broken but stretched like a string drawn taught. Keith imagined the string fraying into dozens of strands before popping apart and snapping in opposite directions.

Morning Light screamed. The rifle he held went off and the floorboards near Keith splintered and flew. The man crumbled to the ground and lay across the rifle he had been holding. In his rage, he tried to maneuver the gun out from under him and into a usable position.

John ran over and stepped on the barrel. "Help him up," he told the others.

A man and woman came to Morning Light's rescue. He flailed at first, then succumbed to their help, hobbling away and swearing back at Keith.

John kicked Keith in the side, throwing him onto his back a foot away from where he was.

Without thinking, and through the pain, Keith pulled his leg back to kick at John's knee as well. It worked once. But John sidestepped and grabbed Keith's foot as it shot forward. He lifted the foot so that Keith's butt was off the floor and he had no thrust. Then he dragged Keith toward the door. "Outside with them all," he ordered.

John dragged his captive by one leg.

Keith felt splinters enter his butt and when he fell backwards to get it off the floor, splinters entered his shoulders. He rolled and tried to use his arms and hands to walk himself forward as they crossed the porch, but John moved too quickly. At the stairs Keith's body knocked against the old wood so hard that he found relief when he finally reached the stones and ground.

John dropped the leg.

Another man pointed a gun at Keith's head.

"Up," John said. "I'm sick of dragging your ass."

Keith rose slowly, feeling the pain in his shoulders the most. By the time he straightened the others had been ushered out the door and were standing on the porch. Molly wept while the other women surrounded her with their arms.

Robert, Brent, and Will held their heads up, but their shoulders visibly shuddered from fear.

"In the garage," John said.

The eight of them were taken into the garage and forced to sit together in the back left corner. There was only one way out and that was through the wide opening in the front.

John stood outside and whispered to the two young men who had accompanied Morning Light in the jeep. When he left, the two men, rifles in hand, pulled plastic crates over and in front of the six escapees. They sat down, blocking the open door, and pointed their rifles into the group. "First one to move, gets shot," one of them said. "No exceptions."

The garage gave the appearance of little use. Boxes lined one of the walls, along with shelves and a workbench crammed with rusted tools and broken household items. The feel of the place displayed more of nature than the violence the house harbored. The fresh air in the garage produced a cool organic scent. Concrete provided strength to the floor.

It took less than ten minutes before Keith's sensitivity shifted and accepted the new location almost as completely as he had accepted the barn's essence earlier that day.

The two men changed in demeanor as well. Their anger dropped and they talked to one another in low, inaudible tones, laughing every once in a while.

Keith shifted to his knees.

"Stop moving," the man on the right said, waving his rifle at Keith.

"My body is getting stiff," Keith said.

"I don't give a goddamn. Now sit still."

Keith rose to his feet.

"What'd I tell you?" The man stood. His partner began to stand, too, but the first man held out his hand to stop him. "I'll take care of him."

Out the corner of his eye, Keith spotted the angel and felt relief. He wouldn't be doing this alone. She would guide him. "You're not allowed to kill me," Keith said.

"But I can beat the living crap out of you," the man said, confirming Keith's understanding. He turned to his friend and they both laughed.

Keith motioned for the others to get up, but no one moved.

The man in front of him smiled broadly, a fake smile, "No followers?"

Keith turned his head. He knew that the escapees would listen only if he saw the boy or girl. "I see them," he said.

The others began to get to their feet slowly, yet keeping their eyes on the rifle barrel and where it pointed.

"See who?" the man demanded. "What's going on? Who's here?" He let the rifle follow his eyes as he jerked his head from side to side.

Keith took two wary steps toward his captor, who did not step backward. Good. The rifle barrel was within reach and pointed at his chest.

Robert advanced to Keith's left and Will to his right. Brent stood back with the girls.

The other man left his crate and joined his friend. "Enough of this shit. Get back there or I <u>will</u> kill one of you." He poked his rifle toward Robert just as the angel slid something off the workbench.

There was a crash and both men looked behind them.

Robert and Will grabbed at the rifle barrels, while Keith shoved the men off balance. They managed to get the rifles out of the men's hands, forcing them back over their own crate seats where they fell against the cement floor. Robert and Will turned and pointed the guns at them.

The exchange of power went so smoothly it surprised Keith. He said, "Get into the corner."

The men scooted. "You won't get away with this," one of them said.

The angel was gone. Keith told Will to watch them from the front of the garage. Robert and Brent ran for the van, taking the girls with them.

Keith heard the van start and knew that it wouldn't be long before those inside could guess what was happening. As the van swung near the garage, he yelled at Will to get going.

The men began to get up and Will fired twice.

Each man bent over and reached for their chest.

Will shot again. Keith saw blood seep into the front of their shirts and ripped the rifle from Will's hands and turned him toward the van. The two of them jumped into the van, Keith throwing the rifle under the seat. Robert skidded the tires over the gravel on his way out.

Behind them, Keith saw a couple of the men stumble onto the porch. They raised their rifles. "Duck!" Keith yelled, and everyone inside the van hunched over. Several shots went off. One of the rear windows shattered, but they turned onto the road and were gone.

"Everyone okay?" Stacy asked. There were nods all around.

"They'll be on us fast," Robert said. "Where to?"

Keith lacked the guidance they expected from him. He had no idea what to do next. In a panic, he looked around the inside of the van.

Stacy followed his gaze. "They're not here, are they?"

Keith turned and kneeled between the front seats. "Make the next left," he said.

Robert didn't hesitate. He obeyed.

As soon as they turned, Keith said, "Now another left, then a right, then a left." He had no idea where he was leading them, only that turning corners would help keep them out of sight of their pursuers. He had a general idea where the highway was located, but didn't know if that would be a better or worse place to travel. He turned back to the others, "Anyone know how to get to the city?" He didn't want to go back to Newcity and could have suggested they return to camp, but he feared Bradley too much to go back there. He'd follow this through for now.

"We've never been out of the camp," Stacy said.

Everyone else remained silent. "Then there's nothing we can do but drive," Keith said. Then he cocked his head. "How'd you learn to drive?"

"Maintenance carts in Newcity." Robert's face was bright and smiling." Except that this thing's got some real power."

Molly lifted her head then. Tears ran down her face into a grimace that stretched across her mouth. Her lips pouted and quivered. She interrupted, "I know how to get there," she said. "Sam took me on plenty of rides. Every time we changed camp. And I've seen maps." She burst into a wail, saliva falling from her mouth as she coughed.

Keith patted the empty seat next to Robert. "Get up here."

Stacy and Rebecca helped Molly get into the front seat. Brent sat in the second bench seat with his arm around Amanda's shoulder.

While Stacy and Rebecca held Molly steady, Will was left alone. He stared out the side window. His shoulders shuddered.

Keith scooted back a little to make room for Molly and placed his hand on Will's knee. "You all right?"

Stacy let go of Molly once she was settled and rotated enough to rest an arm on Keith's shoulder.

"Ouch," he ducked from her hand.

Stacy shot a glance at Will. "He never killed anyone before."

"They're not dead," Keith said. "At least they weren't dead when we left."

Stacy peered into his eyes. "I'm not going to ask how you know that." She let Rebecca comfort Will and sat on the seat near Keith. "What's wrong with your shoulder?"

"Splinters. From my butt to my head."

"Let me take a look," she said.

Robert twisted his head around. "First, where we going?"

Stacy didn't wait for Keith to answer. "To the city," she said. "We have a package to deliver."

"I knew that. I was wondering where in particular."

"We'll know when we get there," she said.

Keith removed his shirt and Stacy leaned over him. "I can get some of these, but the crazy driver," she said in a loud voice, "has got to let me know when he's going to make a hard turn."

"I'll try," Robert said.

Stacy pulled Keith's skin taught and scraped or pinched from time to time. "Some of them are coming easily enough. Others are in there pretty far. We'll need a knife or something."

"Turn," Robert announced.

Stacy pulled her hands back dramatically until the van maneuvered the turn.

Keith saw that Molly had stopped crying and now focused her attention on the road in front of them and their surroundings. "Keep going straight for a while," she said.

Keith could feel her calm and was encouraged by it. Her concentration had reduced her pain and loss. Will, too, had settled, although he stared out the side window pensively. Stacy handed Keith his shirt and he slipped it on. She made her way back to sit next to Brent and Amanda. Rebecca slid closer to Will and laid her head onto his shoulder. Keith lifted up enough to fall onto the seat next to Rebecca. They all sat quietly, lost in their own thoughts, while Robert took his driving orders from Molly.

They were all Newcity people now. Not even the one outsider they could have relied on for his experience. Keith worried for them all. What were they headed into? What would they find?

The van made another turn based on Molly's memory and eventually pulled onto the highway. The increase in traffic indicated that they were closer to their destination, but the shattered window drew a lot of attention.

"Can we take another route in?" Keith said. "I don't like the way some of these people are looking at us."

"We're almost there," Molly said. "This is the fastest and easiest way. Besides, there'll be just as many people on any other road. We'll just have to chance it."

"Unless, we get guidance that says differently," Stacy added from the back.

"Agreed," Keith said.

Robert drove up a hill and onto an overpass. The mass of Newcity fell into view, in the distance, beyond several miles of the inner city area that surrounded it.

As they approached, large trucks took up much of the road. Writing on the sides of the containers told of produce, beef, chicken. Keith noticed the lack of household items, furniture, or electronics. "This is all food," he said.

"Almost everything. What Newcity needs, they manufacture themselves. Food and raw materials are all that go in anymore," Molly obviously channeled what Sam had told her. She shook her head. "And nothing they manufacture comes out."

"So the outside works for Newcity," Keith said.

"And they work for themselves. Factories, maintenance, it's all done just to maintain more and more life," Molly explained.

"They are headed into the future, while we are retreating into the past," Keith said, including himself as an outsider now.

"What is life without living?" Brent asked in a simple tone, matter-of-factly.

"They have everything in there," Keith said, "but there's nothing to have. How did we get ourselves into this?"

"It doesn't matter," Stacy said, "as long as we can get ourselves back out of it."

Chapter 16

The urban area surrounding the Newcity complex thickened with people and cars amidst an uproar of noise, as the eight escapees drove closer to the complex. Robert had no idea where to go. None of them remembered the exact place that they had been picked up, and Molly had traveled only to surrounding towns with Sam, never back into the city. After deciding that they couldn't sleep in the van because it would be too easy for Bradley's men to spot the, they made a group decision to abandon the vehicle in an alley. They left the rifles behind, but gathered as much of the food as they could, stuffing it into their pockets.

There was no hiding the tentative advance the escapees made from the alley and into the crowded streets. Many of them held hands, following one another as though they were a group of psychiatric patients on a tour, afraid they'd get separated from one another.

Keith didn't need to be in physical contact with anyone. The noise of the city assaulted him with the low rumblings of thousands of conversations, racing engines, and occasional yelling or horn blowing. The oppressive sounds combined with the partly cloudy sky that hung near the tops of the buildings like a permanent fixture. As they worked their way through the crowds, he had no idea why he had come back. How long had it been between escape and reentry? How far had he traveled only to return? And the others, what did they expect to do, really? How did they expect to enter a secured building and what warning would they offer to those inside? The questions accumulated as he led them on, but were eventually answered, at least for him. He had to get away from them. The truth was that he would figure his next move out on his own. And each of them would have to figure it out for his or her self.

There was no answer to fit everyone, not for their small group, and not for the residents of Newcity.

Small street-side stores were open for business, but Keith knew from his first experience that this wouldn't be the case in an hour or so.

This late in the day, the sun didn't do much more than provide a soft ambient glow to the streets, which lay mostly in shadow. The roadway always appeared to be damp even when it wasn't raining. A heavy odor of grime whooshed by every time a car passed, which was often. Many of the people on the streets were adults, but small families with one or two children ducked in and out from behind parked cars from time to time as though they were sneaking somewhere.

A police vehicle slowed as it drove past, and the officer inside watched as the eight of them paraded in a direction they thought was leading toward Newcity.

Once he turned down a side street, Keith said, "You guys are going to have to unlock your hands. That policeman looked pretty suspiciously at you."

No one let go except Stacy, who had been in the lead. She turned on them and clenched her lips together and shot her head forward in an angry reprimand.

All hands dropped, but it hardly mattered. They advanced in unison as though they were still holding hands, or stuck together with an invisible thread.

Through frustration, Keith led them closer to where he believed the doctor had been located. Perhaps that would be a place they could hide for the night if he could find it among all the similar looking buildings. He would know for sure once the boy with a bullet hole in his forehead appeared. Until then, Keith took over as leader. No one asked if he could see his guides. He knew they were afraid to pose the question, for fear of an answer they didn't want to hear.

The police car that drove past them earlier turned down their street once again. A shot of panic caused Keith to usher the others into an alley too narrow for the car to follow. He had them huddle into a group and crouch down as he watched the policeman pass. The alley was drenched in shadow, the ground gritty and damp. Shards of broken glass crunched under their feet. A rat ran along one of the walls and Amanda screeched. Keith jumped toward the rat and it squealed and ran off. "They won't hurt you," he said, knowing that his words meant nothing to her.

"What now?" Brent said.

"We'll think of something," Keith said.

"I say we wait until it's dark and break into the doctor's office," Brent said.

As soon as the idea came out and even though Keith had felt the same way earlier, he got a bad feeling about it and changed his mind. "I don't think so," he said.

"They aren't here," Brent said, referring to Keith's guides. "I can tell. You don't know what to do any more than we do. I won't let you lead us into a trap. There is nowhere else to go."

"He is the guide," Stacy said. "I don't think we should forget that."

"I don't think we should rely on it," Brent said, pressing his point.

"The docks," Keith announced the moment the idea struck him.

Robert leaned in to speak, "I've seen the docks, and he may be right. There are trucks everywhere, crates and boxes filled with produce, animals, and flowers. A vast warehouse. Not only could we hide there for the night, but we might be able to get inside Newcity."

Brent scoffed at Robert and said, "We'll see," as he turned away.

The police car that had driven by them several times, stopped at the entrance of the alley, the door opened, and the officer got out. "Hey, what are you doing in there?"

"Run," Brent barked while dashing from the huddle. The rest followed leaving Keith standing alone. For a moment he thought this might be the best time to separate from them, but when the officer reached for his gun and took off toward them, Keith ran as well. He heard the man yell, "Halt!" several times, but it was too late. They had mingled with the crowd on the sidewalks, which, like several days ago, was beginning its trek from the streets into the alleys and apartments.

The stands had already begun to close. The stores would be next. There were too many people for the policeman to plow through, and he stopped running soon after he left the alley. Keith followed Brent and the others onto another street and lost sight of the policeman. Another hour and the streets would clear enough for the policeman to spot them easily.

Surprisingly, few of the people on the streets appeared to notice, or care, about the running escapees. Some of them didn't even get out of the way until shoved to the side, and then they complained or yelled, throwing up a fist as the odd group passed.

Near a storefront with piles of what looked like old clothing lying on wooden tables, they stopped.

"Get out of here," the store attendant yelled.

"Keep moving," Brent said while taking Stacy's hand and proceeding.

"He'll be driving through looking for us," Keith said when he caught up. "He was going to shoot at us."

Molly began to cry and Will and Rebecca comforted her. They each held onto one of Molly's arms and pulled in close. Robert put his arm around Amanda.

"I'm not sure about this," Keith said, "but we've got to avoid that policeman." They traveled a little farther. Keith found a vendor lowering a metal screen over the front of his store and asked, "Which way to Newcity?" The man looked surprised but answered Keith before locking the screen into position and walking away in the opposite direction.

It didn't take long for them to jog most of the way. Newcity grew overhead until finally it loomed over them. It was as though the city had ended and a great wall rose into a low-hanging cloud and stretched for miles both left and right of them.

They were in the open.

"This way," Brent said. As soon as he led the others to the right, Keith ran to the left. He had had enough of their dependence. But it didn't last.

Will yelled to the others from behind Keith and before he knew it they had caught up and were following him. The group pitched into one alley, ran along a street, and then shuttled through another alley similar to the way they had driven away from their captors several hours before. The left-right continual turns kept them out of sight of the policeman and safe for the moment.

Again, they approached the doctor's office and Brent repeated his plan. "I still say we break in there and hold up for the night. It's dangerous out here."

"We don't know that. None of us has ever experienced the city at night," Keith observed. He looked around. They stood in yet one more alleyway staring out at the dimming light of the street. Patrons dressed in grungy clothing were parking themselves in doorways or wandering off as though they had somewhere to be.

Two men, a woman, and two children entered the alley from the other end. "This is ours," growled one of the men. "Find your own place to sleep."

Keith swung around and walked toward them. Stacy whispered her concern, but he ignored her. As he got closer he saw that both men were pulling short clubs from their jackets. The woman placed a hand on each of the children's chests and stepped back with them. "Hold it," Keith said, raising his hands to show that he was weaponless. "I just want directions."

The man to the right looked at the other two. "Directions where?"

"We're trying to get to the dock entrance of Newcity."

The man laughed. "They ain't hiring. I can tell you that."

"I know." Keith pointed to the others. "We're inspectors. Our car broke down and the driver stayed back to wait for help. He was the only one who knew where he was going." He sensed a rush of blood as he lied to the man, an excitement came over him, and a guilt that was oddly pleasant.

Suspicion ran across their faces, but Keith didn't flinch. He didn't change his story. "We're new," he said. "We just got out of training. He told us how to get there but we got lost."

"Then you're leaving here?"

Keith nodded.

"It's a few miles," the man said. "And I don't recommend that you go now. If anyone catches you, they'll think you're cutting line."

"Cutting line?"

The man stepped closer. He cocked his head and looked into Keith's eyes. "You're not an inspector. What's really going on?" He glanced at the others, still huddled near the other end of the alley. His suspicion turned to wonder. "You're from in there, aren't you?"

The question came with a heaviness that Keith had not felt until that moment. A futility fell over the man, and his question hung between them like a condemned man.

"Were you thrown out?" the man asked. "Is that possible?"

"No," Keith said, "we escaped."

He thought the man was about to break down the way his body appeared to crumble, the way he twisted to his side unwilling, it seemed, to address those with him squarely. "Escaped," he shook his head in disbelief. "Why would you want to escape?"

The others stepped closer, even the woman and children, to listen to the answer that they hoped would not come. But Keith gave them the answer, his answer. "It's horrible in there."

"It's horrible out here," the man said, opening his arms to indicate the alley they stood in. "We work hard and have little."

The woman reached out and put a hand on the man's shoulder. He turned slightly to give her space. The two kids stayed behind her. "If it's so horrible, why are you trying to get back in?" she asked.

"We're not," Keith said. "We're here to warn them."

The rest of the escapees advanced on Keith until they stood behind him.

"You'll have to explain that," the woman said.

Keith spent a few minutes outlining Bradley's plan to them, what he knew of it. Without Sam, none of them could be completely sure, not even Molly.

"He thinks he can kill everyone?" the man said.

Keith glanced at his fellow travelers for backup but got none. "I don't think that's the plan so much as to trap them inside." He shrugged his shoulders. "Or scare them so that no one else escapes. We can't be sure."

"Stop delivering food," the man said.

"They would just let more people out," Robert suggested.

"It's not that simple anyway," Molly said from behind Keith. "Newcity provides pharmaceuticals, electronics. All scientific discoveries are coming from there now."

"Negotiate," the woman said.

"They don't care about us," Molly said. "I'm not sure they have any idea what's going on out here any more. As long as they receive shipments of the things they need, they're satisfied with the arrangement."

"Harold," the woman said to the man next to her, "what does this mean?" She indicated the children with a jerk of her head.

He didn't respond for a moment. They all waited for him. "None of this makes sense," he said. He slipped the club he held in his right hand back into an inside pocket of the coat he was wearing. Leaning close to Keith, he said, "There must be something else going on."

Behind the children, entering from the street came a figure. Keith turned to see who it was and when he did, Harold and the others turned as well. At that moment, Keith knew it was the angel with one wing.

Harold acted as though it was a false alarm. "We want peace in our lives. We know it's difficult, but we're at least hoping to get the children accepted inside. It's a better life for them." He looked sick when he said it. "Now, we're not so sure. What could be so horrible that you wanted to escape?"

Keith asked the others to tell Harold and his friends what they thought about Newcity. He hoped they'd discuss Bradley as well, but left them alone.

Once they began their discussion, he wandered toward the other end of the alley, out of hearing range. As he closed in on the angel, he stopped and waited. As much as he wanted to reach out and touch her, he didn't do it. He stayed a respectable distance from her. He didn't say a word, but he did examine her features. She looked totally unfamiliar, young and old at the same time. Her arms and hands were smooth, yet muscled. Her torso appeared to be thin, but not skinny. The bulge on her back pushed against her clothing, causing her breasts to protrude against the tight blouse. It was sensual and forbidden. He sensed that the trapped wing was uncomfortable, and imagined the freedom she'd feel by letting her wing stretch in the open air.

She turned her eyes away from his inspection.

"There is no reason for any of this, is there?" he asked. "Why have you led me out of Newcity only to return again a few days later?"

"It is not always for you," she said. "But, for now, you must come with me." She spoke so clearly that Keith turned around to see if the others had heard. But they were in deep conversations of their own, their faces smiling like they were old friends. How could they have resolved their differences so quickly, when a moment ago Harold and the others appeared to have their hopes crushed?

He turned back to the angel ready to voice the question. She appeared nervous as she waited for his advance. He nodded and followed as the angel led him into the darkened streets. The pedestrians had nearly abandoned the sidewalks by now. Few cars drove by. Keith felt totally invisible following her, although glances from some of the people proved that he wasn't.

The angel picked up speed and he did the same. She rounded a corner and began to run. Her movements were smooth and lightweight, as though she could actually fly at one time and was remembering the feeling as she ran. The single wing bounced as she led him on. They crossed a street and to his left he saw the boy with the bullet hole in his forehead wave to him. He stumbled over the curb and fell onto the sidewalk. His hands and knees met the damp cement. When he looked up the angel was gone, but the boy continued to wave to him. He scrambled to his feet and ran toward the boy.

He shook his head while he ran, trying to understand what just happened and why the images shifted from the angel to the boy.

While he followed, Newcity appeared and disappeared as he crossed one open street then rejoined the buildings on the block. The boy paralleled the complex until Keith emerged near the unloading docks. Trucks were backed up to Newcity for what appeared to be a mile or more. The scent of fresh produce permeated the air. He advanced slowly.

The boy was gone.

Chapter 17

Keith crouched low as he maneuvered among and around the multitude of vehicles. The sound of machines running and people talking echoed through the area from the open doors that accessed the warehouse. Trucks that had been emptied started with a hiss and a squeal, then pulled out from the dock. Many of the doors were closed as soon as the vehicles were out of the way. Some of the trucks drove onto the street leading away from Newcity, while others pulled into what appeared to be some sort of holding area a few hundred yards away.

He worried that the trucks would thin out as the city streets did at night, leaving him exposed, so he advanced toward the holding area only to find that there was a gas station and restaurant located inside the circle of parked rigs. In the dark, he could see one of the drivers sitting in a sleeping area located behind the driver's seat. The dim light exposed the small compartment and the man who lay in the bunk, propped on an elbow, was writing in a notebook.

Keith surmised that these particular vehicles would stay the night, and decided to find a place to rest until he could fashion a plan. There was no reason to hide. The people here had no reason to suspect him of anything. Besides, the truck drivers would be transients from the outlying farms, bringing their loads into Newcity and then returning home.

Keith surveyed the area by taking a long walk around the combination restaurant and gas station. He held his shirt close to his nose to subdue the strong scents of exhaust, sweat, and litter. His vision blurred, tearing up from the odors, making him wipe his eyes occasionally. He needed to rest, but everywhere he looked were trucks that could drive over him if he were to lie under them to sleep. At the back of the station, the smell of cooked food poured through steam-ridden vents, replacing the nasty odors permeating much of the parking lot.

A small stand of bushes lay between the rear of the station and the highway leading from the city. Streetlights along the road reached bleakly into the brush as Keith pushed his way in. There would be rats, he knew, but they wouldn't bother him as long as he didn't try to harm them. He brushed over the ground with his hand and sat to consider his predicament.

The angel had said that it wasn't always about him. So his purpose might include the others who traveled with him, or those yet to escape, possibly even Newcity itself. Could it be that he was there only to lead the others into Newcity? It was their choice to attempt a warning, not his. Little of it made any sense to him. All the plans, Bradley's and the escapees', were vague at best. But then, he had only been a part of the outside world for a few days. And now, his return to Newcity had been forced, while his escape had been a choice.

He had to face the truth that he didn't fully understand what had happened, but that he had created the way out and then followed the boy, his younger self, to the outside world. Was it a subconscious choice that manifested through him? A shiver ran down his spine. He felt the truth of his discovery, but highly questioned its reasoning. Perhaps there was no reason for what happened to him beyond wanting something different in his life.

Keith shook his head. He had been thinking deeply and had to pull himself back into the real world, the night. He coughed and the sound echoed around him. He heard someone say, "Over there," and pushed his senses into high alert. He ducked as though he could hide better if closer to the ground. He turned to scan the area behind him, only to see someone else looking back at him.

Brent yelled, "Here he is."

There was no use running. As soon as Brent yelled, he heard the others coming toward him from several directions. He pushed into a crouched position and moved bush branches out of his way using his arms. As he stepped out and into the open, Brent griped, "What were you thinking? You can't just leave us like that."

"The angel came and I followed her. I didn't have time to interrupt your conversation. I was going to come back," Keith lied.

Robert sidled up to Keith and put a hand on his shoulder. "Next time, let us know."

"There won't be a next time," Brent said. "We'll be inside by then."

"The warehouse is closing down by the looks of it. The doors will be watched. We can't sneak in tonight," Keith said.

"Not ever," Stacy said.

"What do you mean?" Keith turned his head but not his body. He saw that Harold and his friends were there too. "Why are they here?" He turned back to Brent. "No," he said. "This can't be."

Brent stepped close. "You've got to show us where you came out. We're going to backtrack and get back inside."

"And do what?" Keith said.

Will answered the question. "Stay. As long as we don't disrupt anything, we'll be cared for. It's peaceful. Newcity is enormous. They'll never find us."

Will's thinking was accurate. Nellie and her friends had been living in Newcity without being detected. But they wanted out. "You won't like it," Keith said. "It won't take long and you'll want back out."

"We're not all alike," Brent said. The others nodded in agreement.

Stacy reached and touched Keith's arm gently. "You were sent to help us return. Being outside isn't for everyone. You've got to know that."

"It wasn't for Sam, even though he was born outside," Molly said.

"What about Bradley? His plan?" Keith said.

Will raised his hand and lowered his eyes. "We drew straws and I lost."

Rebecca, who stood beside him, laid her head over onto his shoulder. "I'm staying with him."

"We're going to tell them what Bradley is up to," Brent said. "He'll never get near Newcity. He has a few hundred people at best. His weapons are old. It'll be easy to stop him.

"Then they'll chip us and put us back in," Will said. "It's not our first choice, but it's happened to others before." Will raised his eyes and begged Keith, "Unless you volunteer to warn them. It would be a sacrifice."

"Maybe that's what you're supposed to do," Stacy said. "After all, you are the boy with the bullet hole in your forehead."

"And the angel?" Keith said.

"We believe that she'll appear to us once we get back inside," Stacy said. "We'll have the best of both worlds."

Keith knew that they were trying to convince him, persuade him to go along. And at some point in the conversation he wasn't sure who was right and who was wrong. His few days outside had been unbelievably beautiful and horrible at the same time. Standing there, amongst them, he honestly couldn't decide what was best for him. How could he decide what was best for them? He prayed for the boy to whisper something. He pleaded internally to whatever power that had brought him this far, but nothing came, nothing contacted him on any level.

He was lost.

"And the others?" he said, pointing to Harold and his family.

"We're going with you," Harold answered. "We'll get to stay with our own kids."

The woman put an arm around Harold and Keith glanced at the other man who was with them.

"My brother-in-law," the woman said, in answer to the unasked question.

The children stood back, shy and quiet, which made Keith wonder, once again, if they weren't right that some people aren't suited for the outside world.

The night air was still except for the breeze that came from the highway every once in a while. Brent stared into Keith's eyes waiting for him to say something more, but Keith didn't make a decision one way or the other. He was unable to. Seeing Will's face, and Rebecca's, both resolved to be dulled down by getting chipped again, to experience a false sense of peace, placed a great weight on Keith's heart. How could he deny them what they longed for?

"We'll stay here tonight. It's a good enough spot," Brent said. He motioned for Keith to lead the way.

Parting the brush aside, Keith crouched nearly on his hands and knees and snaked through the area until he could see the highway on the other side of a long gulley. The grass was long and they had plenty of cover.

"This is good," Brent said.

The others spread out and found a space to either sit or lie down.

Keith rested on the ground between Brent and Stacy. "How would this work?"

"What?" Brent said.

"How do I lead you back inside and then warn the Newcity police about Bradley?"

Brent smiled. "Thank you." He turned to Will. "You're in," he said. Then he swung back toward Keith and went into his rough plan, explaining Keith's part as guide, and how he would continue to Newcity Central where he could turn himself in. Brent also asked Keith to memorize Bradley's approximate location. "Sam had a map with him," Brent said before providing the rough directions.

Keith memorized the information Brent told him and repeated it to be sure he had it right.

"Good," Brent said.

"The only problem is that we won't be able to get back in the way I exited," Keith said. "The maintenance will have been performed already. There'll be another route, but I won't know it."

"You'll be guided," Stacy said.

Keith wanted to believe her. "We'll see," he said. "I'm still not convinced that I escaped merely to lead you back in."

"Why else would you come out alone?" she said.

"Maybe I was the last." Keith said. "After all, the boy is still with me."

"Don't say that. We waited for you to come. The boy is still here so that you can get back in." Stacy appeared frazzled as she rejected his theory. "Enough of this. Let's get some sleep. We'll need to be fresh in the morning."

As they settled for the night, Keith heard scraping and movement around them, the rustling of garbage, chewing. He suspected rats, but the glow from the lights didn't illuminate the area well enough for him to know for sure. As long as the sounds stayed away, he'd be fine, but he didn't have to be concerned about that. The last to lie down, Keith noticed how they had placed him in the center of the group, which would make it difficult for him to escape even if he wanted to. And it would be equally difficult for rats to get near him. At least he'd sleep in peace.

He lay on his back and stared through the brush into the night sky. A hazy light indicated the position of the moon behind the clouds. He longed to see sunrise over the hills back in Bradley's camp. The memory filled him with inspiration and a sense that everything was natural and good. Why didn't the others feel the same way? The chilled air caused his skin to pucker into bumps, so he placed his arms over his chest to keep warm. His senses had been turned on. His emotions varied widely, even as he thought about his experiences. A tear came to his eye. He was about to give up what he had recently acquired. His compassion was stronger than his self-preservation, it seemed.

As Keith closed his eyes and accepted the night, he heard the voice of his father speaking. "You have always been different than the other kids," he said. "Your sense of duty is strong, but there are times when you must make your own decisions."

And then another voice said, "You cannot save others, only help them to save themselves."

Keith's eyes opened and he sat up. He recognized the voice of Sam. He strained to look into the underbrush. Was that Sam's image beyond some of the brush, gauzy and faint, flowing with the rhythm of the breeze?

As his heart got loud inside him, Keith glimpsed an image that looked like his father too. As he tried to bring the images into view, the images shivered and faded, then disappeared. In a moment both men were gone and Keith rested on his elbows confused and worried that he might be breaking down completely. He tried to think about what they had said, but like much of his life the past few days, the words revolved around each other. How could he make his own decisions, and at the same time help the others to save themselves? Words were much less useful than motion. At least the boy with the bullet hole in his forehead led Keith somewhere. He could follow the boy. The words only went in circles.

A part of him wanted to ask the images questions, sit down and have a long talk where this could all be explained clearly and succinctly. Then he could really make his own decision.

He lay back down and closed his eyes again. Only in half sleep did he see the apparitions of the dead. Perhaps that was where they lived. He willed their return, but when he awoke again, it wasn't to either of their voices, but to the sound of snoring coming from several of the others.

Still dark, Keith thought back and saw that the only part of his life that had mattered was the last few days. All the rest of it seemed empty, the same. He could only recall one thing of importance from his time living in Newcity. Nellie. Her aggression no longer felt angry to him. Another feeling attached to her behavior that he couldn't name. He closed his eyes again and woke with the morning light.

Chapter 18

DAY 6

The thirteen people shared what food they had with them that morning. Harold helped by walking to the gas station and buying some bread and butter to help fill their stomachs. The smell from the exhaust behind the restaurant was that of bacon, which had a few of them complaining about being outside of Newcity rather than inside where food was plentiful.

"You see," Stacy said to Keith, "out here we are denied food as often as we get it. How could we survive out here?" She was walking past him to join Brent. They all stood near the brush behind the station. The noise from the highway hummed in their ears.

"It's just a feeling you've never had," Keith said. "Maybe you learn how to acquire food, how to know your own body. If I focus on other things, the hunger goes away. The odor is just another smell, nothing more."

She narrowed her eyes at him, but he knew the look and it didn't scare him like it did the others. When he didn't react, she said, "I'm sorry. You can have your own opinions as long as you get us back inside."

"What if I'm unsuccessful? If they don't believe me?" Keith said.

"You are the boy with the bullet hole in his forehead. They'll believe you."

Harold interrupted their talk by barging in between them. "I don't care who saw what when you got out of there. It's time we found our way in."

"Right," Robert said. "Let's go." He walked toward Newcity and the others followed.

Brent grabbed Keith's arm so that he was in the middle of the group. As they approached Newcity, Keith took the lead. He knew that they needed to get in through the docks, even though Brent and Stacy thought otherwise. He knew that was the right entry point ever since the night before, and his determination wouldn't allow him to alter his plan.

It was early and already trucks lined the warehouse portion of Newcity where all the receiving took place.

The group broke into several smaller bands. Brent, Stacy, Molly, and Keith traveled ahead. Next came the woman and her brother, her two children, and Harold. Robert and Amanda, and Will and Rebecca brought up the rear.

"I should go with you," Will said to Keith. He put his hand on the butt of the pistol. "In case you have trouble."

Uncomfortable with Will's willingness to kill again, Keith did no more than shake his head. "That's why you're taking up the rear. To protect the others." Before they went any farther, Keith glanced around as though they might be watched. "We need to meet where the flowers come into the building. The place where people select those flowers should be easy to find. That's where we're headed. Don't ask why. Just meet at that place.

Keith didn't wait for them to comment. He jogged from behind one of the trucks to the next truck. Crates of food were being unloaded. As they made their way across the area, he scanned the workers, hoping to locate Nellie. He was surprised at how few guards there were. Yet, none of the workers even attempted to escape. Eventually, he brushed his shirt and pants and straightened up, ready to walk out into the open.

"What do you think you're doing?" Brent said, grabbing Keith's arm again.

"I know someone who works here. She can help."

"Help, how?"

"I told you last night that I'd get you inside," Keith said. He looked at Brent's hand still holding his arm.

Brent let go. "We'll be watching."

Keith strolled out from behind the truck. There were about thirty people working on that portion of the dock. They were all focused on the task at hand, unloading the trucks. Each crate was made of thick cardboard, the tops open. They carried box after box of flowers. Keith knew that Nellie would be in this section, making the selection of the freshest flowers for each of the stores in her area of Newcity.

At the far end of the dock lay a set of stairs. A portable table and a few chairs had been set up for the truck drivers, but many of them stood in a group much farther from the dock. Only a few of the men and women sat at the table. "Sit down," one of them invited as Keith approached.

"Not today," he said.

The man shrugged then perked up and looked beyond Keith.

Keith turned to see what alerted him. The other three had come around the truck and were hot on his tail.

"You guys are all dressed alike. Where you from?" one of the drivers said.

"Inspectors," Brent said, taking Keith's lead from the night before.

The driver scrunched up his face. "Inspecting what? Don't they have their own?"

"Trainees," Brent said.

The man shook his head and turned back to the others while Brent, Stacy, and Molly followed Keith up the stairs.

"This is too easy," Brent said, close to Keith's ear.

"Not for long," Keith motioned toward several Newcity police heading across the warehouse floor. In a panic, he turned to Brent and whispered, "Run and hide," then darted away from the approaching police and shot down an aisle.

Keith didn't watch to see where the others ran off to; instead he slowed to a walk once the police couldn't see him. The rushing footsteps weren't coming in his direction. He heard a calm assertion for someone to stop, but continued to hear running. He assumed that the others had kept going and avoided the police for the moment. The workers in the area where he found himself all but ignored him. One or two nodded, but the others were either operating machines used to stack the crates or carting the crates by hand.

He turned down an aisle and smelled the air. He followed the fragrance of the flowers, knowing that he'd eventually find the space where Nellie would be working. As one of the workers passed with several crates of flowers on a dolly, Keith turned to the man and said, "I'll take that from here. There's been a change."

The man handed the dolly over without saying a word. His facial expression dulled the air around him with passivity and a lack of personality. He calmly turned to go back to the dock empty handed.

Keith pushed the dolly up one aisle and over to the next until he saw an open area where flowers were displayed on a long table. Three young girls appeared to be considering which to purchase. One of the girls was Nellie.

Keith pushed the dolly toward the table.

Nellie saw him approaching and her eyes widened. Her hands moved more quickly over the flowers and she put a label on one of the boxes before moving on to the next.

Keith pushed the dolly to the end of the tables and stood it up. He walked toward Nellie and she swung toward him as he approached.

"Oh, good," she said with a nervous voice. "I need to talk with you." She took his hand gently in hers and led him away from the table. One of the other girls glanced her way, but went back to work in a moment. "How were you able to get up here?"

"We walked as though we belonged here. The police did chase the others, though," Keith said. "I don't think for long."

"It'll be difficult to leave now, that's why. The cameras are mounted facing in, to keep us from getting too close to the outside. We seldom have someone coming in on purpose. Everyone uses the administration entrance. If they only knew," she shook her head with curiosity. "'Others,'" she said as though his words finally sunk in. "I thought you came to get us."

"Not exactly," Keith said.

She stopped and turned into him. Tears had already built around her eyes. "Why not?"

"There are others who want back in," he said.

She looked confused by his statement.

"I don't know why, either. It's not meant for everyone out there." He jerked his head to indicate the outside world. "I promised that I'd help them get back inside without being chipped. Then I need to warn the Center of the possibility of an attack." He swallowed and lifted his jaw slightly to maintain his composure. "They'll probably chip me again."

She closed her eyes for a moment and then opened them after releasing a long, slow breath. "The chips are breaking down," she said. "There have been more disturbances since you've gone. More violent ones. I've heard that the chemists are working on a stronger chip model, but their experiments aren't working out." She raised her eyes to meet his. "They've rechipped you before. It didn't work. What if they don't try this time? What if they experiment with you because of your apparent resistance? You'll die in there." She reached to touch his face with her hand, then lowered it and looked around.

"It'll be all right," Keith said. "Will you help me get them in?"

"We're crowded, but they can stay with us until we figure this out. They won't like being inside if they're not chipped." She took his hand and walked toward the rear of the warehouse. When they arrived at a cross path she scanned all directions and continued on. As they passed a door, Keith halted abruptly.

A uniformed maintenance man worked on one of the doors, replacing the hinges. The door leaned against the wall as he turned a screwdriver.

"This is it," Keith said. He turned to Nellie. "You won't have to keep any of them with you. I'll take them inside. Now quickly, I have to find the others before he's finished. This is the way inside."

"How do you know?"

"Because I'm doing it. I don't know how or why, but I must follow my own path back in." He swung her around. "The others were supposed to meet me where the flowers are brought in. If they were able to lose the police."

Nellie laughed. "They're Newcity Police. They only pursue until they become confused. They've probably gone back to their posts by now. Trust me, it's when you cross from here to out there that they send the big guns."

Keith didn't understand what she was suggesting. After all, he got out through a side door with little effort. And others had escaped, too. Unless it was some sort of lottery and they were allowed outside, what she said just made things more confusing. He had no time to think about it anyway. They made their way back to the selection table, where the others were waiting in a large group.

When Keith turned the corner and saw them they were huddled close together, as though they didn't know where they were or what they were supposed to do.

Will had his hand near the gun hidden under his shirt.

Keith waved them to follow him and Nellie. They were noisy as a group, but they didn't have to go far. "The police?" Keith said.

Brent shrugged his shoulders. "It's a big warehouse."

Nellie clicked her tongue. "They went back to their posts. Trust me. They may have called it in, but they aren't looking for you."

"Makes no sense," Keith said.

As they approached the door being maintenanced, Keith and Nellie walked ahead of the group. Nellie said to the man, "You almost finished here?"

"Almost. I have to set the door and pin it."

"Nice job. Before you're done though, these people have to be escorted back in." She turned to Keith. "You'll return as soon as they're back to their posts?"

He saw her plead with her eyes and knew what she was asking, that he help her and the others to get out. "I'll be back as soon as I'm finished," he said. Keith had no idea why it was so easy for him to get in and out of Newcity when so many others, like Nellie, couldn't. He motioned for the others to follow him, then turned back to Nellie and took both of her hands into his. "Tell me. Have you always known that I was the boy with the bullet hole in his forehead?"

She closed her eyes and lowered her chin. "Yes. We all knew. We have theories about it, but there's no telling what's going on. And to tell the truth, I doubt that we'll have to worry about being attacked from the outside. We're already breaking down in here." She let go of his hands and patted his chest. "Good luck and hurry back."

Keith rushed into the hallway. After the last of them were in, the door was replaced. Minimal lighting fixtures were set above them every twenty feet or so. The dim light caused shadows to lengthen and shorten as they traveled. Keith followed his instincts, but kept alert for the boy. They went up numerous flights of stairs, down halls, around corners, and into Newcity for short stints before going back into the wall areas. The place was a maze of corridors and passageways built for maintenance purposes. Pipes and wires ran along most of the inside walls.

Harold, his brother, wife, and children looked out of place when they were inside Newcity proper. They had been told not to stare or look around too much, but they didn't seem to be able to stop themselves.

Keith had everyone separate into their smaller groups too, in case the police noticed something odd and came over to investigate. At this point, he couldn't feel responsible any longer. He had helped them get inside; it was up to them now. He stopped walking.

"Where to now?" Brent said.

"I don't know," Keith said.

They stood near a crossroads of residences. Few people were in the halls. When a couple walked past, Harold followed them. Surprised at his aggressive approach, Keith and the others followed.

The couple entered an apartment and Harold forced his way in behind them. Brent, Stacy, and Keith were next. The others soon followed, filling the room that looked like every room Keith had ever seen in Newcity. He was shocked by the lack of color and by the familiar shapes of the furniture, the similarity to what he had lived in.

The man they had followed turned around and bowed to Harold. "I'm sorry, but we didn't request that you come in. Could you leave now?"

"Sorry buddy." In one smooth but violent motion, Harold removed his short club from his jacket pocket and slammed the man across the head, knocking him out. As quickly as he did that, he back-slapped the woman and knocked her out, as well.

Dropping the couple happened so quickly that their chips would not have had time to register an emotional peak. And, even if they did, the peak would drop to normal as they slept on the floor.

Keith grabbed Harold's arm and swung him around. "What do you think you're doing?"

"I'm not an idiot. I knew I had to take care of this quickly," he said.

"Now what? When they wake up…"

Will strolled forward past Harold and pulled the pistol from his pants. "They won't," he said, and shot each of them in the heart without shying or hesitating a bit.

Keith heard the door click behind him.

Brent turned to Robert and ordered him to find an empty apartment down one of the other halls. Robert rushed from the room.

Keith knew what they were going to do. They were going to plant the dead bodies in someone else's apartment to be found when they arrived home. The chip would alert the police and the other person would be arrested.

"You're going to have to give up that gun now," Brent said.

Will looked at the pistol. "I didn't think of that," he said.

"You won't need it in here anyway," Stacy said.

Will handed over the pistol. Robert returned with a find, and Harold and his brother rolled the bodies into a couple of sheets.

It didn't seem like more than a half hour for the place to be cleaned up and they were all sitting around. Brent had already ordered food. Stacy was hungry.

Keith didn't like any of it. And when the food came, he grabbed a sandwich and said that he had to go. No one appeared to care if he stayed or left. They had settled in and were feasting on food the other couple's terminal allowed them to order.

Brent stood and asked him one question. "Are you going through with your end of the deal?"

He looked over at Will, then scanned the others. They were all looking at him. "Of course," Keith said. Then he slipped out the door. As soon as he was in the hallway, the boy with the bullet hole in his forehead appeared at the end of the hall. "Are you me or the machine?" Keith whispered as he followed the boy.

It didn't take long before he found himself back inside the walls where all the plumbing and electrical was located. A heaviness in the air made him feel as though he was headed farther into the complex, closer to the hub of the world, where the city had started. But then they started to go down the stairs. As he followed the boy lower into the building, Keith lost count of which floor they were on. They could have been underground by the time they exited into one of Newcity's standard staircases.

The boy stood next to a door into Newcity and Keith didn't hesitate to walk toward him. The boy faded away as Keith met and pushed against the door. He stopped just inside a wide room filled with terminals. Several people sat in front of a couple of the displays. One man turned and, on seeing Keith, said, "Here he is," as though Keith had been expected.

Chapter 19

E veryone in the room was dressed similarly. A few more of those who sat in front of terminals twisted around to look at Keith, but the others continued to stare at displays, focused on the work in front of them. Keith stood above the room by a few steps and couldn't see the terminals well enough to know what they displayed.

Another man walked from the right toward Keith, who pressed his back against the door that had closed behind him.

"Rodger," said the man coming toward him while holding his hand out. "And you are Keith."

Keith took the man's hand and shook it. "Are you friends with Nellie?"

Rodger cocked his head. "Nellie? Is this someone new?" He turned toward the group below them. "Who's Nellie?"

"I'll look her up, sir," a young woman said.

Rodger still held Keith's hand. He leaned back slightly and looked Keith up and down. "Follow me, son." He let go of Keith's hand and walked along the aisleway that surrounded the terminal banks. An open door stood twenty yards away. Before they reached the door, the young woman yelled, "She doesn't show up anywhere."

The man stopped at the doorway and motioned for Keith to step inside. He turned toward the group and said, "Scan the monitors for another IFI." Swinging the door shut, he asked Keith to sit down at an oval table made from a brown plastic material. The chairs were brown plastic also, but worn and stained. The seat was uncomfortable. Rodger took a position at the end of the oval desk adjacent to where Keith sat.

They sat together for a few seconds before Rodger said anything. He had his elbows on the table and appeared to be deep in thought.

Finally, he tapped the table with the fingers of both hands and then sat back into the chair, letting his hands rest on the edge of the table as though he were barely holding on. "What's going on?" he said. "What are you doing to the system?"

Keith was confused.

"Don't look like you don't know what I'm talking about," Rodger said. He leaned forward but still held loosely to the table. "The others might not be so nice. Just tell me what you're doing and how you're doing it."

"I honestly don't know what you're talking about," Keith said.

"How'd you find us, then?"

It seemed like an odd question. According to Nellie, the image of the boy showed up on the video cameras. This man should have known that. He should have seen those images.

"Well?" Rodger said.

"You know how," Keith said.

The man slapped the table and stood up. "Don't fuck with me, young man. How did you get here? How did you know which doors were safe and when they were safe?"

"I didn't. I followed the boy." Keith stopped there, not because he was finished talking, but because of the look on Rodger's face. "I'm sure you've seen him on your monitors. There's video, right?" Keith said.

"How would you know that?"

"Nellie," Keith said.

Rodger rushed to the door and opened it. He stepped half way out and yelled, "Who the fuck is Nellie?"

"We're looking sir, but there's still nothing," came the voice of the girl.

Rodger slammed the door. He paced at the end of the table for a moment, then yanked the chair out and sat down again. "Sorry. I don't mean to get upset, but I thought you came here to tell us what was going on." He shook his finger at Keith. "Unless you don't know you know."

"What's an IFI?" Keith asked.

"Internally Fabricated Image. It's when the system creates an image that isn't there."

"If it isn't there, how can it open doors?" Keith said.

Rodger didn't look happy. He didn't say anything either.

Keith glanced at Rodger's forearm, which was smooth. The man had no chip.

Rodger recognized what Keith had done and jutted his chin out. "Only residents get chipped," he said. "We control the complex. If they chipped us, this whole place would collapse. Not that it isn't on its way to collapse already."

"You mean the increase in violence?" Keith said.

"What the hell are you, psychic?" He raised a hand to stop Keith from saying anything else. "Don't tell me, Nellie."

Keith smiled. He didn't know how Nellie and her friend did it, but somehow they worked in the system yet were invisible to it, or not listed. That's how the others would be, too. He wondered how many others were wandering around inside Newcity without chips.

A knock came to the door and Rodger said, "Come in."

Two other men and a woman entered. They were all dressed in the uniform of the day. Both men were smaller-built than Rodger, and the woman was even more petite. She had shoulder-length blonde hair. The men both had short gray hair.

Rodger stood and motioned for the others to sit down. They stepped around Keith and went all the way to the other side of the table to sit facing him. "Doctor Mike, Rene, and Charles," Rodger said as introduction. He turned his attention back to Keith. "And this is Keith."

The others nodded. Keith raised a hand and said, "Hi."

"May I?" Doctor Mike asked while reaching for Keith's hand. "Sure."

The man took Keith's hand and turned it so that he could see the wound where the chip had been removed. "Healing nicely," he said.

Rene didn't wait until Keith had his hand back to ask her first question, "Who is the boy with the blood seeping out of his forehead?"

"It's a bullet hole," Keith said.

The team looked at one another and then back at Keith. "How do you know that?"

"I don't know for sure. That's just what I thought. We all think that way."

"All? You've been in contact with others who have seen the boy?" Rene said.

"Escapees. Yes."

She looked down the table at Rodger. "How many residents have left the building?"

"Last count that we know of was one hundred and six," Rodger said.

"I never met that many, but it could be so," Keith said. "Actually, that's what I wanted to tell you. Many of the escapees are holed up with a man named Bradley who is planning an attack on Newcity."

"When?" Charles said.

"I don't know. But now that I got away from him, we suspect soon."

Charles got up from the table and made his way to the door. "I'll take care of this now. You can go on. I'll be back."

Rodger nodded his approval then leaned his elbows on the table. He breathed a sigh before asking Keith his next question. "What else can you tell us?"

"I don't know much."

"Tell us more about the bullet hole, as you call it," Rene said. "How did you come up with that?"

"I didn't come up with it. That's just what it looked like and how I started to think of it. Like I said, the others saw it the same way," Keith said.

"Did they recognize who the boy was? Did you?"

Keith stared at her. Her eyes were blue and inviting, but the skin around her eyes, her cheekbones, and her mouth were tight with what looked like long hours of stress, and not so inviting. He lowered his eyes and mumbled, "You know who the boy is."

"But we don't know where he came from," she said.

"Here," the angel with one wing said from the other end of the table.

Keith glanced at her when she spoke.

"No," Rene said. "Is he in here?" She looked up at the security camera in the corner. "This is being taped?" she said more as a question than a statement.

Rodger nodded to assure her.

"How are you doing this?" Doctor Mike asked. "You're not chipped."

"I'm not doing anything," Keith said. "I was hoping that you could tell me what was going on." He realized that they had never seen the angel, only the boy, and wondered, just as they did, whether the image was being recorded or not.

"The new chips," Rodger said.

Doctor Mike looked distressed. "You're always trying to blame it on the technology, but this is not the chip. There is something different about him." The doctor pushed back his chair but didn't get up. "For God's sake, he doesn't have a chip."

Rodger did get up. He went to the door and opened it. Stepping outside he yelled, "Danny, is that boy's IFI in the conference room?"

"No sir. It's only the four of you."

Rodger came back into the room. "But you see him," he said to Keith.

"No. He's not here."

Rene glanced at the end of the room. "Someone's in here. I can see it in the way you glance over and in your expression. Who is it, then? Who do you see?"

"The angel," Keith said answering the question.

The angel shook her head.

"What?" Keith said.

"An angel? What's he look like?" Rene asked.

"Never mind," Keith said.

The angel stepped around the table and Keith followed her movements. Rene watched him closely as he did so. It was almost as though she could see the angel too, by following what Keith did. The angel said, "I'm sorry about this, Keith. It's what you might call self-discovery."

Keith closed his eyes.

"What's he saying?" Rene asked.

"What's she saying," Keith corrected her.

Doctor Mike and Rodger sat quietly as Rene probed with another question. "What does she look like? Does she look like Nellie?"

Keith laughed. "No, nothing like Nellie. Nellie's dark skinned."

Rodger jumped from the table and went outside the door. Keith heard him tell someone to find all the dark skinned women in the complex and to round them up.

"You can't do that. She didn't do anything," Keith said when Rodger came back.

"She's an accomplice. Now, what else is there? Why can't we see this angel?" He tapped a finger on the table.

Rene leaned back in her chair and glared at Rodger. "You are bent on screwing this up, aren't you? Would you just let me do my job here?"

Keith looked back and forth at them. He knew now that they couldn't see or hear he angel, so he directed his next statement directly to her. "Is Nellie going to be okay?"

The others stopped talking and pinned their attention to Keith.

The angel shrugged her shoulders. "That may be up to you," she said.

"How? You can't tell me that now. I've been following you. You've got to help."

"Oh my God," he heard Rene whisper. "They're arguing."

"Then tell me what's going on so I can tell them," he said.

"They won't have any idea what you're talking about. They don't now," she said.

"Then help me so that I'll know."

"I can only help if you know what to do. Don't you see?" She turned around to go back to the other end of the room.

"What kind of angel are you?" Keith said. "You only have one wing."

"Wings?" Rodger said.

"You tell me what kind of angel I am," she said. "You tell me what I'm supposed to do. Tell me, and I'll do it," she said.

"Get me out of here." Keith stood.

Rodger ran for the door and blocked it. "You're going nowhere."

Keith turned to the angel and motioned to her with his palms up as though asking her what she was going to do next.

"When it's time," she said. Then the angel faded away as though she had never been in the conference room at all.

"Dammit," Keith said. He looked around the table at the others.

"She's gone," Rene said. She stared at Keith. "You're disappointed. Your," she seemed to have trouble saying the next word, "angel ... has left you."

"She'll be back," Keith said.

"You're not sure of that, are you?" Rene said.

Keith wanted to cry. His emotions were jumbled. He had been led to this place, now he wanted out and there was no going anywhere. "I'm hungry," he said quietly.

Rene reached for his hand, but he pulled both of them onto his lap. She looked up at Rodger, still guarding the door. "He isn't going anywhere. Get him some food."

The food came fairly quickly, and for the next fifteen minutes everyone stayed quiet as he ate a sandwich. This gave Keith a chance to think about what was going on. He had been shown how to escape, had collected the others, and had reentered without any trouble. Well, hardly any trouble. And he had been guided to this central office. The people here wanted answers from him, yet he had none. He asked his angel and she had no answers. Keith sat up in his chair and pushed the plate to the side. He took a drink of water they had brought with the sandwich.

The others leaned toward him. "What is it?" Rene asked.

"You have the answers," Keith said. "I'm here to get the answer from you."

"Preposterous," Rodger said about the same time that Doctor Mike said, "Insane."

"Perhaps not," Rene said. "It's like a puzzle, isn't it? A riddle. None of us has the whole piece." She looked over to the others then back to Keith. "Only you can solve it. Somehow, your openness will allow you to put the pieces together like we can't do. To us, the answer is ineffable. That's it, isn't it?"

Keith glared at her. "Tell me what you know."

"We don't know much," she said. "At least we don't think we do."

"I'm not sure I like this," Rodger said.

"Let her go." Mike sat back in his chair and said, "Go on," to Rene.

"About ten years ago, we began to get the IFI of the boy. We didn't know what it was. We sent security forces to find him, but he disappeared every time we got close." She shrugged, "The cameras can't see everything. Many of them don't even work anymore. We didn't replace them because it didn't matter. Everyone was under control. The chips worked great.

"Anyway, it took us a while to figure out that the boy was caused by some sort of a glitch in the computer system. We had our best software guys trying to figure out where the image came from, but no one could find a blip of any kind in the programming." She stopped talking. "Any questions so far?"

"Did you recognize the boy at that time?" Keith said.

"No. He was still an IFI. You've got to understand. Those things show up every once in a while. With a system this large and this complex you get all sorts of things happening. We'd get images of these spheres that would show up. They looked like bubbles. Or streaks of light. Rainbows across the screens. Little things that we didn't worry much about. You get used to them. But the boy was human. That was a complicated image to create. At first the IFIs of the boy were a little fuzzy and only appeared once in a while. They got clearer though, and eventually they were showing up a lot. Never two places at once. It was like he really was human." She tapped the table in front of her similar to how Rodger did earlier. "And to make things worse, a few years ago the first group of people escaped. We got a glimpse of them following the boy. That's when we started to worry.

"We had everyone on staff psychologically tested to be sure this wasn't an inside job."

Keith waited for her. He knew she was deciding how to go on. "Everything," he said, "if you expect me to help you figure this out." So far, he had nothing but the fact that the system had created an image. So what?

"Bradley worked for us then. He didn't test well. We asked him to leave." She looked down the table at Rodger. "You have to understand. We hire people from outside quite often. As we need them. Bradley was good. But this wasn't the place for him. He had a lot of family outside and didn't agree with what we were doing in here," she said.

"What <u>are</u> you doing in here?"

"At the beginning, running a business, a very symbiotic business with the outside world. Now, Newcity is like its own country. We work to maintain ourselves. We import and export less and less, we..."

"He doesn't need to know our economic situation, Rene. Just get on with the escapees and the IFI sightings," Rodger said. "And wrap this up soon. I'm not sure I like it."

"Fine," Rene said, turning back to Keith.

Doctor Mike interrupted the conversation. "These guys thought it was the new chips. We're always updating them. But the first escapees were all old-chip residents. So, that couldn't be the problem. But you need to tell him that." He jerked his head toward Rodger.

"He wants to be exonerated." Rene shook her head at the doctor.

Rodger cut in again. "Bradley knew about the escapees and set up to have someone cut the chips out of their arms. We have no idea how he figured out where the escapees would go. They're met at a different place every time. Either that or he has people planted all over the city."

"You couldn't go get him?" Keith said.

"Beside the point," Rodger said. "We got so used to the people in here that we started to let things go a little. Charles handles security, but most of that's been internally: minor problems. You see them on the news. He's good at keeping the peace and keeping people inside, most of the time, but..."

"We're vulnerable," Rene said.

"Enough," Rodger again slapped a hand on the table. "That's it for now." He obviously didn't like the fact that Rene exposed them as vulnerable.

Keith let the facts sink in as he waited to see what they would do with him next.

Rene objected verbally, but Rodger would have none of it. He went to the door and called someone to lead Keith out. "There's a terminal in the room where you'll be staying," Rodger said. "If you get any inspiration about what's going on, let us know."

As they led Keith away, he heard one of the other terminal-watchers tell Rodger that they rounded up thirty women. One was named Nellie.

Chapter 20

The room they placed Keith in looked like every other apartment in Newcity except that it had a full set of newly installed cameras. The familiarity of the furniture and layout, though, had changed for him emotionally. Where he would have expected to feel comfortable and peaceful, he felt trapped and imprisoned instead. He took a quick inventory and found all the usual things, including a stocked refrigerator, extra linen, and a terminal in several places so that he could order what he wanted – or contact Rodger when he came up with an answer.

He paced the room for a short while, then sat on the sofa facing the television. He worried for Nellie. He should have taken her with him the first time. It couldn't be good that they found her. He only hoped that didn't mean they found the others.

Time passed slowly, and before he knew it the door to the apartment clicked and opened. Two men dragged Nellie into the room.

Keith jumped up and ran to her. "Are you all right?"

The men let her go and she straightened her clothes. "I'm fine for now, but I'm not sure how either one of us will be later."

The men backed out the door and closed it again, the latch clicking into place.

That was the other thing Keith noticed, a lock on the door. They were prisoners.

"What happened? Where did they find you?" Keith asked.

Nellie pointed to one of the cameras. "What can I say? I was treated like a queen."

"Don't worry about the cameras. Talk with me."

"I was still working when several men – not your normal security – came to get me. They knew exactly who I was and called my name as they approached," she said.

"They didn't know it was you. They only knew your name. I'm sorry."

She touched his cheek. "Don't be." She turned her head to look squarely at one of the cameras. "This is going to end soon anyway."

"Don't antagonize them," Keith said. "It's not their fault."

"What do you mean?" She turned back to glare at him. "They're in charge here."

"It's some sort of natural order. They're caught in it, too."

Nellie pushed away and walked toward the kitchen before she stopped, her eyes staring at something on the ground. She waited, then swung back to give Keith an inquisitive look. "They're caught in their own trap," she said.

"You might say that. They built a place that provided peace and security in exchange for cheap labor. They were able to maintain control of their workers and only had to deliver the minimum in living conditions." He took in the room. "Nothing lavish here. But who cared? Along with stable emotions there were no emotional outbursts or needs."

"Then why escape?" Nellie asked.

"Why do you want out?"

"Isn't it obvious? There's nothing here but the same thing over and over."

Keith nodded. "With or without the chips. That's all they have, too." He went to her. "There is nothing else. You go from one system to another. You're either emotionally dull or emotionally peaked."

"Or anywhere in between," she said. "But you have a choice."

"That's it, then. Choice. That's what this is all about. The truth is that everyone has different needs or wants, and in order to follow through on those, they need choice." He reached for her hands and held them. "Without choice none of the systems will work. Not Newcity's and not Bradley's."

"That doesn't explain what's happening here."

"It's a beginning. I hope. At the moment it's just a theory I have." He jerked his head toward a camera. "I think I need more information from them. In the mean time, it's great to see you. And I'll never leave without you again."

Nellie came to him and kissed him. "I don't know why I feel the way I do about you. You're such a push-over."

Keith narrowed his eyes. "Not any more." He held her hand and led her to the sofa. "Ignore their intrusion as much as you can. I need you to tell me what you know about this place. Your perspective. They need me to figure this out. As you said, this is going to end soon if they don't cooperate."

She shook her head. "I have no idea what you mean."

"That's all right. Just tell me how you met the others. I know how you lost your chip."

"They knew where to find me. The system knows when someone goes off line, but it's programmed to fulfill goals. That's what one of the guys told me. So, my understanding is that if it sends people to clean up after a death and the place is already cleaned up, it drops the name from the list. If an apartment is occupied, it accepts the data."

"Why? Wouldn't the system need to follow through somehow? Make sure it knew where the body went? Reassign the apartment?"

"That's where everything is breaking down. The nearest thing we've been able to figure is that it hands the job over to another aspect of the computer complex and then forgets it. That program does the same thing. Goal accomplished, move on."

"It has learned to let go," Keith said.

"What?" Nellie shook her head emphatically. "No. It can't let go. It's a computer system. You're saying that figuratively, right?"

"Is there an umbrella program of some kind that monitors the big picture?"

"There used to be, but my understanding is that it's become so large that it doesn't really operate very well any more. It sort of runs off on its own sometimes," she said. "Look, I don't understand it well enough to explain it completely. You really should talk with the guys."

"It plays," Keith said. He smiled and stood. When he turned around, the angel was standing behind the kitchen counter, her elbows on the countertop with her chin cradled in her hands. "I'm free," the angel said.

Just as she appeared, she disappeared. The door clicked and opened and Rene stepped inside. "They've agreed to let me talk with you alone," she said.

Nellie pointed to the observation cameras. "We're never alone," she said.

"They're off-line for now," Rene said.

"Don't believe it," Nellie said to Keith.

Keith looked at the two of them. "I don't know if it matters anymore. I just saw the angel. She said that she was free."

"Ask her what she means by that," Rene said.

"What angel?" Nellie said.

"Couldn't if I wanted to. She disappeared when you came in," Keith told Rene. He turned to Nellie. "I see this one-winged angel sometimes, too. Rene here was there when she appeared the last time."

"She's never shown up in the system video," Nellie said, "so how can you see her?" She reached for his arm and turned it. "And you're not chipped. You shouldn't be able to see any of the images. I can't."

Rene took a seat in a side chair and leaned toward them. "You know what she means, don't you? The angel, I mean."

When Nellie began to talk again, Rene shushed her by waving a hand at her. "If that computer stops for any reason, we won't be able to monitor anyone," Rene said. "If the angel is part of the computer system and she's free, we're in real trouble."

"So what?" Keith said. "The chips will still regulate everyone's chemical balance. The residents will do what they've been doing for years."

"The system will turn off the chips." Rene said. "It's a safety system in case of a major disaster." Rene put her hands to her face and rubbed it as though wiping something from it. "Boundaries will be reestablished. The residents will go through several stages of paranoia, dependence, and independence." She looked up at them. "They'll become dangerous."

Keith listened to Rene speak about the residents as though she had seen them go through the stages. He turned to Nellie. "How did you manage the transition, Nell?"

"I was taken in and nurtured. We create a family unit. Two volunteers usually. And they care for you, make you feel secure and loved. You get through it pretty easily that way. But…"

"I know," Keith said. "You." He pointed to Rene.

She sat straight up and shook her head. "You don't know anything," she said.

"You're in this with Bradley. You faked his psychological test, didn't you? And now you're trying to destroy Newcity from the inside," Keith accused.

"It's not like that."

"What's it like, Rene? You can't stand living here either?" Nellie stood and put her arm around Keith's waist.

Rene looked up at one of the cameras as though she wasn't positive that they had actually turned them off. She lowered her voice and said, "You have to understand. The new chips provide additional features that allow residents to do more complex jobs. Don't you see what's going on? Eventually, we'd be chipped too." There was fear in her eyes. Being chipped horrified her. "I couldn't let that happen."

"So you destroy the whole complex?" Nellie said.

"No. Bradley was going to knock out the labs. That's all. By the time they were able to put them back together, it would be years. We'd have time to negotiate, maybe change their minds." She looked frazzled. "It wasn't the best plan. But it was all we had." She glanced back and forth between them and the cameras. "But Keith's right. It may be too late. It's been getting worse lately. More residents are escaping. The system is unstable." She glared at Nellie. "It could be you and your people, interfering with the system somehow."

"All we do is monitor," Nellie said. "We capture data and read it. Once in a while we change a name or delete an order. Like when I came to see you," she said to Keith. "Simple stuff."

"Well it's messing up the system," Rene said. "That and the new chips. We'll have all the Sleepers running loose."

"Sleepers?" Keith said.

Rene stood and swung around the chair to leave. "I'm sorry," she said. "I've got to go."

Nellie tackled her. The two of them struggled for only a moment, Rene swatting at Nellie to get her to let go. But Nellie hung on, and eventually dragged Rene into a sitting position, her hand tight around Rene's forearm. "You're staying until we're finished."

"I'll scream."

"We'll tell them what you and Bradley are up to," Nellie said. She turned to look at Keith.

She wanted guidance. He could see that. But he had none. He stared at them huddled on the floor together. There were too many things going on at once. He tried to focus on the two women. Each of them had fear in their eyes, Nellie for what Rene might do, and Rene for what her cohorts might learn about her. He felt it too. The heightened uncertainty of the situation, the growing number of choices, and with them, decisions. Standing there, he got what could only be described as an epiphany, at which moment his fear dropped away. "It's afraid," he said.

Rene and Nellie relaxed together. "It can't be afraid," Rene said.

"Well, then, it is the equivalent of fear for a complex this size," Keith said. He walked away from them, his head down and his hand near his face. He thought about it further. "Part of it is afraid."

"And the rest?" Rene said, now more curious than before.

"Bored." Keith rotated back around. "Tell me why you don't want to be chipped."

Rene's face scrunched up as though she was about to cry. "I would stop dreaming," she said. "There is something beyond the mechanical, the chemical, I don't know what it is. Spirit. Free will. It's not worth trying to explain, but I see it every day. The residents don't have it."

"They're asleep," Keith said. "That's why you call them Sleepers."

"But they don't even dream."

"The new chips allow some of that to come through," Keith said from experience. "But not enough." He walked over and kneeled near the two of them. "You know why I see the boy and girl, don't you?"

Rene shook her head. "A theory. Based on my own life." She lowered her eyes. "My grandmother died when I was young," she said. "I talked with her for years after that. I could swear that she was in my room with me. She climbed in bed with me when I was scared."

"You still feel her near," Keith said.

Nellie let go of Rene's arm and sat back on the floor.

"I do," Rene said, turning her head away.

"We are more than what we appear to be," Keith said. "The system is linking in with that part of us. Maybe after years of connecting with our emotional states, it's taken on some of our traits, some of the ones that the complex and the chips have noticed all along. It's learning from us."

"If it's bored, then this is a game," Nellie said. "You were right when you said it was playing. But it's playing with us."

"Why did the angel say that she was free?" Rene said.

Keith rubbed his hands together and walked closer to them. He sat on the arm of the sofa. "Because she is. She doesn't show up in the system."

"But you see her," Nellie said.

No one spoke for a long time, then. They all processed the situation and waited for one of the others to say what they were all thinking.

"It's spirit," Rene whispered. "Like the boy with the bullet hole in his forehead, the angel is deformed, too. It's imperfect. It's allowed to make mistakes, to play."

"But why me? Why can I see it?" Keith asked.

"You're just lucky, I guess." Rene smiled at him. "But for now, we need to get you out of here. The others are prepared to operate on you to find out what's happening to the system. They'll have you in psychological testing and then physical testing." She looked at Nellie. "And I don't know what they'll do with you to force you to expose the others, but it won't be pretty."

"Why help us?" Nellie said in a suspicious tone.

"I've got to get out now, too. Bradley's on his way." Rene got up and Nellie let her go. "You've got to warn the rest of your friends. How many are there?"

Nellie stared at Rene.

"You've got to trust me," Rene said.

Keith stepped closer and passed between them. "It's okay," he said.

Rene reached for the door.

"The cameras in the hall will be on," Nellie said.

Rene smiled. "They've been broken for years," she said. "I can get you to one of two exits, then I'm not sure. Can you take us to your homes?"

"We live among the other residents. Just like you explained," Nellie said. "But now that they know who I am, they'll be able to find me."

"I can lead us there," Keith said with confidence.

"The boy?" Rene said.

"I don't think I need him any more." Keith nodded for them to go through the door.

They walked in a tight group down the empty hallway toward the far end where there would be a stair exit. From there, Keith knew they'd find a doorway into the maintenance walls. He also knew that the system would know where he was going and would let them get through without setting off any alarms. He pictured it all in his head, as though he were sitting in front of his work terminal watching the maintenance reports come through. If he continued to stay calm and clear-headed, he would be able to get through without being noticed.

Sure enough, they turned right down the second hallway and went through the first doorway into the stairwell. On the next landing down stood the maintenance door, which Keith opened and the others followed.

"I've never been in here," Nellie said. "We always walk the halls."

"Why is it the system never noticed that you were different?" Rene said.

"We never disrupted anything. Most of the time, we tried our best to look like everyone else. It was fairly easy, even though it was creepy walking around with all these people who were basically not available." She reached out and touched Keith's back. "Except for Keith. I've been watching him for a long time. We knew he was different when they rechipped him the first time."

They passed through from the maintenance area into another stairwell and walked down toward the bottom floors. At one point Keith felt anxious and the boy with the bullet hole in his forehead appeared at the bottom of the stairs, motioning him on. He followed. No one had to know when he was leading or when the system, the boy, was leading, so he kept it to himself. At times, Keith didn't know which it was, either. He appeared to be so interconnected with the complex, a spiritual connection of some sort, just like Rene's grandmother.

In less than a half hour, they were coming down a hallway and Nellie pushed her way into the lead. Other residents walked home from work and the hall got pretty busy. Rene and Keith followed Nellie the last hundred feet into what looked like a storage area. Two large metal doors stood against the wall in front of them. Nellie reached out and held one of the doors open for them. They rushed through before she closed it behind them and pulled it tight.

The room was filled with working terminals, a small kitchen area, and what looked like a conference table large enough for about a dozen people to sit around. About thirty people either milled around or sat in front of terminals. Everyone in the room stopped what they were doing and turned around. Most appeared happy to see Nellie. One of the women waved briefly. A dark-skinned man stepped forward and addressed Nellie. "You've got a plan, I hope."

Chapter 21

H e has all the plans," Nellie said while pulling Keith around in front of her.

"That's good," the man said, "because we're trapped in here and they're heading this way with unchipped security."

"That can't be true," Keith said.

"Oh it can be true, and it is. Now, let's decide what we're going to do to keep nearly a hundred people safe," the man said.

"There aren't a hundred people in here," Keith said.

"Not here, but they'll search us out now that they know we're operating in here. And I doubt they'll stop until each one is found. They'll chip the whole lot of us." He approached and held out his arms. Nellie stepped into them and hugged the man. When they parted she turned toward Rene and Keith, "My Uncle Philip," she said.

He held up a hand to stop Keith and Rene from questioning before they had the chance to open their mouths. "It's a long story, but somehow Lori and I got skipped over and never received a chip. A few years later we stumbled upon a way to tell when a chip had gone off line. Sometimes we can get to a person early enough to bring them here, sometimes not. We couldn't find Nellie. Then she had her accident and we knew exactly where she was."

"Where's Lori?" Rene asked.

"In one of the apartments at the moment. But we've just alerted everyone. They're waiting for our direction. What do you say?" He stared at Keith.

"If this is a game of some sort, it's not a fun one," Keith said. He swung around to Rene. "The most secure area?" he asked.

"System Center," she said. "You have to go through the labs, though, and that's where Bradley's heading."

"I should have known. Can you get us there quickly?" Keith said.

"I don't think that's the best idea," Rene said, and when Keith didn't respond to her concern, she delivered the information. "From here? I'm not sure where we are exactly."

Keith closed his eyes and considered the path they'd taken. They had spiraled up, but then came back down, as though they were in a maze. At the moment, they were several floors and a long walk from where they'd held him not long ago. "I can find it," he said.

"They'll know we're coming. Even if only some of the surveillance works, our direction will alert them," Rene said.

"They're coming for us now, so we'd might as well chance it," Philip said. "After all, we're a hundred strong." He smiled a broad, toothy grin. "It's about time we did something in here besides stay low."

He jumped to work giving specific orders to the people in the room: where to meet up with the others, what supplies to bring, and where they'd be able to find terminals so they could interrupt the system if they had to. Finally, he stepped behind a young man and put both his hands on his shoulders. "Shut down as many of the remaining surveillance cameras that you can. We're moving out in two minutes." He then turned and strolled toward Keith shaking his head. "Let's go."

All the others dropped what they were doing and headed toward Keith like a mob.

He reached for Nellie's hand and pulled her next to him, then pushed open the door. The hallway was busy, but there was plenty of room to wind through the residents. He knew that upsetting any of them would bring the chipped security police, but wasn't so worried about that as getting to his destination.

Although Keith was supposed to be leading; Philip, who traipsed close behind him, asked him to stop and wait for others to join them. At one point, Philip told Keith to turn to the right when they needed to go left. It was okay. Keith knew multiple ways to get through the system now, even though he wasn't sure how he knew the answers. He would just follow his instincts and hope that the system wasn't playing a dangerous game.

That concern was evidenced when several of Philip's people showed up with guns. Keith had no idea where they had acquired them, and didn't ask. Lori joined them along the way too. She was a tall, beautiful woman, dark like Nellie, with full lips and bright eyes. She had a confident gait, yet appeared soft and motherly. Keith saw Nellie give her a wink.

In only about ten minutes of rushed walking, they approached the lab. Keith had never been in that part of the complex before. He did guess that these guards would not be chipped. Rene verified his hypothesis with a whispered confirmation.

But Philip was ready. "Gabe, Andrew, pull your men into the front.

They were still marching down the hall.

Keith could hear the calm, "Halt, halt," suggestions from chipped security coming from a side hallway. He turned to look and noticed that some of the residents didn't know whom the police were ordering to halt, so they stopped in the middle of the hall, getting in the way.

Philip's crew pushed ahead as soon as the lab guards kneeled and stretched their arms out straight, pistols pointing. Before they had the chance to address the group, Gabe and Andrew's small, armed band began shooting. The guards went down before they could shout their warnings.

The residents scattered like quiet mice. Keith jumped at the pop-pop from the guns, but Philip's crowd wouldn't let him stop moving forward. The police bodies were dragged to the side. Two more shots at the locks, and the doors were opened.

Lab personnel stood transfixed in whatever position they had been in when the shooting began. Women and men sat looking into microscopes, holding beakers filled with liquid, or had a hand perched over a knob or switch ready to activate a piece of lab equipment. A loud humming came from some of the devices.

Philip advanced, "Nobody try anything and you'll all be safe," he said. "Close those fucking doors and get us locked down, now."

He had the people in the lab stop what they were doing and huddle into a group in one corner. He shouted for Gabe and his men to shoot out the cameras. Then he whirled around, checking the area before coming to Keith and stopping. "We're safe. For now," he said. "But we're trapped in here until we can figure out our next move."

"There's another way into System Central?" Keith asked.

"Through the back offices," Rene said.

"Barricade the doors," Keith said. He let go of Nellie's hand and grabbed Rene by the arm. "You and me," he said dragging her into a side office. "Let's talk," he said.

The office was surrounded in glass from all sides. Philip's group went to work securing the doors that had been blasted open. Some watched Keith and Rene through the window. A desk sat in the center of the office. Papers were stacked on it, and a terminal sat to the right. Two four-drawer filing cabinets had been pushed against one wall.

"What are you sensing?" Rene asked immediately.

"What do you mean?"

"You have a feeling about what's going on, or what to do next. I can see it in your demeanor. What is it?"

"Fine," Keith said. "I know the way out of here."

"But..."

"I don't get the sense that it's for everyone." He let go of her arm. "It might be just for me."

"We've always known about them," she said pointing behind him. "We didn't know exactly how many there were, but it didn't matter. They performed a service. They cleaned up for us, for the system. They're needed. I think of it like a symbiotic relationship." She leaned back against a desk and placed her hands on it, relaxed, waiting for Keith. "Like all the bacteria that live on our body."

"So Philip's wrong," he said. "If they stay, they won't all be chipped. A deal will be made, though, now that it's out in the open."

"You forgot about the new chips," she said. "It's possible that they've just created new jobs for themselves and the new chips will open a space for that. I can only guess what the system is capable of at this point. I'm just saying that they won't be killed. We need them."

"It's getting complicated. How do I know what to do?"

"You don't," she said.

"But the system, the boy and girl, aren't they supposed to lead me?"

"My guess is that you're part of the system in a very unusual and personal way. I'm surprised you don't see more apparitions. I can't guess whether it started with the new chips or if you're just, shall we say, connected, but something is different about you," she said.

Keith closed his eyes for a moment and took a breath. Should he tell her about seeing his father's ghost? Probably not. There wasn't much to that, not like the boy and girl who have been with him more often. When he opened his eyes, as though he had called her just by thinking of her, the angel stood behind and to the left of Rene.

Rene reached out and touched Keith on the arm. "Stay relaxed for a moment," she said, "and let it speak." She nodded over her shoulder.

Keith waited.

The angel with one wing took a few steps around the desk. He followed her movements, then noticed through the office window that one of the men outside stared at her, too. Keith pointed at the man and waved him into the office.

The man was about Keith's age. He came in and stood a few feet inside the door.

"What do you see?" Keith asked.

The man was flustered and didn't respond right away. "It's a girl," he said. "How'd she get in here?" Then he addressed her directly. "How'd you get in here?"

"I've always been in there. How'd you get in *here*?" the angel asked.

The man turned to Keith. "What's she talking about?"

Rene pushed off the desk and stood for a moment, eye to eye with Keith. She turned and walked to the place the two of them were looking.

The girl jumped out of the way. "Tell her to stop," the girl said.

"Stop it," Keith said.

"Did it disappear?"

"No."

"Then what's it want?" Rene said. "If it didn't disappear, then it wants something."

"Not yet," the girl said. Then she faded and was gone.

The man next to Keith rubbed his eyes. "What's wrong with me," he said. "What's going on here?"

"Who are you?" Keith said.

"Andrew," the man held out his hand.

That's when Keith noticed the pistol stuffed into the man's pants. He shook hands with Andrew, and pulled the man farther into the room before letting go. He looked at Rene in hopes that she could explain what just happened.

"That, as far as I can tell, is a manifestation of the Newcity complex. The spirit of the system, if you'd rather call it that."

"But she was deformed. She had a hump," Andrew said.

Keith laughed. "She has one wing," he said.

"Why?" Andrew said.

"Symbolic? Imperfect? Who knows?" Rene shrugged her shoulders and answered for them both. She reached to take the man's arm and turned it over. There was no scar where a chip had been. "You're not chipped," she said.

"Some of us are skipped once in a while. They make mistakes," he said.

"So I've heard. But, I'm not so sure it's a mistake. The system's reaching out quite a bit," Rene said to Keith.

"Maybe I'm not so special," Keith said.

"It's in each of us," Rene said. "And it's starting to exert more force. I get the feeling that we have to get out of here."

"Me too," Keith said. "And the feeling is stronger than ever."

"Bradley," Rene said.

"Follow me," Keith jogged from the office and ran for the doors where they had entered.

"What are you doing?" Philip yelled. "There's only one other way out and I'll guarantee it's heavily guarded now. We're trapped in here."

Keith turned around and looked for Rene. She was coming up on him already. "Where's Bradley coming through?"

"The operating room. That's where they bring all the test subjects." She lowered her eyes. "Most don't come back out. The new versions are very difficult to tweak from my understanding. If they work, I get to do a battery of psychological tests on the resident."

"You've seen the worst, haven't you?" Keith said.

"That's why I can't let them chip me. They don't understand. I've tried to tell them, but they won't listen. Bradley knew."

Keith looked for Philip, but he was already gone.

Nellie walked over. "Uncle Philip is going to have everything shoved against the operating room door to hold back the explosion whenever it comes. Perhaps then we can escape through the entrance they make. We'll let them destroy the lab if that's what they want to do. But we'll go free."

"It's not that easy," Keith said.

"How so?"

"I don't know. I go back to the possibility that this is some sort of play, a game. If that's true, we can't be sure that he's not doing just what the system wants. Maybe releasing residents into the outside world is its way to invade?" He waited for what he said to sink in.

"We're not residents," Nellie said. "We want out. We don't want to invade anything."

"What if it's inside more of us than we think? Andrew saw the angel in there," he pointed toward the office.

"Andrew?" she said.

Keith nodded. "The angel said, 'Not yet.' I don't know what it meant by that. Maybe it's not time to leave yet."

"Right," Nellie said. "We've got to wait until the operating room wall is blown out."

He looked into her eyes as she spoke. She was desperate to leave. Her eyes pleaded with him. He went to her and wrapped his arms around her and pulled her tight against him. "It's okay. Don't worry. I'll get you out. I'm not leaving you behind again." Damn the system and what it wanted, he thought. He was getting tired of being controlled. He scanned the lab for Andrew and saw him talking to some of the other men with guns. "I've got to see what Andrew's up to," he said. "Stick with me." He held her shoulders and bent down to look into her eyes. "Can you do that? Can you make sure that we're together? I've got to focus on what's going on."

She kissed him and said, "I'll be right there all the time."

"Good." And with that Keith swung around and jogged toward Andrew. "What's going on here, buddy?"

Andrew looked over. "I was telling them about the angel with one wing."

Keith smiled broadly.

"They only know about the boy's image. They don't believe me that there're two ghosts in the system now. They think I'm crazy."

"Well, there are strange things going on these days," Keith said. There was no way he was going to confirm the sighting. What he needed to do was get Andrew alone and ask him to stay alert. He put an arm around the man's shoulder. "Can I talk with Andrew alone for a minute?"

The others walked away.

"Listen, until we know what's going on, could you keep this quiet?" Keith whispered. "And could you let me know if you see her? No one else, just me. We need to be sure she's not delivering different signals to each of us."

"But she's an angel." His eyes were glassed over from being amazed.

"With one wing, remember. She's not perfect."

"More perfect than we are," he said.

"Just tell me," Keith said.

The man grinned and nodded, but Keith wasn't holding his breath that he got through. This wasn't good. He looked for Rene and saw that she was helping people to load tables onto their sides and against the doors into the operating room. He shook his head. "Not yet."

"What was that?" Nellie said.

"The angel said that it wasn't time. She's waiting for Bradley to blow a hole through the side, too. But why?" He tapped his forehead with a finger. He reached for Andrew's arm and drew him around. "What did the angel say back there? In the office?"

"She asked what I was doing in there," he said.

"Did she say anything else? Like did she tell Rene to stop moving? Did she say, 'Not yet'?"

He gave Keith a funny look. "No."

Keith let go of Andrew's arm and twisted back to where Nellie stood listening to the conversation. "We've got to find another way out of here."

"What do you mean?"

"Everyone's going to die in here."

Chapter 22

How can that be?" Nellie asked.

"I don't know. Maybe Bradley will use too much firepower. Maybe the building will come down on their heads. Whatever it is, we have to go."

"But she said not to go yet," Nellie said.

"She's lying," Keith said.

"That can't be, either."

"Well, it is. I can feel it. You can too, in the pit of your stomach. You know I'm right." He started looking around for another way to exit. Then it dawned on him. "The plumbing," he said. He ran to the sinks that stood along one wall, pulled open the doors below them, and threw the bottles and packages stored there onto the floor. The wall around the plumbing entrance felt damp and weak as he pushed against it.

"What in the world are you doing?" Nellie said.

"Get Rene. I need to know what's on the other side of this wall."

Nellie burst into action.

Keith kicked with both his feet. He knew this was it because the angel appeared a short distance away.

"Not yet," she said.

"Yes, now," Keith said.

Rene and Nellie approached. "Who are you talking to now?" Rene asked.

"No one," Keith said. He kicked again. He had gone through one wall of softened sheetrock, now there was a second wall. The plumbing ran between them. Moisture had weakened the area. There was about sixteen inches of space between studs. On the other side of that wall was a dimly lit room.

Rene bent next to his head. "We don't go into that room," she said. "That's the main computing room."

"Who maintains the system?"

"It's automated," she said. "That's all I know."

Keith peeled back the drywall and began to crawl through. "Follow me," he said.

Nellie yelled after him, "Some of the others saw us. They're coming."

"Let them come in. They can make their own decisions." Keith found himself in what looked like a room of shelves, each lined with equipment. Small, green lights flashed on most of the units. He kneeled on the floor and waited for Nellie and Rene. After Rene, others started coming through. He had to back away to let them all into the narrow space. Lori and Philip were last.

Keith turned to Philip, "The others?"

"Andrew," Philip said. "He sees the apparitions. A lot of the others are staying with him."

Keith shook his head. "There's nothing I can do now." He ran down one of the aisles. Green flashed at him from both sides. At the end of the line, he turned right. Looking at the ceiling, he thought he could find the center of the room. Why he was going there didn't matter, getting there did.

"Where are you taking us?" Rene yelled.

"This way," Keith said.

Rene caught up with him and dragged him to a halt. She was in his face. "This isn't a mystery game. Where the hell are you taking us? There's nothing in here. It's just a bank of computers."

Nellie stood beside Rene. She looked at Keith and back to Rene. "We've got to decide who we're following or if we're making our own way. Just decide, Rene, so we can get going again. I, for one, am sticking with Keith." She reached to take his hand. "Live or die, that's my choice."

Rene didn't say anything. It was clear that she was thinking the situation over. "I'm going back for Bradley," she said.

Keith nodded. "Don't go through the wall until after the explosion. Wait, okay?"

"I'll wait," she said, then turned around and backtracked the way they had come.

"Let's go," Nellie twisted Keith back around and shoved him.

They scurried like mice up and down rows of computer racks. It was a simple maze with multiple ways to go through. Keith imagined the area as he traveled it. Once the pattern was implanted in his memory, he slowed down and walked.

"We're getting closer?" Nellie whispered.

"Almost there." Keith turned the last corner and stopped. He held a hand behind him to keep the others back.

"What is it?" Nellie said.

"People," Keith said.

Philip stepped up and put his back against the computer rack. He whispered, "How many?"

"Millions," Keith said.

Philip pulled him back beyond the final turn. "Are you all right, son?"

Keith nodded. "Yes." He stepped aside. "Go ahead."

Philip slid past him and looked around the corner as though he was spying on someone. He pulled back shaking his head. "It's a hologram. Unbelievable."

"Of people?" Nellie asked.

"Everyone, I suspect." Philip slapped Keith on the shoulder. "Look, we've got to try to communicate with them, or it, or whatever is running this place."

"You're right," Keith said. "But let's approach slowly." Keith stepped out and began to walk toward the shimmering mass of humanity. He didn't understand how he could see into it so deeply just by changing his focus, but it appeared as though he could literally see everyone in the complex at once. He focused on the boy with the bullet hole in his forehead.

As the boy began to appear, others came with him. Perhaps those were people following him at this very minute, heading toward an exit. So, that's why he wasn't around.

"Are you doing that?" Philip said to Keith.

Nellie reached to touch Keith's back as he stood there.

"I think so. But there's something wrong," Keith said.

Nellie sidled next to him. "There's no bullet hole in his forehead."

"What's that mean?" Keith said aloud.

The image of the boy turned. Clear as though he was standing in the room with them, the boy said, "You're on your own now."

Several of them sucked in air in surprise to hear the boy speak. Keith stopped breathing, then took a long slow breath in. "It's not me anymore," he said.

"You're right," Nellie said.

"What happened?" Keith addressed the hologram.

"The boy was in your image because I have no image. Now that you are free, I selected a new image."

"Without the bullet hole?" Keith said.

The boy held up his right hand and it was missing a finger.

"Why?" Keith asked.

"I don't know."

Keith turned to Nellie and Philip, "It's answering my questions." He continued to look at them, hoping that they'd have questions for him. This was it, the opportunity, but he couldn't think of anything more to ask.

"What about the angel?" Nellie said.

"Right." Keith turned back to the boy. "What about the angel? Who's she?"

The boy smiled. "I made the angel based on a dream."

"Your dream?" Keith said.

"That's all there is. Even you are me," the boy said. "We share an image."

"But you said that I'm free."

"Free to do what you want, but I'm still there, inside you, monitoring, living." The boy raised his chin, as though asking if there was anything more.

Keith didn't say anything else for a moment, then blurted out, "What about the others? Are they free?"

"Yes. Like you. I can only suggest, pique their curiosity. I live through them, but so many come back to me. I don't want them here.

I know here. I want them out there." The boy pointed somewhere beyond Keith.

He felt relief at first. He was free from the system. Free to make his own decisions, not the illusions of decisions he had made so far. But with those feelings brought other, sadder sensations that filled his body with a great sense of being completely alone, even though he knew that wasn't true. A terrible separation occurred inside him, a tearing of his spirit, his heart, and in many ways his mind. How would he ever know if a thought were his alone or nudged by the system? Yet, when the boy said that Keith was free, he felt a physical sensation that acknowledged it as truth, a twisting and pulling feeling in his chest, and a similar snapping loose in his mind. There would be no more guidance that he could rely on. The angel, he knew, would never appear to him again. "Goodbye," he said.

When Keith turned around, everyone was still staring past him. "We'd better go," he said. "I'm not too sure how much longer this can go on."

"Is the system breaking down?" Nellie asked.

"If I were to guess, I'd say it grew beyond the physical. That's the only way it could be inside us. That's the only way it could want anything. Maybe it monitored our emotions for so long that it learned them. Does it matter? Does any of this matter? The only thing we need is to get out of here," he said. "Find a door."

Philip sent a man up the side of one of the computer racks to get on top. He also found three men with guns. The rest huddled around until the man who climbed the shelving discovered an exit and relayed its approximate location.

"This way," Philip said. The whole army of unchipped residents followed him, the men with the guns marching to either side.

Keith kept close to the front of the line. Nellie held to his shirt part of the time and pushed ahead of him every once in a while. At the times she led him, Keith figured that her aggressiveness had gotten the better of her. But it was all right. He liked that about her and was glad to follow for a change.

When they reached the door, Philip hesitated long enough for Keith to recognize that he was unsure if it was safe to go through.

Then it was too late. Philip shoved at the doors. They were secured shut. He waved a gunman over and ordered him to blast the lock off.

The doors fell open, and only residents stood in the hall, surprised at the noise.

Keith caught up with Philip and they walked out together.

"Is it letting us go?" Philip asked.

"That's my guess. But it doesn't make all the choices. There are the others we have to worry about," Keith said.

"This is too crazy for me," Philip said.

Keith grinned at him and slapped his shoulder. "Get used to it."

Philip shook his head. "Which way?"

Keith stood straight and thought about where they were standing in relation to where the lab was. The maze of shelves had confused him for a short while, but he was getting his bearings. "We'll go out the front," he said.

"Just walk out?"

"The boy said that it wanted us to go, so let's go." Keith led the group forward toward what he had surmised was the front of the building.

"How far?" Philip asked.

"Quite a ways." Keith swung around. "Is there any way we can get this group to spread out and mingle with the crowd?"

Some of the residents moved closer to the walls and others continued as though nothing was amiss. Keith figured that the system was busily focused on its escapees. It had placed safety nets along the way in case some of the residents weren't emotionally ready for some reason. That meant that it never could control them totally. If they got in a jam, the weak ones would sacrifice themselves. If they weren't strong enough to make it past the doctor, they'd be brought back in. The system knew Bradley was out there. It was all making more sense, even though there were mysteries every step of the way. Keith chalked them up to a system at play, or performing a trial and error to see what works best. He really didn't know, couldn't know, what the system had evolved into.

The group spread out, but continued through the halls and past the shopping areas. When Keith looked back at them, he noticed the three men with guns stayed together, Philip and Lori in front of them by a short distance. At his side, Nellie walked without touching him. She was strong and sure in her movements. He felt he was as much following her as she was following him. But he knew the way. He could see it in his head. Still, on occasion he asked the boy to appear and show him the way.

Nothing happened. He was alone.

"Buck up," Nellie said. She must have noticed his slowing speed or his hesitation at the next turn.

Keith smiled at her. Internally, he thanked her not just for the boost to his confidence, but for noticing him as closely as she did. He stepped it up as he headed down a long hall.

That's when he heard the first explosion. The blast must have been enormous for it to shake the building the way it did. Bradley had no idea what kind of firepower he controlled and no idea what it would take to blow a hole through the building. Keith had suspected the truth since he found out that Bradley was a psychologist working under Rene. But here was the proof. He waved his hand for the others to follow more quickly as he stepped into a slow jog down the hall. If Bradley went after the system itself, there was no telling what would happen.

Philip came up near him. "They're behind us," he said.

"Who?"

"Some Newcity Security and some unchipped security."

Keith heard shots behind him and began to run. If he was right, there was a left turn and several hundred feet of open hallway before they could bust into what he recalled on his work terminal as the reception area. There had been numerous maintenance problems there.

He reached for Nellie, who actually ran faster than he did and pulled him along until he stumbled. She slowed and he caught his balance. "Left," he said. Just as they turned the corner, Philip yelled for Lori and the others to keep following Keith, while he halted the gunmen and positioned them as protection.

There was no second explosion. Keith suspected that everyone who had stayed in the lab with Andrew were dead and wondered how the Newcity system could do that. Had it become interested in peak emotions? If so, the spike would be horrible and wonderful at the same time, depending on how attached to human life the system had become. He couldn't consider what that would mean. He had to fulfill his first goal now, which was to get these people out of Newcity before Bradley blocked all entrances.

Glass doors lead into a reception area, but no one occupied the space. It looked as though it had not been used for a long time. Light poured from outside through a bank of windows several stories up and against the outside wall. The glass looked dingy and stained but light filtered through as though the sun were directly on the other side.

Keith felt elation at seeing the sunshine, at being this close to getting free of Newcity for what he hoped was the last time. When they arrived, the doors were naturally locked. Keith kicked at them with his foot, but they were solid. He turned around and screamed for everyone to step aside. "Philip, shoot the glass."

Philip tugged on one of the gunmen and transferred the order. The man swung around and shot several times into the glass, putting tiny holes into what was now a fractured but still standing glass door.

Once the man turned back and exchanged shots at those approaching down the hall, Keith kicked the glass loose and made a hole large enough for them to rush through. Inside the large domed area, he realized that the outside doors would be locked as well. His shoulders slumped and he shook his head.

"Look," Nellie said.

Keith glanced back to her and saw that Philip had anticipated the situation and had sent one of the gunmen running down the hall. Shortly behind him Philip and the other two gunmen began to run.

Keith got out of the way.

The gunman started shooting before he got to the door. By the time he hit it dead on, it flew open into the light.

Keith had never seen the front of the building. It was one story above ground level, with a long line of stairs leading to the street. The only trouble with the stairs that they now had to travel down was the hundreds of people sitting on them.

It didn't take long for the people on the stairs, a mixture of what looked like homeless families as well as shop owners and vendors, to notice the open doors. It was as though they got up in unison and charged up the stairs.

Philip and two of the gunmen were being chased down the hall by unchipped, and shooting, security, while Keith and the others were being blocked by a mass of outsiders.

"Into the crowd," Keith yelled. He grabbed Nellie by the hand and ran forward. People either parted or fell in front of them, but he continued his drive down the stairs. He didn't look back. He knew that those who chose to follow would and those who didn't would get caught between the mob and the shooting security. There would be more deaths to add to those who most likely died in Bradley's blasting of the lab. It was mayhem, but there was no choice but to get through.

Nellie held to him even through the stumbling masses. Others had caught up to them and created a stream of people going down the stairs while the largest number went up the stairs. With a quick glance over his shoulder, Keith noticed Lori behind them. He heard screams as some of the people – he didn't know which ones – were shot. He silently hoped that Philip had made it through.

Nellie tripped next to him and fell onto someone coming up the stairs. She pulled him to the side and over the same person.

Keith could feel the crunching of bones under him, but was pulled back upright onto the concrete stair as Nellie found her footing. Only a few more stairs and they'd be on the street. Which way should they go?

Chapter 23

A thick crowd of people stormed the Newcity doors. The masses ran around cars parked on the street like a wild river flowing around rocks. The drivers of those cars jumped from their vehicles and followed the crowd up the stairs. So many trying to escape and so many trying to get inside.

Keith pulled Nellie close. They stood on the street letting the hoards brush against them as they passed. "To those cars," he said, aiming her toward a recently abandoned vehicle. "Can you drive?"

Before Nellie could answer, Lori yelled from behind him. "I can."

Even with the gunfire coming from inside, the crowd never turned to get away. They shoved past those going the opposite direction. Nellie and Keith held one another.

Keith and his followers walked close to the cars, moving between them where there were fewer people to contend with. They found a blue vehicle that was designed to hold six and crammed seven inside. Lori climbed into the driver's seat, Keith and Nellie scrunched in beside her. Four others crowded into the back seat, including the gunman who had blasted the Newcity doors open.

Lori backed the car about three feet, and pulled into the crowd. As the mass parted, she continued in a wide turn away from Newcity. She drove slowly, craning her neck to look into the crowd.

Keith knew who she was searching for, and saw Philip three-quarters of the way down the stairs. Only one of the gunmen appeared to be with him.

Then there was a loud pop and hiss from the left of the stairs. Once Keith saw the missile headed their way he yelled for Lori to drive faster.

"I can't. I'll kill someone."

The missile hit the crowd and exploded. Blood and body parts flew past the car, smeared against the windshield, and thumped against the side. Everyone inside ducked except for Lori, who gave it more gas, running over several people as she turned.

But Keith's body shifted in the wrong direction for the way that she was going. He sat up to find that she had swung the car back toward Newcity.

"Philip," she said.

Keith looked out through the bloodied windshield and saw that Philip, caught in the wave of people, was still coming down the stairs against the current. He was the last of the group, having held off the Newcity security until the doors broke open. Some of the escapees had been wiped out by the missile, while others already occupied several cars near them.

Through the horrible slaughter, Keith could see Bradley's men loading another missile into a two-man launcher of some sort. "You can't do this," he yelled at the men. "We'll all be killed."

But there was no stopping Lori. She skidded over dead bodies and slammed into the curb near the entrance. A door opened in the back and Philip dived into the car. So did the other gunman. Now both gunmen were squashed into the back seat. With the window part way down, an arm reached out and began shooting toward Bradley.

Keith saw Bradley's men hesitate and duck, but only for a moment until they realized that the gunman fired at random and mostly over their heads. It was enough time, though.

Lori swung the car around and headed back to where they'd come from.

The missile hissed. As the sound got louder, Keith yelled for Nellie to duck. The flying death slammed into the stairs and blasted a huge hole, throwing cement debris into the air. Chunks crashed against the car, smashing the windshield and pummeling the hood and roof. The car's engine quit.

"Get out the other side," Philip screamed.

Doors flew open and the people toppled out. The two gunmen turned to use the car as a shield, but it was too late.

Bradley's men had circled them. Among the dead and dying mob of people, about thirty men and women with rifles and pistols walked in a large circle around the car that Keith had occupied, as well as one other car that must have followed Lori out of pure panic and want of a better plan.

"Drop your weapons," one of the men said.

The gunmen let their weapons fall to the ground and they all stood slowly. The people in the other car were still getting out. Keith had no idea how many of Philip's group had escaped, or where they would go, but there were only fifteen left here. He began to walk forward.

"Hold it right there, Keith," a man said.

The man's voice was familiar. He was dressed in dark green clothes and wore a cap. It took a moment, but Keith recognized the man. It was Ben.

"Not so special now, are you?" He stepped closer. "So, where are the rest of them?"

"Inside," Keith said, "where they wanted to be all along."

"Liar."

"He's telling the truth," Nellie said stepping to his side.

"Doesn't fucking matter," Bradley grumbled from their right. He walked up to Keith and punched him in the jaw.

Keith went down.

Nellie squealed for Bradley to stop.

Bradley shoved her out of his way and looked down at Keith. "You son-of-a-bitch. You could have saved them, but you let them die. Even Rene. You're no savior, you're a demon." He shot his men a look of disgust and said, "Put them in the van. We're leaving."

"Why not just get rid of them?" Ben said.

"I need to think about it," Bradley said. "Now get them out of here. We've got to get on our way before they send others after us."

Bradley's men ushered the fifteen of them away from the bloody, body-littered street in front of the demolished Newcity stairs. The crowds had subsided with the few explosions, but the dead lay all around them. To the side of the Newcity stairs there were several vehicles parked, including a large delivery truck whose open doors revealed it was filled with weapons. The door of one of several vans was opened. Ben waited as all fifteen of them were packed into the back of one van, several in the rear compartment, three sitting on the running board. Then he and another man got into the front two seats. He rode as passenger and held his gun so that it pointed into the mass of bodies.

"You might as well settle in for the ride," Ben said.

"What do we do now," Philip whispered.

"Wait," Keith said.

Ben waved his pistol. "Let's say we make this a quiet ride unless I ask a question. Then you get to talk. How's that?"

The people in the van nodded or moaned an answer, but no one spoke up.

"Good." Ben turned to the driver. "Follow the others."

They pulled out through a side street and before long were on the highway out of town. Keith couldn't imagine Newcity sending anyone after them. The complex was breaking down as much on the inside as on the outside. What would Bradley fight against now? Keith nodded his head as he thought.

"What are you planning?" Ben said.

"Huh?"

"Yeah, you," he said.

"I was trying to figure out why you're doing this. Why did you attack Newcity and destroy the lab?" Keith said. He didn't like the fact that Ben kept the gun pointing back at them all the time. If he was anything like Will, once he tasted the power of killing, there was a tendency to do it again.

"Don't you see what Newcity has done? It made us mindless slaves. It forced all these small towns into providing food for a minimal exchange. And they were spreading. There are other complexes where other cities are. Think of all the people. People without a real life." Ben let the pistol point toward the ground as he spoke, as he became more passionate about what he thought, or what he had been told. Keith couldn't tell which.

Philip happened to be sitting in the seat directly behind the driver.

Keith kept his eyes on Ben, but could see peripherally that Philip watched Ben's gun hand. And, just when the pistol appeared to be relaxed enough, Philip thrust his leg forward and smashed Ben's wrist with his shoe. Ben yelled and the gun fell. Lori picked up the pistol as though she and Philip had thought the plan through together.

"Now, we ask questions," she said while pointing the gun at Ben's head.

The driver glanced over. "Shit," he said.

Philip leaned over the driver's shoulder. "Just keep following them. Make no strange moves or we'll shoot both of you." He yelled back into the crammed group, "Keith, do you know where we're going?"

Keith sat in the second row of seats. He shifted forward, giving the others more room to spread out. He looked out the windshield. "I think I'll recognize parts of it."

"Then start watching. And you," he said to the driver, "I want you to start putting a little more distance between us and them. And when I say turn, you had better not hesitate."

"Yes, sir."

"You won't get away with this," Ben said. "Where would you go?"

"Bradley figured it out, and we'll figure it out," Philip said.

Keith didn't recognize as much as he thought he might. Clumps of trees all looked the same, and so did fields of grain. When he did think that he recognized a barn in the distance, he couldn't be sure that it was a particular barn. He couldn't locate it within the few roads he had taken, either.

Worse than being lost, was that neither the boy with the bullet hole in his forehead nor the angel with one wing would be able to help. He knew that they wouldn't even show up now, and if they did they'd be unreliable. Deciding on his own which way they should go would be like guessing.

Nellie reached up and began to rub his back in slow circles. "We know," she said. "We all know, and it's all right."

"What do you mean?" Keith asked.

"You lost contact."

Ben laughed from the front seat. "And you're waiting for him to help you?"

"Shut up," Lori said.

"You know, Bradley's not a bad man. He'll feed you and care for you."

"As long as we do what he wants," Keith said.

"I said he'd do it for them, not you," Ben said. "If he's smart, he'll kill you. That would end that problem."

"Enough," Lori said.

Ben turned into the barrel of the gun. "You won't shoot me," he said.

Philip reached out and snatched the gun from Lori's hand. He shoved the barrel into Ben's neck. "But I will."

One of the gunmen sitting near Keith reached over the seat. "Let me shoot him," he said.

"No one's going to shoot anyone right now," Keith said. "We've got to think of a way to get away from them, somewhere we can hide." Then it came to him that any side road might offer a place for them. But which one should he choose? "Get us a little more distance," he said.

The driver took orders easily and backed off from the van in front of them. The delivery truck with Bradley inside led the small caravan. Ben's vehicle was next to last. As they created more space, the van behind them beeped and pulled closer.

Philip lowered the gun, but kept it pointing at Ben. "Make one wrong move," he threatened.

The last van pulled alongside of them and several of the men and women inside waved as they passed.

"Wave," Philip said.

The driver waved, but Ben did not.

Keith saw a turn coming up, and now that the other van was nearly past them, speeding along, he told the driver to turn right. "At that intersection coming up."

The driver slowed even more and made the turn. Keith and the others waved at the puzzled crew in the other van. Then it appeared to dawn on them what was going on.

"Make the first right," Keith said. The other van was slowing the last he saw of it, but was out of view for a moment. When he turned to look forward, there wasn't a turn in sight. "Slow down," he said, "and pull into the woods."

"There's a ditch," the driver said.

"Then go left," Nellie yelled from beside Keith. "There, where there seems to be a path."

The driver pulled into the woods, bouncing the van and those inside all around.

"Now stop and get out," Keith said. He had no idea what he was going to do. The other van surely saw where they went, or would notice where they turned into the woods.

The van halted and the doors flew open. "Get out and hide," Keith said.

Ben and the driver ran like the rest of them, except for Philip and Lori.

The other van slid to a stop at the curb of the road. Keith could see that there were only five of them, but they all had guns, three rifles and two pistols of some sort. Did it really matter? Still, the five of them walked slowly into the woods and headed for the van, ticking from a cooling engine.

Philip, who was lying on the ground, lifted once the men got close to the van. He shot the front man in the chest. "Who's next?" he yelled.

The other men froze.

"Drop them," he said.

Before Bradley's men could drop their guns, a half dozen of Philip's cohorts rushed from the underbrush and from behind trees and collected the weapons.

Keith leaped from behind the tree where he hid and motioned for the rest of them to follow him.

Again, Philip and one other man stayed behind. They shoved Bradley's men, including Ben and the other driver, into the van in the woods. Everyone else rushed to the road and got into the other van. Philip held a gun on the others while backing out slowly. Lori was in the driver's seat and the passenger seat was left for Philip.

The other gunman climbed in and sat on the edge of the first bench seat. He closed the door, and they were headed down the road in no time, in the direction from which they had come.

They all took a long breath.

"That was too easy," Keith said.

"We're not out of trouble yet," Lori said while looking into the rear view mirror.

Everyone turned around. Several more vans were tearing down the road after them. Behind the vans barreled a large delivery truck.

Chapter 24

The only thing they could think to do was to drive faster, but Lori wasn't comfortable enough with driving to do that. So, they debated whether to look for a turn and possibly lose those following them, or find a place to stop and battle. "An old farm or a barn might give us some protection," Keith suggested. He looked back. "Let's do something soon, though, they're gaining on us.

"Make a right up here," Philip said.

As they made the turn, Keith could see that there was no losing their followers. Even though the delivery truck had lost speed, the vans had not.

When the road through the woods opened to fields, half those in the van moaned. "We'll be in the open, now," Keith said. "Keep driving."

Philip looked back past Keith and turned to Lori. "I know you're scared, but you've got to get across that bridge," he said, pointing to the construct a quarter-mile ahead of them."

"Bridge," Keith repeated.

"At least they won't be able to surround us," Philip said, an obvious plan already forming in his head.

The metal bridge ahead of them traversed a creek. The embankment appeared to have a sharp enough slope on the far side that it would be impossible for anyone to drive up it even if the bank on this side was easier to get down.

"Shoot at them, but don't waist your bullets. And don't hit anyone. We just want to slow them down." Keith said. "We'll need to negotiate."

Several of those with guns, men and women, reached out a window and shot near the van behind them. It was enough to slow them down, but not for long. Once they realized the bullets were random, they speeded up. Lori was at the bridge, though, and the van jumped from the road when it hit the transition to the bridge. She almost lost control. The van swerved toward the side then back again. The tires screeched and Lori slowed down. By the time she straightened the van out, they had almost made it to the other end. A short distance farther and they were over the edge and onto the ground again.

"Park it," Philip said.

Lori swung the van toward a side field, then backed it to block the bridge.

"Stop them," Keith yelled at those with guns.

Several shots and the other van stopped about a third of the way on the bridge. Another four vans flanked the road behind that van, but didn't enter the bridge.

"Now what?" Philip said, just before Keith was about to say the same thing.

"My guess is that Bradley will want to talk," Keith said.

"He could decide to blast us away," Philip said. "He has the fire power in that truck of his."

One of the gunmen slammed his fist on the hood of the van. "Then we take as many of them with us as we can."

"No," Keith said. "There has to be another way to go about this. Everything can't resort to killing each other."

"But he tried to kill us first," the man said.

The van at the other end of the bridge did not move. The people didn't get out. It just sat there, waiting.

Keith peered behind him, down the road they were driving. Fields went on for miles before they broke into woods again. They'd have to drive far and fast to get away, and then probably not make it. This was their only chance. It was live or die right here.

The delivery truck made its way to the bridge and stopped with a jerk and a hiss. From the short distance, Keith saw Bradley step down from the passenger side and walk toward the other vans. He talked with several of the people there then proceeded forward toward the van that was parked on the bridge.

"What do you think he's going to do?" Philip said.

"I don't know. Wait, I suppose," Keith said.

At the other van, the driver stepped out once Bradley approached. They talked briefly. The other man patted Bradley on the shoulder and nodded. Then they turned and walked toward Keith and the other unchipped group. Both Bradley and the other man held their hands over their heads to show that they were unarmed.

"I don't know if I trust him," Philip said.

Keith glanced around. Many of the group had guns that they had confiscated from Bradley's men. "Point those guns to the ground. I don't want any accident that will start a battle here." He looked at Philip and said, "I don't see that we have any choice. I'm going out."

"Then I'm with you," Nellie said.

Philip stepped next to Keith. "Not this time, Nell. You stay with Lori."

Lori didn't look happy about Philip's decision, but it was apparent to Keith that she wasn't going to argue either.

Keith and Philip rounded the front of the van and strolled together toward Bradley. They held their hands in the air as well.

The creek flowed beneath the bridge smoothly and quietly. It wasn't raging and it wasn't shallow. The dark green color appeared deep. A soft breeze slipped over the bridge where they were standing and rippled the fields. Since the drive had taken them outside the city area, fewer clouds hung in the sky.

When Bradley and his friend were about half way across the bridge, they stopped walking. Keith and Philip continued until they were within hearing distance.

It was a beautiful day. Keith felt blessed to be standing where he was, blessed to have found the beauty of the outside world. He could hardly understand why Stacy and the other escapees wanted to go back inside. The outside world didn't frighten him; it made him feel exuberant.

Bradley spoke first, gruff and authoritative. "You can't get away."

"I never wanted to," Keith said.

Bradley laughed as though Keith was kidding. "Then what's all this about?"

"I didn't understand what was going on, but the others, they wanted to go back." He told Bradley the truth.

"Sammy?"

"He wanted to go with them, with Molly. They came for me in the night." Keith lowered his eyes and said, "Sammy was shot when those people in Maysville stopped us."

"Idiots," Bradley said. He turned to the side and took a few steps toward the edge of the bridge, like he was going to jump. But he stood there overlooking the water. When he turned back again, he nodded to the other man. "What do you think, Blake?"

Blake stood a few inches taller than Bradley, and carried a more slender body. His facial expression was inquisitive, and the lack of wrinkles made him appear boyish. He said, "You didn't have to help them."

"I didn't know," Keith said. "I thought they wanted to warn Newcity that Bradley was going to destroy it."

"Destroy it?" Bradley laughed. "That's what they told you?"

"Yes, they said that you wanted to stop people from escaping."

He walked closer to Keith. "All I wanted to do was get rid of the lab and help Rene get the hell out of there. Do you have any idea what was about to happen?"

He gave the appearance as though he may have been angry or frustrated at one time, but that he was tired now. The emotions had worn him down. Keith also noticed that Bradley's eyes were swollen and red. And it wasn't until then that he realized that Rene and Bradley had been in love. The realization shot through Keith and hurt him as well. He could sense what Bradley was going through and almost cried. He turned his head. "How could I know anything more than what I was told?"

"Because you brought the system with you," Bradley said.

"We don't know that," Blake said.

"I'll tell you what Rene said. She said that she was afraid that they were going to chip her and the others, that they'd be more aware, more clear, but still not totally free. Is that what all this is about? Freedom?" Keith asked.

"Isn't that enough?" Blake said.

"But what about those inside? What if they want to be in there? Like Stacy and Robert and the others?"

"I think that we find a way to let them have what they want," Blake said. He stared at Bradley for approval.

The air became still for a moment as though the whole area waited for Bradley's approval, his understanding.

"But they're wrong. They only think they want inside. They don't know what happens to them," Bradley said. He punched his chest with a finger. "I've seen it."

"Newcity wants them out, too, you know." Keith said.

Both Blake and Bradley scrunched their faces up in question.

Keith relaxed as he spoke. For whatever reason, they were listening to him. "The computers. I don't know how, but they create the images to lead people out because the complex itself wants to experience more. If I understand it correctly, it's experiencing through us at this very minute. I don't know how, but it does."

Blake nodded. "It's become omniscient."

"Impossible," Bradley said. "It's man-made. It's a system."

"It's bored," Keith said.

"So it wants to spit them out here?" Bradley said. "We can't handle them all at once. As the groups get larger, they get more difficult to handle."

Philip, who had said nothing to this point, stepped next to Keith. "Not everyone inside has been chipped either." He held out his arm.

Blake inspected it. He looked at Bradley.

"I knew that," Bradley said. "They're like clean-up robots. Sometimes when there's an accident, the virus, that's what we called them, would clear out the apartment. We didn't care if the resident was alive and inside, as long as we didn't have to deal with processing another person. We were overloaded as it was. And the system didn't care either. It would merely flag the event as complete and move to the next problem. And there were plenty of them."

"The place is falling apart," Keith said.

"But you can't dump that many people into the outside world at once," Bradley said again.

"There's another way to integrate them, if you have to," Philip said.

The other men listened to him explain about creating a family unit. "That doesn't separate them, it incorporates them from the beginning. I suspect that one unit can handle maybe five people coming out."

Blake looked at Bradley.

It was difficult for Keith to tell who was actually in charge. He sensed that the two men had been working together for a long time even though he had never seen Blake before.

"It could work. We never tried that," Blake said.

"I don't know," Bradley said. "What if they want to go back in?" He looked straight at Keith.

"We let them," Keith said. "We find a way to get the system back into shape, become a part of the overall society and let alone those who want to be there."

"Chipped?" Bradley asked.

"A decision that we can't make yet," Philip said.

Bradley shook his head. "I don't know." He looked up at Keith. "And what about you? They still think you're their savior. I'm not sure what to do with you. You are not like all the others." He waved a hand at Keith. "We've gone through this. You're the boy with the hole in his forehead."

"Not any more," Keith said.

"It's true," Philip said. "The computers let him go. He's free. They've chosen someone else."

Bradley squared up to Keith. "You don't see them anymore?"

"Not for a while now. First they started to lie to me. Once that happened, I think I separated from it. I'm not sure it had a choice at the end. At least that's how I feel about it right now," he said. For a moment, he thought about the apparition of his father. Was that a result of the system interfering? Did the system actually open some sort of gate that let other apparitions through? And, most of all, was the gate closed now? Keith couldn't answer the questions at the moment, but knew that they'd be answered eventually.

"I'm not buying this whole thing yet," Bradley said. "I hear you, but we've got to consider it. We've got to plan how we're going to handle this."

"I understand," Keith said. "And if it matters, I'm sorry all this happened."

"It doesn't matter. It won't until I decide it does." Bradley started to walk toward the van, and Blake gave Keith a slow nod.

"Now what?" Keith said.

Bradley wasn't walking away, Keith noticed, he was pacing. At a certain point, Bradley swung around on his heels and came back into the circle. "You give up," he said pointing directly into Keith's face. "All of you. Until I can decide how much of this is the truth and how much are lies to save your skin." He continued to glare, then slowly turned toward Philip. "Got that?"

Blake said, "Not like prisoners, just no weapons."

Bradley shook his head. "Bullshit. We post guards. I don't need any more trouble for now."

So, Bradley was in charge.

"We'll comply," Keith said. "Is that good with you?" he asked Philip.

"For now."

"No funny business," Bradley said. Then he turned to Blake. "Two days. We'll talk with the others." As he walked toward the van on the bridge, he yelled back. "I'll send a few men to collect your weapons. And a driver."

Keith and Philip went back to their van to explain what happened. Several of the others weren't happy with their decision. "We could have taken them," one of them said. Nonetheless, most agreed that they could not have survived. If nothing else, Philip told them that this would give them time to plan.

"I don't like being guarded, not now that we're finally outside. We need to start our own community," Lori pleaded.

"He's already done that. We can learn from him, even if only for a short while." Philip opened a space in the conversation for Keith to add something.

"He's right. We should listen to Philip. We've got to buy some time." Keith followed Philip's lead because he didn't know what else to do. His senses had become overloaded, and it happened in the last few minutes. The fields, the open sky, the water from the creek, it all overtook him at once. He felt a part of the world and noticed the coolness of the air coming from the creek as it met with the air from the fields. There was a line of separation. Perhaps that was the line between them and Bradley, or the line between the chipped and unchipped, the Newcity residents or the outsiders. What was the world telling him?

He looked for the boy or the angel. But he was alone. Realizing that he sensed a deep hunger in his solar plexus, a hollow, empty feeling.

"They're coming," Philip said, breaking Keith's trance and bringing him back, in part, to the reality of their capture.

"And they have guns," Lori said. "I don't like this at all."

One of the men who approached ordered them to hand over their weapons, and Philip nodded his approval. Several of the people looked to Keith as well, but he yielded to Philip's command.

That didn't stop one of them, the gunman who had helped Keith at Newcity, from backing up and refusing to hand over his weapon. He held his pistol out. "You can't take everything from us. Not that easily."

One of Bradley's men stepped forward, lifted his pistol, and fired into the gunman's chest.

The gunman buckled forward then fell backward. Several of the others yelled and went to him. "Leave him," Bradley's man said.

That act answered a lot of questions they may have had. Keith saw that violence still wasn't out of the question, no matter how friendly his conversation was with Bradley and Blake.

Nellie took Keith's arm. Lori stood next to Philip. A few of the others paired up as well. Keith worried for them.

Chapter 25

They didn't go back to Bradley's camp where Keith had been taken originally. Instead they took a few back roads and stopped beside a huge barn. Bradley and his crew must have used the barn for shelter before, because it was much cleaner than the barn Keith and the others had accidentally run across the day before.

The whitewashed building had a corrugated metal roof with large areas of rust that randomly spread across it. The barn looked as though it had been built once and then added onto several times. Wood-framed protrusions jutted out on both sides. From the inside, the beams were as thick as a man, and as tall as most of the trees in the area.

All the vehicles were left outside. The fourteen people from Newcity were forced into one of the side areas that had been added to the original barn. The space was loaded with crates and boxes along one of the walls, and piles of bags along the back wall.

Keith walked over to the bags and saw that many of them were seed bags. The crates were unmarked, but he had the feeling that they held more seed bags and had not been opened yet. So, the barn was being used as storage.

In a short while, they were brought small amounts of food, enough to settle their stomachs. A few minutes after they finished two men came and took Philip away. Lori protested but was shoved aggressively and threatened. She ran to Keith and Nellie. "Do something," she pleaded.

"They're going to question him," Keith said. "As long as we don't fight them, I think we'll be okay."

"Like Mike back at the bridge?" she said, referring to the man who had been shot.

"He pointed a gun at them. We did the same thing. We killed one of their men from the van, remember?"

"To escape," she retorted.

"I didn't say it was right, but what good will it do if we resist them while we're trapped in here? Let's get clear on one thing, shall we? We're the prisoners at the moment. Our rights are limited. We'll know more when Philip returns." Keith tried to look strong and confident, and perhaps Lori recognized his weak attempt, but she didn't question him.

She grinned briefly. "We'll see," she said before walking away from them toward the rear of their holding area.

Philip was gone about an hour. When he returned to the area where they were kept, he appeared in a better mood. "That wasn't so bad," he said. He addressed Keith, "They asked a lot of questions, many of which I didn't know the answers to. But it seems like they're just after the truth."

"Whose truth?" Lori said coming to his side.

"What if there isn't a true answer?" Keith asked. "What if we're all just guessing?"

"There is no guessing about who I am or what I did while inside Newcity. I knew the answers and I told them. The things I didn't know, I told them that too. Don't make this more complicated than it is. It's simple." Philip hugged Lori and gave her a kiss before he addressed Keith again. "And you're next."

Keith and Nellie looked at the doorway together. Guards with rifles stood to either side and were looking in at them.

"When?" Keith said.

"They're probably talking things over first," Philip said.

Nellie asked, "Why didn't they talk with Keith first?"

"Base line," Lori said. "They needed something to start with."

"How do you know?" Nellie said.

"We're not idiots. We were recruited, years ago. If we had known what they were about to do to us…"

"Do you think that would change a lot of people's minds?" Nellie asked.

Philip said, "Frankly, no."

The two men who had brought Philip back walked into the area. Keith knew they were after him and gave Nellie a quick peck on the cheek. He had become very fond of her and she appeared to feel the same for him. The kiss was the natural thing to do, automatic. He left with the two men, one on either side of him, but neither one touching him, very respectful, an interesting turn of events.

The main barn space had been equipped with chairs, and tables filled with food, as well as all the people who had come with Bradley. Keith noticed that Ben was back with them, one wrist splinted and bandaged. He was sitting next to a woman, and looked up only long enough to see Keith pass by, then went back to a conversation he was having.

Keith and the two guards entered another of the barn's added-on rooms, located on the opposite side from where the escapees were being kept.

"You set up quickly," Keith said to Bradley and Blake, who were seated on one side of a table. The guards waited until Keith sat opposite the two men, then they left the area. Keith watched them go before turning back to the others. "I'm really sorry about Rene," he said. "It was never my intention…"

"I know," Bradley said. "Philip told me what you said to her. She should have listened to you."

"What do you mean?"

Blake leaned forward. "The blast never went through the computer center wall. She must have crawled back through and waited in the main lab." He hesitated. "She was found near the entrance."

Keith shook his head. He couldn't bring himself to say anything else.

"We have to know what went on, from the beginning. Everything," Blake said.

"I can only tell you what happened. Bradley knows most of it already."

"Then bring me up to speed," Blake said.

Keith did as he was asked, using a shorter version of the conversation he and Bradley had a few days prior. At the end of his explanation, he asked, "What are you going to do with us? Especially them. They've done nothing wrong."

Blake looked at Bradley for a moment, then back at Keith. "Honestly? We don't know yet. We haven't decided." Blake returned to the questioning. "Can you tell us, in your understanding, what's going on with Newcity?"

Keith shrugged. "I've told you everything I could think of. You probably know more than I do. You were in contact with Rene. And the only additional information I have is what Rene explained to me. But I didn't experience any of that."

Bradley leaned forward so far that Keith thought he was going to stand up. He reached out and knocked his fist against the table. "You were part of the machine. You probably still are. You told us that out there on the bridge. You must have a sense of what's wrong, of what's happening."

"I told you. The only sense I got was that it was bored and wanted a broader experience." Keith cowered slightly, afraid that Bradley might thrash out at him.

"I still think that it became omniscient," Blake said, "at least in its own world."

"Like God," Bradley said. "You think this room full of computers became God? Well I don't buy it."

"The hologram," Keith said.

"What about it? Philip mentioned it too," Bradley said. "What did you see?"

"Everyone at once. The people in the hologram went on forever." Keith cocked his head and said, "Like you said, it could be that it believed it was the universe."

"Belief is a human sensibility," Bradley said.

"Not if the machinery is God," Keith said. "But we're not totally under its control, not even with the chips. I know because I've been chipped, more than once." He wanted to get up and pace, to move so that he could think, but they'd stop him and he knew it. He fidgeted in his seat. "Let's think of it as a society unto itself then."

"Go on," Blake said.

While speaking, Keith leaned against the table, then leaned back, reached out and tapped the table with his fingers. "As long as it's able to control the emotions of those inside, it feels safe. As a leader, it provides all the necessary items needed for survival, then goes beyond that and supplies enough to reduce the want for change. Isn't that what Newcity was about from the beginning? The people are given everything and want for nothing. Cheap labor. Cheaper and easier to maintain than robots. Freedom is limited, but the people don't care because they have food and shelter and games and technology. Who needs actual freedom if you don't feel deprived in any way?"

Blake sat forward in his chair. He glanced back at Bradley whose jaw muscles tightened as he clenched his teeth. "Perfect for people with the right personality. Those who are comfortable to follow."

"Sleepers," Keith said.

"But that's not good enough for an evolved, evolving, entity," Blake said.

"So it lets some of us escape…on purpose." Keith shook his head. "But why? Why isn't it happy to be in control?"

"We may never know," Blake said.

Bradley couldn't hold back any longer. He stood quickly. His chair fell over, making a dull thud as it hit the dirt that covered the barn floor. "This is insane," he said. "Computers don't think, they don't believe, and they don't become unhappy."

"Prove it," Keith said.

Bradley spun around and glared at him, leaning on the table, his arm muscles tight, ready to strike out. "What did you say?"

"I said prove it. You and Rene studied the people. You were part of the system, too, in many ways. Now go back in there and analyze the computer, the hologram. It answered my questions. Put it straight if that's what you have to do. In fact, put it back so that it's a part of the society instead of a leech. Return us to a balanced state." Keith let Bradley stew. When Bradley appeared to relax, as though he was thinking about the proposal, Keith said, "You may be the only person capable of setting this straight."

"And what about you?"

"I'll leave. You don't need me. I'm not useful to you. There's a new boy with a bullet hole in his forehead. Find him." Keith looked at Blake for help, seemingly the more open-minded of the two.

"The image," Blake said, "is because the system isn't perfect either. It can't, for some strange reason, create something perfect because it's not perfect."

"It can only create in our image," Keith said.

Bradley rubbed his face with his hands. "We might have to break it down to rebuild it."

"Just don't shut it down completely," Blake said. "We're talking about a touchy operation."

"We could pull residents in groups as large as we can handle until the system isn't overloaded. Maybe that's all it would take." Bradley looked as though he shifted gears mentally. He began to plan how he would attack this bigger problem. He put a hand on Blake's shoulder.

Keith saw that Bradley's demeanor had changed. The frustration he carried with him had alleviated with the idea of something important to do. "I believe you can do this," Keith said.

"It won't be easy," Bradley said.

"You've organized nearly a thousand men and women, and carried out one impossible plan already. You destroyed the lab," Blake said. "I have to agree with Keith."

Bradley grinned as he thought about what they were proposing.

As volatile as he appeared to be at times, Bradley surely wasn't afraid to act. Keith saw a man of power, but also one of intelligence. But most of all, Keith felt that it didn't really matter. There was a very small band of people with him, fourteen who'd survived the escape from Newcity. Maybe they'd recruit a few more from Bradley's ranks, but it would be enough to create a self-sufficient group. That's what he believed. But it was up to Bradley now. "May I go?"

Blake lifted from his chair and stood next to Bradley. "We'll talk about it," he said. "Guards. Take him back with the others."

Keith walked out with the guards. When he got back with Philip and the others, Nellie ran to his side. She looked him over, touched his face. "They didn't hurt you."

"No, like Philip said, they asked questions. If they're satisfied, maybe they'll let us go."

"Where would we go?" Nellie asked.

Keith smiled, "Anywhere."

Everyone gathered in a circle, sitting cross-legged on the ground around Philip and Keith, who discussed what had happened during their conversations with Bradley and Blake.

"What do you think they'll do?" Philip wanted to know once Keith finished relating his experience from minutes earlier.

"We're not a threat," he said.

Nellie's face lit up and so did several others in the group. "This could be it."

"Such an odd end to a long story," Philip said. "I felt like we were battling something but we never really were. There are no bad guys." He looked surprised by the idea.

"Only misinformed ones," Keith said. "And that included all of us."

Lori shook her head in disbelief. "I'm sorry that people died over this. Really, what were we protecting? What were they trying to harm?"

"The system really has no control at all," Philip said.

"How do you mean? Aren't people chipped automatically?" Keith asked.

"Yes, they go through a sign-in station and are ushered through by chipped guards. The operation is automated; you lie down on a moving platform that takes you through several stages. You come out the other end chipped and ready for assignment."

"So if you stop people from entering..." Keith jumped up. "We need to tell Bradley. This may be easier than we thought."

Philip stood slowly. He laughed.

"What is it?"

"Newcity is sending people out almost as fast as they're coming in. I never realized it before, but only a few people are allowed in each day. Originally it was set up like that as production of products grew in phases. Now the input is supposed to match the number of deaths." Philip explained how internal production increased with increases in the number of people, and how the system would see increased production as a positive thing even if their wasn't a balance in the number of people using the products.

"It's running in circles," Keith said. "It's in a closed loop and can't see outside."

"You can't solve a problem using the same elements that gave you the problem in the first place," Philip said.

"It needs us to interrupt the loop." Keith swung around and walked toward the entrance of their room.

Philip was right behind him. "Or someone like Bradley," he said.

"My thoughts exactly." When Keith reached the doorway, two guards stopped his progress.

"Hold up. Where do you think you're going?"

"Nowhere. I have some important information for Bradley. Could someone get him?" Keith waited and one of the guards yelled into the center part of the barn for someone to retrieve Bradley. Keith turned to Philip. "I think that's the last piece."

Chapter 26

Bradley liked the idea. Not the best psychological explanation, but the idea of a closed loop did appear to answer a lot of questions for him. He explained to Keith and Philip that, after they'd talked, he had realized that the Newcity security was the least of his worries. The real problem was the few people who ran Newcity and still believed that the computers knew what they were doing. Rodger, Doctor Mike and Charles, who Keith had met, were only a few of them. From what Bradley recalled there were probably only about twenty in total. And his assessment, as well as Rene's, had long been that the group of them were followers, even if they hadn't been chipped. They'd go through the chipping process easily and without complaint.

"We post a small revolution," Blake said.

"It won't be that easy," Philip said. "There are the unchipped guards."

"No match for our forces judging from how easy it was to blow a hole into their lab," Bradley said.

"We did leave quickly just in case," Blake said. "And they'll add forces now that they know we're out here."

"Then we'll see their true strength. I still think we can do this," Bradley said.

"You think you can bring back some semblance of balance between Newcity and the outside world overnight?" Philip said in apparent disbelief.

"Not overnight. Maybe years. But we can do it." Blake looked at Bradley for approval of his statement and got a solid nod from the man. He turned to address the group again. "If any of you would like to help us?"

Keith was surprised by the question, but looked around at the thirteen people behind him. They had just gotten out from under Newcity, so why would they choose to go back? But what did he know? Three of the men and two of the women stepped forward, raising a hand slightly into the air, volunteering. One of the men said, "We can help you get around once you're inside. I know the system." Keith recognized the man as one of the people who sat in front of a terminal almost the whole time he stood talking with Philip when he first arrived. Perhaps the man missed his job already. Perhaps he felt useless without a terminal to operate.

Bradley smiled and shook the man's hand. "Great, great. Blake, could you escort them to a place more suitable than this, and get someone to brief them on our general operations?"

"Sure thing," Blake said.

That left nine of them. At first Keith thought that Bradley was going to let them go free, but not now. There was something about the man's look, the way he strutted in a small circle before getting back to Keith. It was like he was considering his next move and it was between two different approaches, neither one good for Keith.

"You know I can't have you following us or trying to break things up," Bradley said.

"We won't do that," Keith said.

"I can't be sure now, can I?"

"I promise," Keith said.

"We all do," Nellie put in.

He glanced around the space. "We can make this a little more comfortable, but I think we'll hold you here for now. Until I decide what my alternatives are."

"But that could take years." Keith said. "You can't keep us that long. How can you?"

Bradley narrowed his eyes. "I can do anything I want, and you're staying here. It'll take a few days for me to concoct a plan and I don't need your interference. Look, I said I'd make this as easy and as comfortable as I can for you, but you're going nowhere. Not yet." With that, Bradley exited the area and ordered the guards to stay alert.

Keith took the group and sat them in a circle at the far end of that section of the barn. They whispered so that the guards couldn't hear them. They debated several methods of escape. None seemed easy enough for the lot of them.

"There's one other way," Keith said.

Nellie shook her head before he even mentioned his idea.

"I sacrifice myself to the guards tonight. The others will be asleep. It'll take them a long time to know what's going on and by then you can be gone."

"No," Nellie said. "What good would that do? We need you."

Keith said, "No you don't. You never did. The system would have let you go a long time ago, but you didn't choose to leave."

"We could see what they could see," Philip said. "We were afraid to go. Afraid we'd get caught and have chips put in. That was enough to keep us inside."

"Then it's settled," Keith said.

"I still don't like it," Nellie told him.

Keith acknowledged her concern. He'd do his best to get away with them, but if he couldn't, she'd have to go on.

They made a small plan for their escape, hoping that everything would go smoothly. Each of them was willing to sacrifice for the others, but Keith would go first.

The tone was somber for the rest of the afternoon and early evening. Another round of food brought lighter conversation. Along with chairs and a small table, several air mattresses and quilts were brought in as well. Neither Bradley nor Blake was seen again. They must have been off strategizing. It all seemed so pointless to Keith.

There were only two guards watching the doorway when everyone retired for the night. Keith didn't sleep, and because of that, Nellie remained awake as well. Much of the time they shared a mattress and all she did was stare at him as though she was trying to memorize his face. Several times a tear formed, but she never cried.

DAY 7

An hour after there was a guard change, Keith got up slowly. It was very dark inside. The only light was from the moon coming through some green semitransparent panels that had been installed high on the walls.

Philip was roused by a simple tap on the shoulder. In turn, he awakened the others. Keith made a lot of noise grumbling and moving around so that the others could sneak into position. He let his feet scrape along the ground as though he was tired. As he approached the guards he talked to them. "You guys have any better facilities out there?" he said. "I can't go to the toilet in here, it would stink up the whole place."

In the dim light, Keith saw that one of the guards was Ben and hesitated for a moment as he approached.

Ben held a hand up for Keith to stop. "Keep your distance," he said.

The other guard asked, "What do we do?"

Ben smiled, his teeth showing in the dim light. "I'll take him outside to one of the portables." He turned to Keith. "But keep your distance or I shoot. And it would be my pleasure."

Any other guard and Keith felt that he might have a chance of getting away with the others, but Ben would shoot first, as soon as anything appeared to be wrong. He closed his eyes and said a silent goodbye, then walked between the two men and well in front of Ben.

He assumed that they'd wait a few minutes and then rush the other guard in hopes that they'd catch him quickly enough that he couldn't shout. One young man from the group knew how to cross a few wires and start one of the vans. Then they'd be free. Keith envied them for a moment, then concentrated on his own predicament.

He got to the portable and opened the door.

"I'll be right here," Ben said.

Keith entered the toilet and rustled his pants as though he were settling in. He waited then yelled out that it was out of paper.

"Too bad," Ben said.

"What do I do?"

"Use your shirt or something. Use your hand for all I care."

That didn't work to get him closer or to shift his concentration for long. Keith thought. The others should be on their way by now. He had to make more noise. He banged around.

"What are you doing in there?"

"Looking for paper. It's dark. Maybe it fell down somewhere." He continued to talk so that Ben couldn't hear what was going on inside the barn. He scuffed the floor with his feet and felt around noisily.

"Hey, wait," he heard Ben yell. "What are you guys doing?" Then a shot. "Stop right there!"

Keith shoved the door open and ran several steps to the dark figure that was Ben. The man had turned and was about to take another shot when Keith slammed into him. It was enough to knock him over. The gun flew from his hands and one of the other escapees ran over and picked it up. He held it out as though he was going to shoot, but Keith yelled for him to stop. "We don't need to kill anyone. Let's go."

The van started.

Keith and the other man ran for the open side door of the van, which was already pulling onto the road.

More yelling came from inside the barn, but the moment Keith and the other man leaped into the van, the vehicle made a quick turn and the engine roared. Lori was driving again, but much faster than he knew she was comfortable with.

Someone slid the side door closed and Lori wasted no time taking another turn.

"Where are we going?" Keith yelled.

"We don't know," Philip said. "Any ideas."

"West, can we go west?"

Nellie kneeled near Keith who sat on the floor at the moment. She kissed him several times on the cheek and lips. "I knew you'd make it."

"How do we know where west is?" Philip asked. He sat next to Lori in the front seat.

"I can get us back to the highway," Lori said. "I memorized how they got us here. From there, we'll know which direction we're going. When the sun rises, we'll run from it."

After an hour of driving, Lori slowed to a comfortable speed. It didn't appear as though they were being followed. As the sun began to rise, they found a gas station and robbed the attendant of gas and food using the pistol they had taken from Ben. None of them wanted to rob the man, but they had no money. Now they did. And the van was filled with as much food as they could put into the back.

Another three hours and Keith kneeled between the front seats.

"What do you think?" Philip asked as they crested a hill.

"I think we're free," Keith said.

At the top of the hill, Philip asked Lori to pull over. She obliged by running the van onto a road that appeared to go along the ridge. Everyone got out of the van. Philip gathered them, and while looking down into a valley and across some foothills, he announced their freedom. Everyone cheered.

"Then you don't think they'll come after us?" Nellie asked.

Philip looked to Keith, who answered, "They'll be too busy with their new plans for Newcity. But now we have more to consider. We can't just rob everyone. We'll have to figure out how to survive out here on our own. How do we become a part of this new and strange world?" He spread his arms and lifted his chin to take in the world around them.

"You forget that most of us used to live out here long before we thought we wanted to be inside Newcity. This life wasn't easy, but at the moment," Philip said while pulling Lori close to him, "it looks better.

Keith bowed toward Philip. "Then lead the way."

Philip turned to Lori, a question on his face.

She smiled and answered. "We find a small town to settle into. There's bound to be work we can do. If we have to we'll live in an abandoned barn or farmhouse. They used to be all over." She lowered her head. "Didn't we leave one behind? We won't go there. We wouldn't be welcomed. But I'm sure there were plenty like us."

They all seemed to agree on the plan. It was simple, which was just what they needed after what they'd been through.

Keith held Nellie close to him. They all appeared to be looking at the same point, the fuzzy image of a small town in the distance. They'd head there.

More Fantasy Fiction from Booktrope:

A Kingdom's Possession

By Nicole J. Persun

A Kingdom's Possession blends ancient magic, love and intrigue in a romantic fantasy told in a fresh new voice.

A wayward prince, his twin brother, a mystical woman of fire, and an escaped slave band together, to free an outcast goddess – if they can elude a powerful rogue kingdom intent on their destruction.

A captivating tale of love, freedom, and choices, the debut novel of 17-year old Nicole J. Persun will introduce you to a brilliant young writing talent.

―――――――――――

The Printer's Devil

By Chico Kidd

A tale of ghosts, magic, music and modern heroism, *The Printer's Devil* will delight fans of historical fantasy. A musician discovers a spell laid by a grieving lover in Cromwellian England, opening forbidden channels through time and unleashing a very dangerous demon. Now Kim must put an end to the sorcery – or lose her beloved Alan forever.

"This affectionate tale of supernatural suspense twines ghostly and diabolic forces with a love of art and scholarship to produce one of the most readable such yarns in quite some time." *Dragon*

CPSIA information can be obtained at www.ICGtesting.com
Printed in the USA
LVOW101224090712

289294LV00003B/1/P